"In *Beyond the Valley*, talented author Rita Gerlach once again delivers a heart-pounding tale that takes readers back in time to an era when life was a blend of adventure and hardship. Through the eyes of characters who are strong-willed and courageous, readers will experience the testing of faith, the sorrow of loss, and the joy of new love . . . all woven into a tapestry of magnificent frontier vistas."
—Loree Lough, bestselling author of 100 award-winning books, including *A Man of Honor*, #3 in the First Responders series

"The author skillfully weaves through the exquisitely written pages the message of hope and freedom and redemption. It's a message the world desperately needs to hear today, that despite tragedy and hard times, new life and hope are right around the corner. Rita's writing flows over you like a gentle breeze. It's beautiful, poetic, and her words have a way of transporting you back in time, making you feel as though you were there among the early colonists of our great nation."
—MaryLu Tyndall, author of the Swashbuckling Romances Anchored in Faith, including *Veil of Pearls*

Other books by Rita Gerlach

Surrender the Wind
The Rebel's Pledge

The Daughters of the Potomac Series

Before the Scarlet Dawn
Beside Two Rivers

Beyond the Valley

Book 3

The Daughters of the Potomac Series

Rita Gerlach

a novel approach to faith

Nashville, Tennessee

Beyond the Valley

ISBN: 978-1-4267-1416-0

Published by Abingdon Press, P.O. Box 801, Nashville, TN 37202

www.abingdonpress.com

Published in association with Hartline Literary Agency

Library of Congress Cataloging-in-Publication Data has been
requested.

Printed in the United States of America

1 2 3 4 5 6 7 8 9 10 / 18 17 16 15 14 13

To all those who tread over difficult paths

Acknowledgment

To the staff at Abingdon Press, who worked on the production of this novel and the entire series, from the edits to the book cover. You have my deepest gratitude.

Dear Reader,

I hope you will enjoy reading the third book in the Daughters of the Potomac series, *Beyond the Valley*. It is a novel that stands on its own, even though it is the last book in the trilogy. What inspired me to write the series was the love I have for the Potomac River Gorge and the rich history in the area in which I live. Book two, *Beside Two Rivers*, took me beyond the river to England where the story all began in book one, *Before the Scarlet Dawn*. I hope if you have not read the first two books, you will, and thereby gain a deeper look into the lives of the characters and the events that affected their lives and all those around them.

Fondly,
Rita Gerlach

Part 1

Yea, though I walk through the valley of the shadow of death,
I will fear no evil: for thou art with me;
thy rod and thy staff they comfort me.

Psalm 23:4

1

Cornwall, England

Autumn 1778

*S*arah Carr would never look at the sea the same way again, or listen to the waves sweep across the shore while in the embrace of her first love. Drawing in the briny air, feeling the wind rush through her unbound hair, now spoke of danger and loss. Basking in blue moonlight under the stars and having Jamie point out the constellations was now a thing of the past that could never, in her mind, be repeated.

Tonight a hunter's moon stood behind bands of dark purple clouds as if it were the milky eye of evil. Along the bronze sand, deep green seaweed entwined with rotted gray drift-wood. The scent of salt blew heavy in the air, deepening the sting of tears in her eyes, and tasting bitter on her tongue.

She had pleaded with Jamie not to go down to the shore with the others when they beat on the door and called out that a ship had wrecked in the harbor. But an empty pocket and a growling stomach influenced him to go. For over an hour, she waited for him to return and then she could bear the anxiety no longer. Sarah slipped on her worn leather boots and hurried down to the beach, working her way through the tangle of frenzied scavengers in hopes of finding him.

People rushed about her, some with torches, others carrying glowing tin lanterns. There were calls and shouts over the howl of the wind and the noise of the sea. They carried sacks, barrels, and crates, which had been tossed in the surf and washed ashore; others were taken perilously from the sinking vessel. The groan of its timbers caused Sarah to shiver, as she thought of the poor souls trapped aboard. She could make out its black hulk in the moonlight, its main mast shooting up through the boil of waves like a spear.

"Have mercy on those left behind, O Lord." She shoved back her tangle of hair and watched the hapless ship go down into the dark depths of an angry sea.

A bonfire threw sparks over the sand. The foamy edge of the surf seemed a ribbon of gold near her feet. The few sailors who had survived looked on wide-eyed and drenched to the bone. They shivered in the cold, with no weapons to fend off the looting.

A firm hand moved Sarah back and she gasped. "Come on, girl. This is no place for ye to be." She turned to a man in untidy clothes. His wet hair corkscrewed around his ears and hung over his forehead. He had turned up his collar against the drizzle and wind. She recognized him as one of the villagers, a fisherman by trade, but did not know his name.

"You must leave this place before it gets too rough, Sarah. We'll take Jamie to the chapel with the others. Come with me."

She shook her head at his meaning. "Jamie? Where is he?" she shouted over the blast of wind as she glanced at the chaos around her. "Why must we go to the chapel?"

The man did not answer. Instead he shifted on his feet, frowned, and glanced away. Then, still silent, he took her by the arm again and led her across the sand. Her hair, the color of burnt umber, floated about her eyes, where the mist blurred her vision.

"Are we gathering there to pray?" she asked. "We need to pray for those poor souls caught in the sea." She lifted her skirts and stepped unsteadily. Her limp made it difficult to navigate the beach.

"Ah, let me help you." The man threw his arm across her back. "Over this way. Watch your step. Steady now."

He took her to a place where the rocks made a barrier between the village and the sea. In the orange firelight, Sarah saw bodies stretched out on the sand in a row, their clothes soaked and splattered with sand. Faces were ashen in the torchlight. Their arms were crossed over their chests. The worst of her fears exploded into reality. She trembled and felt her knees weaken.

Upon a blanket lay her husband, Jamie, his youthful face whiter than the wet shirt that clung to his lifeless body. His eyes were closed. His dark hair, soaked, clung to his throat. Sarah gasped. "Jamie!"

She shivered from the cold wind that shoved against her, that pounded the waves upon the beach, from the grief that struck a merciless fist against a breast once content with love, thinking it would last forever.

"No!" She fell beside him and threw her arms across his chest, wherein lay a silent heart. "Lord God, do not take him from me. Bring him back!" She shook with weeping, and someone pulled her away.

Four men wrapped her lad in the blanket and lifted him. She followed. Her skirts twisted around her limbs as the wind gusts grew stronger. A storm had battered the Cornish coast, and another whisked across sea and land behind it. Within moments, clouds smothered the moon and stars—the bonfire and a few lanterns the only lights to guide their steps up to the centuries-old stone church.

To rally her strength, she took in a deep lungful of air. Instead of relieving her, its mix of smoke from the bonfire and the brackish wind choked her. Behind her, she heard the waves break over the rocks, rush over the sand and pebbles, and suck at the shipwreck. A few lights in the cottages afar off glimmered in the darkness. She stumbled, regained her footing, and brushed away the tears that stung her eyes.

Fifteen sailors from the shipwreck and five villagers were laid to rest in the parish churchyard the next morning. Four somber widows walked away in silence with their fatherless children, made poorer by their loss.

Sarah drew her shoulders back, determined to rise above her grief and face what life had just thrown at her. But her heart ached, and she knew no amount of fortitude could stop it. She tipped the rim of her hat downward to hide her tears.

"What is done cannot be undone," she said to the woman who walked beside her. "God asks of me to go on. And I shall for my child's sake."

Her neighbor, Mercy Banks, placed her hand over Sarah's shoulder. She was as tall as Sarah, and lean, with a pleasant countenance and large brown eyes. Known for her kindness to those in need, Mercy's touch comforted Sarah.

"You must come home with me, Sarah. The least we can do is give you a warm meal and a bed for the night. It would be too lonely in your little cottage without Jamie."

Sarah glanced down at the three children as they walked alongside their mother. Their heads were as blond as sand, their eyes like Mercy's. Two clung to Mercy's skirts. The oldest boy walked ahead and swung a stick at the geese in the road.

"Thank you, Mercy. But I am leaving Bassets Cove." She could not impose on her neighbors who had young mouths to feed. "My landlord is not a rich man. I can expect sympathy, but not charity. He and his wife need a paying tenant. So I have told them I am leaving."

Mercy's face crinkled with worry. "You are leaving this minute? Let me speak to my husband."

"Do not worry. I will be fine."

"But where will you go, Sarah? You have no family, no parents, brothers or sisters. Have you a distant relative who would take you in all of a sudden?"

"I am going to Jamie's sister, Mary, and her husband. November is around the corner and the cold weather will be here. I must go while I have the chance."

Mercy pressed her lips together then let out a long breath. "To the Lockes? It is said Lem Locke is a smuggler, that he will stop anyone by any means if they get in his way. It isn't as if he is helping any of the poor in Cornwall, for it is also said he hoards his goods in the caves along the coast, and sells rum and brandy at a high price to the gentry. You should reconsider."

"I have nothing to fear, and nowhere else to go. I am sure it is only a rumor you have heard about Lem. Jamie told me if I should ever need help to go to them. Why would he say that if they were bad people?"

"Perhaps Jamie did not know Lem Locke as well as he should have. Not only that, they must have heard the unfortunate news by now and will come for you if they have any Christian charity in them at all. But why are they not here already?"

"I had no way of sending word. Paper is so precious, and I had none. I imagine they may hear from others before I reach them, but only of the wreck."

Mercy cocked her head. "Have you met them before?"

"Only Mary. It was a few days before Jamie and I were wed. She was quiet but not completely cold. Yet, I do not think she approved of our marriage, and would have rather seen her brother marry a fit woman. She never said where Lem was."

"Away smuggling, no doubt. I pray he is kind to you, Sarah. It is what you need right now."

Once they reached her cottage door, Mercy kissed Sarah's cheek. "I wish you well, and will keep you and your child in my prayers. If you should need to return, come to my door before anyone else's. Understand?"

"Yes, thank you." Sarah hugged Mercy and watched her walk away with the children in tow, down the sandy lane that led into the heart of the village.

Before stepping inside, Sarah glanced up at the gray sky that whirled above. "If only you would clear the clouds away, Lord, I might feel better if I were to see the sun. But if not today, then tomorrow."

Pushing the door in, she stepped over the threshold and paused. The sparse little room seemed neglected, as if no living soul lived there anymore. They owned little, and few things were left of Jamie's—his pipe, and Bible, and one change of clothes. She packed them in a sack with her own scant possessions—brush, comb, and one pair of stockings. The rest she owned was on her back.

Determined to be strong, she wiped away a tear and heaved the bag into her arms. After she shut the door behind her, she took the path to the rear of the cottage and slowly climbed the grassy slopes. It would take her longer than the average person to reach the moorland above, for having been born with one leg slightly shorter than the other hindered her gait, enough to cause her stride to be uneven. It had been the source of ridicule growing up, orphaned and living in a workhouse for children. Told her mother was dead, her father unknown, she wondered if she were an abandoned child, an embarrassment to some gentry family for being flawed and possibly illegitimate.

Abused and starved, she had kept to herself and barely spoke to anyone, until a good-looking young man came down the lane that bordered the field she worked in. The wheat had been scythed and she, along with other able bodies, stood in a line to gather it into bundles. He leaned on the fence rail and watched her. The next day, he offered her water from his canteen. Given ten minutes to rest, he approached her on the third day, sat beside her and told her his likes and dislikes.

"I hate the smell of wheat," he told her. "It makes me sneeze." She remembered how his comment had made her giggle. "I'm a net maker, but I hate eating fish. Don't like the bones."

"What *do* you like?" she asked in a quiet voice.

"Bread and butter . . . and pretty girls like you."

She hid her face in the sleeve of her dress, for she felt the burn of a blush rush over her.

By the fourth day, he suggested she leave with him. "I live in Bassets Cove, not far from here," he told her. "It's a beautiful place. The sea air is good for one's health, you know. I am alone. You are alone. I could use a wife."

Sarah stood and brushed the bits of chaff from her dress. "You could not possibly want me."

"Why not? You're very pretty, Sarah. And I like the way you think."

"Hmm, haven't you noticed my way of walking?"

"Yes, what of it?"

"I am crippled." She leaned down, emphasizing the words.

He jumped up and put his hands on her shoulders. "I do not care. Marry me."

He had been the first man to ask, the first not to care about her *imperfection*. He was a means of escape and the start of a new life, a net maker by trade. She reasoned he would protect her and take care of her, and understood they would never rise above a humble existence. If not Jamie, who on God's green earth would have her?

"Well," she had told him while looking into his blue eyes. "I suppose the Lord has brought us together. You need a wife, and I need a protector. I accept you as you are, not a rich man, if you will accept me as I am—a cripple."

She never forgot the expression on Jamie's face, how his eyes lit up as he gazed into hers. "You may limp, Sarah, but you are healthy. You and I shall not be alone. Not for the rest of our lives. We will have lots of children and grow very old together. And I shall become a wealthy man one day. You will see." And he leaned down and kissed her cheek.

Inside the little cottage, life seemed abundant. Jamie wove the finest nets and mended those of the local fishermen. There was food on the table and rent paid most of the time. But after only a few months wed, he stopped showing her affection and never said he loved her, which began to disappoint Sarah. She never mentioned it to him, deciding she would sacrifice romance for a roof over her head, food in her belly, and companionship.

And so, at age seventeen, she left the wheat fields, with him strolling alongside her as the sun went down. Married only six months, she now found herself alone in the world again.

She came to the little church that overlooked the sea. Sunlight glimmered in the windows. But the gray stone gave it a cold appearance. She stepped over the thick grass, and drew near Jamie's marker, a small narrow stone with his name and date. She stood in front of it and sighed, her cloak fanning in the wind.

"You did not kiss me good-bye, Jamie. You spoke not a word to me, but rushed out the door without a second thought. How I wish you had listened when I warned you not to go. But it was not your way. You showed little attention to my pleas. You made it clear your business was your own and I need not be concerned, only be happy when you returned home with a sack full of goods. Even so, I shall miss you."

She closed her eyes, spoke a prayer for his soul, and moved on. Once she reached the crossroads, she headed south along the coastal road and tried not to think of how hungry she was. Her last full meal was on the night Jamie left to plunder the shipwreck. She thought about how he had gulped down the humble potato stew, grabbed his hat, and rushed out the door at the urging of his mates.

The bag slipped in Sarah's arms. She pulled it up, held it tighter, and glanced back. Leaving the village and the blue cove caused a wave of sadness to ripple through her. She wished some of her long-time neighbors, besides Mercy, had followed, begged her to stay, urged her not to go, and gave her all the reasons why, offered her work, some kind of position to keep her from starving. Then she hoped to see a wagon or coach heading in her direction. But the road remained lonely and windswept.

Her homespun dress opened at the front, and her beige striped petticoat fluttered about her slim legs. The hem was a bit tattered and soiled from wear. Her straw hat lay between her shoulder blades. The blue ribbon, faded gray, looped around her throat. No point wearing it upon her head, for the wind would blow it off or worsen the wear on the brim.

Six miles later, she set the sack down on the roadside and gathered her hair in her hands and twisted it into a braid. Her dress felt tight against her waist. She loosened the stays before going on.

A half-mile further, misty sunbeams shot through the clouds and plunged toward earth and sea. Sarah gazed with awe at the heaven-like spears and the distant patches of blue. For a moment, the sight soothed her soul and eased the pain that lingered in her heart.

She watched sparrows dart across the sky and land afar off. Then she moved on down the sandy road. This time she strove to walk with ladylike grace. But as it had so many times before, it proved to be a task too difficult and wearisome to do.

2

$\mathscr{L}$em Locke's house stood on a green plain of ground above the rugged cliffs of Hell's Mouth in St. Ives Bay. Far below, the sea thundered against sheer cliffs. Gulls screeched and flew in circles against the sky. Gray peppered stones made the old dwelling cold, and the windows were dark and uninviting. The door, also gray due to weathering and in need of paint, had a wrought iron handle and a rope knocker that dangled from a rusty hook, its end a ball of jute. Sarah could not help but wonder if the dreary house reflected the people within it.

Drawing in a deep breath, she trudged up the path and approached the door. She hoped Mary would see her from the window and rush out to greet her. But it wasn't until she raised the knocker and let it fall that her sister-in-law appeared. The same height as Sarah, Mary stood beneath the lintel, slim as a reed. She looked older than when Sarah had last seen her. Her hair, partially tucked up beneath a white cap, hung straight around her ears and temples. Her mouth, lined by a hard life, looked drawn with worry.

A look of surprise sprang over Mary's face. "Sarah? What are you doing here?" She looked down the road. "Where is my brother?"

"Hello, Mary. May I come inside? I must speak with you."

Mary stepped back and waved her in. "Oh, please tell me he did not leave you and you have come to us for help. I will be very put out if he did."

A lump swelled in Sarah's throat. "Yes, he has left me. But not in the way you think."

Mary shut the door and walked ahead of Sarah. A parlor faced the front of the house, and when Mary sat down in the rocking chair in front of the fireplace, she extended a hand to Sarah to sit across from her. At once, Sarah felt crestfallen at Mary's reaction, the way her mouth pressed firm and her eyes narrowed when she mentioned Jamie. They had never been close, only connected by blood, and Sarah had no idea how much she could depend on the compassion of her husband's sister and brother-in-law—if they had any at all. Mercy's words came back to her.

She lowered herself into the chair and gripped the bag on her lap. It hid what was behind it. "You are looking well, Mary. How is Lem?"

"So, what wrong has Jamie done?" Mary ignored Sarah's words and folded her hands in her lap. "I have not seen him in a long time."

Sarah lowered her eyes and drew in a breath. "He has done nothing wrong."

"Then why has he left you? Did you do something to chase him away? Goodness, Sarah. A wife must do all she can to keep her husband in these trying times. What living can you earn to sustain you if you do not have a husband?"

"Mary, please." Tears struggled in Sarah's eyes and she forced them back. "Let me explain."

Mary shook her head. "Dear me. You look as though you are about to cry."

The tears slipped out. Sarah wiped them away with the back of her hand. Then she covered her eyes, bent forward, and wept.

Mary hurried out of the chair. "Oh. Something awful has happened, I fear." A little hesitant, she put her arm around Sarah. "There, there, do not cry."

Sarah felt a bit relieved that Mary showed some sign of sympathy, some glimmer of compassion.

"I cannot help it. Forgive me." Sarah sniffed and straightened up.

"Can I get you anything? A glass of water?"

"No, thank you. Just let me speak."

"Of course. Go on. I am listening."

"There was a shipwreck in Bassetts Cove."

"That is not unusual. The waters there are treacherous."

"Jamie went with the others down to the beach, to take whatever washed ashore."

Mary went back to her seat and held up her hand. "Do not mention it to Lem. He will be envious and no doubt want to pay Jamie a visit. We are down to meager finances and I do not want him going there. He will spend our last coin on any good rum Jamie may have acquired."

Sarah's fists balled and she clenched her teeth. "Mary, you must let me finish. Can you not understand a terrible thing has happened? Jamie went out into the surf and drowned."

Mary's hand flew to her throat. "What? He drowned? Poor Jamie. This is sad news indeed."

Sarah looked toward the door that led to the hallway. "Is Lem at home?"

"No, but I expect him soon. You must realize, Sarah, as hard as it may be, you have to make all the arrangements. Lem will not agree to help."

"You needn't worry. I have done what any good wife would."

She wondered how Mary controlled her emotions so well. She should have cried, but there were no tears. Sarah looked down at her worn shoes as her belly twisted with hunger. By the appearance of the cottage, the fine furniture and rugs, the tapers in brass candlesticks, the bucket of coal and kindling by the fireplace, they were much better off than most. On the table under the window sat a plate of ginger fairings, a pot of tea, bone china cups and saucers.

She set the bag on the floor. Anguish and hunger trembled through her. "I am quite ravenous, Mary. Could you spare something? A little tea perhaps?"

"One must be strong in these kinds of situations," Mary said. "Certainly you are welcome to some fairings and tea. It will make you feel better."

The aroma of ginger beckoned, and Sarah moved to the table. She thought Mary noticed the change in her figure, but she was silent on the subject. She set a fairing on a plate, poured tea, and sat beneath the window. Sunlight flowed through it and alighted on her shoulders to warm her. Beyond the window, she could see the pale blue sky above the darker azure of the sea, hear the gulls and the soft swell of the waves. She would rather sit upon the cliff top in the grass and gaze out at the vast expanse, have the wind whip through her hair and listen to God's voice in it, than to be in this stuffy cottage with a sister-in-law who had not shed a tear over the death of her only brother.

She looked over at Mary and wound a loose thread from her dress around her finger and yanked it free. Sarah had to tell her the rest of her news, unsure what kind of reaction it would bring.

"I am with child."

Mary jerked her gaze back at Sarah and her mouth fell open. "What? Are you sure?"

"There is no doubt. I would not lie to you."

For a moment, Mary said nothing. She stood, paced a little and then paused. "I thought you looked, well, different. How can you take care of a baby when you cannot take care of yourself? At the same time, you cannot expect Lem and me to provide for you and your child. We have so little to begin with."

Sarah set her jaw. *So little?* Mary's clothes were new and pretty. Costly pearls dangled from her earlobes and a gold pendant from her throat. Sarah understood perfectly what Mary implied. "I will not burden you, Mary. I will find work and care for my baby on my own."

Mary raised her chin. "We would never have been able to care properly for a child. It costs money to feed and clothe them, you know. And then, the expense of an education would have been out of the question. Lem likes my figure the way it is, and children would have ruined me. You should think of the hardships this will cause you, Sarah."

"It is Jamie's child. There is no hardship."

"You think that now. In your situation, you should consider getting rid of it. I did, and it saved me a world of grief."

Shocked at this, Sarah sat forward. "You think so? I hear no children pattering about the house. I see no son here to care for you when you are old, or a daughter when you are sick, or to give you joy. Do not make a suggestion like that to me again."

"I do not need children. I have Lem."

"Children are a blessing from God."

"You will change your mind about those pious words after you have borne this one—if you survive childbirth. Consider what I am telling you. Would it not be wrong to bring a child into this world only to have it live in poverty? And would it not be right to sacrifice it if it meant you would live?"

"I fear God more than poverty. He will take care of us." She stood and picked up her bag. "I am sorry I came here."

Then the front door slammed. "Mary!"

Lem Locke's shadow fell over the floor as he strode into the room. His steps were deliberate and firm. He stopped short in front of them, dragged off his hat, and threw it onto the settee. He wore his hair tied back in a queue. Pockmarks marred his cheeks. Sarah considered what Mercy had told her. Perhaps her brother-in-law was a smuggler, mean and self-serving.

"I am starved," he bellowed. "Have you got my supper ready?"

He turned and when he saw Sarah he stood stock-still. "Who may this be?"

"You remember I told you about Jamie's wife. Well, this is she." Mary picked up his hat and set it on a hook by the door. "She's walked all the way from Bassetts Cove. Jamie was careless and drowned."

Lem's glassy eyes widened as Mary spoke. "Drowned, you say? Was he scavenging, girl?"

His voice, gruff and hollow, caused Sarah to fear him. "He was. But does it matter? I have lost my husband."

A corner of Lem's mouth turned downward. "I suppose not. He didn't get anything if he drowned. You buried him?"

Sarah nodded.

"Any debt from it?"

"No. Our minister is a good man and took pity."

"You owe money to anyone?"

"I owe no one. Why do you ask me such questions?"

"Because, I didn't intend to help if you had. Pour me some brandy, Mary. I'm chilled to the bone." He plopped down across from Sarah and stared at her. Sarah felt uneasy. Mary took a bottle from a corner cabinet and removed the cork. Her hand trembled when she handed the glass to Lem. In one swallow, he gulped the brandy down and then he held the glass out for more.

"Not too much, Lem," Mary said, pouring carefully. "You know how it makes you feel fevered."

He laughed. "Fevered indeed, Mary. And you know what kind, don't ye?" He jerked her hand to his lips and kissed it. Then he set the glass on the table and kept his hand around it. He stared again at Sarah.

"Well, you're young, Sarah. Got a pretty face, pretty hair. And lads like fiery hair like yours. Says you got spirit. Someone will marry you. Do it quick though."

As if it were in her power to gain a proposal of marriage.

"No man wants a crippled widow, Lem," Mary said. "Even if she does have a pretty face. They'd have to be desperate, needy for companionship or someone to cook and clean for them and warm their beds. Sarah has a limp. No man likes that."

Sarah cringed inwardly at Mary's prejudice. "I am not thinking of marriage at the moment. Jamie told me to come to you if I was in need. I haven't any money, or a place to live, and I am carrying a child."

Lem slammed his fist on the table. The china rattled and his brandy splashed onto the tablecloth. "You think we should help you, give you a roof over your head, food in your belly and in your brat's belly, for nothing?"

Sarah stood and quickly gathered her bundle. "I will walk on and find work on one of the estates." She looked into Lem's stern eyes. They were a pair of dark brown stones, smooth as the sea-swept pebbles on the beach, cold as the coal ash in the hearth.

Mary set her hand on Lem's arm. "Jamie was my brother, Lem. We cannot turn our backs on Sarah. What would people say?" Mary looped her arm through Sarah's. The change in Mary's demeanor confused her, the soft way in which she spoke to Lem.

Lem leaned on the table. "She can stay a few days to sort things out. But that's all. I'll not have a squalling baby keep me from my sleep. There may be work in Haley for her, Mary. I'll ask 'round at the tavern."

"Do that, Lem. Ask some of the gentry, if indeed any go there."

"Some do."

"A position at a manor would be perfect, but may not be so easy if you tell them she's going to have a child. Say nothing of that."

"I'll not. And neither should you, Sarah. You keep quiet about that."

Mary looked at Sarah with a tilt of her head. "Lem is right. It would be wise to stay quiet. They will take pity on you once they find out."

Unwanted by her husband's family, Sarah pulled away and stepped over to the door. She would have walked out but for the churning in her stomach and the sound of the wind outside. A few days—endure it or go hungry. She could not bear the thought of being on the road on cold dark nights. Where would she sleep? Would anyone take pity on her?

"Come back inside, Sarah," Mary said firmly. "Sit down and eat. We have enough, so do not feel bad wondering whether you are taking food out of our mouths tonight."

Sarah felt her brows press into a tight line. Slowly, she sat and waited with her eyes lowered until Mary returned with three meat pasties. She shut her eyes a second, grateful for the savory meal before her. The aroma of beef, onion, and potato filled the room.

They ate in silence. Lem slopped a slice of bread through the gravy left in his bowl, stuffed the bread into his mouth, and then leaned back in his chair. From his pocket he drew out a coin and flipped it between his fingers. "Look here. A guinea, Mary, for all my troubles today—one guinea."

"'Tis better than nothing at all, Lem."

"I suppose you'll want to feed this girl with it." His eyes drifted over to Sarah and narrowed. She looked away and saw Mary stare at the coin. Lem held it out to Mary, and then dropped it into her hand. She closed her fist over it and tucked it into her bodice.

"Buy something nice with it, Mary, instead of extra food," Lem said. "Sarah will have to do with what we give her. Right, Sarah, my girl?"

She was not *his girl,* and resented him saying so. "I am very grateful, Lem," Sarah told him. "Mary's stew is delicious. I would be thankful for even a bit of bread."

"Good." He cupped his chin in his hand and seemed to study her. Again Sarah felt uneasy. As if he were sizing her up like a piece of merchandise, his eyes roved over her face and down her body. She strove to ignore him.

She set the bowl aside and reached for her bag. "I have something to give you."

His eyes widened. "Oh? What is it?"

"It is all I have of Jamie's. I will keep his Bible. But he would want you to have his pipe and these clothes." She drew them out and handed them to Lem.

Lem looked disappointed. He fingered the clothes, and set the pipe between his teeth. "This pipe is a fine one. Carved ivory. The clothes are good enough—for a net maker."

Ungrateful brute. "Perhaps you could give them to someone in need, if you do not want them, Lem." She then stepped away when Mary motioned to her to follow her out of the room.

Sarah sat at the window in the smallest bedroom in Lem Locke's house. For a long while she gazed at the plain of grass and sand that lead to the precipices above the sea. She heard the gulls crying below her, and the air was filled with the scent of gorse. She missed Jamie and their little cottage. She did not want to be with the Lockes. They had not treated her as she had hoped. But for now, she had to endure living with them until she found a position. She thought of returning to Mercy, but could not bring herself to burden her friend. She had enough mouths to feed and lived in a small house.

In the course of one day, she had become widowed and homeless. Distressed, she turned away from the window and wept. "I must stop this," she said aloud. "I can be stronger."

Without knocking, Mary stepped through the door. "Open the window wider, Sarah, and let the room air out. Nothing is worse for a body than stale air in a room."

Sarah pushed the window open as far as it would go. The wind on her face seemed a caress from the Almighty, soothing her, assuring her all would be made right.

With one movement, Mary swept off the quilt that lay over the bed and handed it to Sarah. "Shake it out over the window. It's dusty."

"This is a fine quilt, Mary. Did you make it?"

"Me? No. I do not like pricking my fingers with needles. Lem bought it for me."

"For a man to purchase a quilt seems unusual." Sarah shook it out the window. A soft veil of dust blew away from it. Then she folded it over her arm, spread it back over the bed, and smoothed it out with her palm. "This is very fine needlework and the color is so rich."

"It is called indigo." Mary smiled proudly. "Lem only gives me quality things. I suppose you think me arrogant to mention my possessions so often. And may even give you cause to envy me."

"No, I am not like that, Mary." Sarah fluffed a pillow and placed it back against the headboard. "I am thankful to sleep under this at night. It is good of you to allow me to. Some people keep their better quilts tucked away."

"Oh, I almost forgot." Mary stepped outside the door and returned with a pail and stiff brush. "It's been a year since this floor was scrubbed. You may see to it."

Forcing a smile, Sarah took the pail and brush from Mary's hands. "It is but a small task to repay your kindness, Mary." Sarah wondered how much longer she could keep up this attitude of appreciation. Mary was making it very hard. She did not mind the chores. She welcomed the distraction they gave. But to be treated like a servant she had not expected.

"We've a little stream behind the house," Mary told her. "It is best to fetch water from there." And with a lift of her head, Mary walked out the door.

Sarah stepped out behind her and paused outside Mary and Lem's bedroom door. Beyond it stood a great carved bed, Eastern rugs, linen curtains, and, upon a dressing table, scent flasks sparkled next to a powder box.

Such fine things were not often seen in such a modest house. But then, Lem was a smuggler and no doubt found the means, either through his purse or through his trade, to set up his wife so well.

"If you would, Sarah, be so kind to do this room as well, I would be most grateful." Groaning, Mary placed her hand against the small of her back. "I have such aches and cannot do it myself."

"I shall try. But if I grow too weary, since I am carrying a baby, Mary, it will have to wait until tomorrow."

Mary widened her eyes. "I hadn't thought of it until now. You are not a burden at all, but a godsend. I shall think of you in that way—until you leave us."

Sarah gripped the handle of the pail tighter. "In what way am I a godsend to you? As a companion or a scullery maid?"

A little laugh slipped from Mary's mouth. "What a silly notion. You know, I have done all the housekeeping on my own. It has worn me down. What I shall do when you leave us, I do not know. Perhaps Lem will change his mind and let me keep you. I will have grown accustomed to your help."

"Lem insists I go. You may have to hire a servant."

"I know, but he, too, will see how well you work and like it. Besides who would hire you in your condition, if you leave us? You best try to endure Lem, be good to him and obedient. In time he will grow used to you."

"And when my child is born? What will happen then?"

"You must find a way to keep the babe quiet when Lem is in the house. You could consider giving the baby away to a good family wishing for a child."

Sarah shook her head. "I could not do that, Mary. This is my child, mine and Jamie's."

Overwhelmed and frustrated, Sarah felt her temples throb. She went down the stairs and out the backdoor. The breeze revived her when she breathed in. The sky turned dark and slate-colored and she could smell rain. Perhaps the clouds would pass and a spangled sky would grace the night.

The stream, narrow enough for one to step across, gurgled. Shoving her hair aside, she dipped the pail into the current and filled it. Trudging back, she heard a man singing and looked up to see Lem walk away from the house. His arms swung at his sides, and the wind blew his coat back.

"*So now I'll sing to you, about a maiden fair,*" he sang, his baritone voice mingling with the sound of the breakers below the cliffs, "*I met the other evening at the corner of the square. She had a dark and roving eye, she was a charming rover, and we rode all night, through the pale moonlight, away down to Lamorna.*"

His poor singing trailed off as he disappeared into the mist that hung above the cliffs. "He is going to the tavern to find a way to rid himself of me. But God shall not forsake me, nor allow me to beg for my bread."

A flutter moved across her belly, and Sarah laid her hand there. She hummed a hymn to her child, the tune giving her comfort. After hauling the pail up the stairs, she got down on her knees and worked the brush across the floorboards with vigor. Her emotions rose with each stroke, first anger, followed by deep sadness, until her eyes stung with tears that fell into the shallow puddles of water.

3

*T*in lamps guided Lem across the field toward the public house. Reaching the pebbled walk, he narrowed his eyes at the figures that moved behind the windows. The words and melody of a sea shanty carried to his ears, and he frowned as he pushed the door in. Tobacco smoke hung in the air. A serving girl stepped by him with mugs of frothy ale in both her hands.

He plopped down in a bench near the fireplace and ordered a pint of stout porter. A fire crackled within the hearth, and the room smelled of burning wood and fish stew. He ran his tongue over his lips when the mug was set down in front of him.

"Fish stew tonight, Lem. Want some?" said the woman serving him. A few flaxen curls slipped out from under her mobcap when she tossed her head back. He did not answer and she shot him an impatient stare. "Well?"

"Go on, Maggie. I want nothing but my drink tonight."

Huffing, she walked away. A man dressed in a caped greatcoat approached his table. "Rumor has it a problem has darkened your doorstep."

Lem gripped the sides of his mug and looked up. "How'd that get around so fast?"

"One of the lads says he saw an auburn-haired girl at your place as he was coming down the road. Pretty lass, he says. He recognized her from Bassetts Cove. Said she lost her husband in the storm."

Lem shrugged. "True enough. But who are you and why should you mention my business to me?"

"My name's Sawyer." The man slid into the bench and leaned his arm upon the table. "I am an office keeper, if you know what I mean."

Lem looked over at Sawyer and narrowed his eyes. "I know what ye are, sir. You take people from this dreaded island to America." He lifted the mug to his lips and drank, then with his sleeve he wiped his mouth. "You kidnap folks, deceive them into thinking they'll find a better life serving some colonial master."

"I wouldn't put it quite that way, Mr. Locke." The man leaned back and drummed his fingers on the edge of the table. "It is like any other business. Smuggling, for example."

Lem laughed. "Except you deal in human beings. I deal in Jamaican rum and French wine. There's a difference."

"But my trade can be more lucrative than yours ever could be. That I know for a fact."

Lem widened his eyes. Money always interested him. "Is that right?"

"It is, sir. Let us say, my captain offers a transportation service when people such as you have an unwelcome person under their roof. We take them to the Colonies, where gentlemen of means pay top prices for a fit servant—especially a young, pretty one."

Lem leaned closer and lowered his voice. "The Colonies? A wretched war is going on over there. Doesn't that prevent you?"

"Not at all. We have ways of unloading our cargo that go unseen. Believe me, business is brisk as it's ever been."

"The girl is carrying a child."

"That makes no difference to me, as long as she is healthy."

"She is, I can promise you that." Lem's eyes roamed around the room then shifted back to Sawyer. He paused a moment in thought, then gulped down his porter. "What do you require?" he said, pushing the empty mug to the edge of the table. "And what's in it for me?"

Sawyer leaned closer. "Well, I know there's a ship coming up the coast laden with rum, china, and silver, and all the casks are watertight. Once it reaches Hell's Mouth, a bonfire will be set up on the bluffs to lure her in. As long as she follows that beacon thinking she's being led into safe waters, that ship is sure to wreck."

Lem's mouth watered and he felt an excited twitch jerk his muscles. "And those casks will wash ashore. You'll be sure to include me in the scavenging?"

"Only if you agree to my terms concerning your *problem*."

Lem swallowed hard. "Well, what are they?"

"Ten pounds and we'll spirit her off."

"Ten? Hmm. Eight and no more."

Sawyer paused a moment, rubbing his chin. "Eight it is. I'll pay a visit to your house tomorrow, late afternoon. Treat me as a guest, so as to make her think I am not to do her harm. Which I shall not do."

"But how, exactly, will you take her off my hands?"

"I will give her a very convincing offer. How can she pass up a position in a fine house with a kind mistress, and a master willing to take her in, even with child?" Sawyer held out his hand and Lem shook it.

⁂

The following afternoon, a carriage rumbled up the lane toward Lem Locke's house. The grating of the wheels drew Sarah to the window. Down the slope it swayed in the distance. The horses' manes whipped back in the wind.

Lem stepped into the room. "One of the gentry is payin' us a call, Mary."

Mary looked up from her box of sweetmeats. "Who, Lem?"

"A gentleman I met last night at the tavern. He is a wealthy man traveling in these parts on business. His name is Sawyer."

"Most likely Mr. Sawyer is visiting family or close acquaintances as well. That is what gentry do. But why would he want to pay us a visit? We are nothing to him."

"He's looking for a serving girl and I told him about Sarah."

Sarah turned swiftly and moved away from the window as a stab of trepidation plunged into her breast. So quick Lem was to be rid of her; she lifted her eyes and met his stare. Her feelings shifted as quickly as a northern gale. She would be glad to leave as long as this gentleman proved a better man, a kinder man, than Lem.

She had changed into a castoff dress Mary had given her— blue-gray with a bit of piping around the bodice, suitable for her station in life. "Should I go to the door, Mary, and let him in?"

Mary stayed her with her hand and locked eyes with Lem. "But, Lem, I need Sarah's help. She's already proven she can keep the house. I hope you will reconsider."

He glared at her. "You're able to take care of the house on your own, you lazy cow. Now tidy up this room before the gentleman comes inside."

A smug look fell over Mary's face. "It is already tidy. If it is not good enough for the gentleman, that is only because he is too haughty."

Sarah looked over at Mary when Lem snarled. Though Mary could fight Lem back with her tongue, she lowered her eyes and bit her lip. Sarah knew she could not abide living with Lem another day, a bully with a temper and a propensity for strong drink. And Mary's selfishness would no doubt grow intolerable.

How could she face having a son or daughter while living with the Lockes? Lem would be a bad influence for a boy, and Mary would require a girl to be a servant, not a niece. Such a shame Jamie hadn't had better judgment in recommending the Lockes.

The clock on the mantelpiece chimed eight just as the horses came to a halt out on the lane in front of the house. Sarah sat down in a chair beneath the window and waited. She decided to hear Mr. Sawyer's proposition, and if it seemed suitable and he a good man, she would agree to his offer.

With a quick step, Lem headed to the front door, and when he came back inside the room, he had Mr. Sawyer beside him. Hat in hand, Sawyer looked smartly dressed in a fine black suit of clothes, almost as smart as a clergyman. Sarah immediately liked him based on his neat appearance. Mary stood, curtsied, and took his hat.

Lem moved closer. "Mr. Sawyer, my wife, Mary."

Sawyer bowed. "Madam."

"And this is Sarah Carr."

Sarah stood and met his eyes.

"She is your daughter, Mr. Locke?" Sawyer's voice was soft and silky, more refined than the Cornish lilt she was accustomed to.

"No, sir. She is the widow of my deceased brother-in-law, God rest his soul. Drowned in the sea. So sad."

Sawyer stepped forward and inclined his head to Sarah. "My sympathies, Mrs. Carr. A great loss I am sure."

She gave him a short curtsey. "Thank you, Mr. Sawyer."

All four found a seat. A frown flashed over Sawyer's face when he noticed her limp. But as quick as it surfaced, the frown vanished, but not before he shot a reproving glance at Lem. After a tense pause, he spoke.

"Mr. Locke and I had a most pleasant conversation last night at the tavern. He tells me you are in need of a position, preferably in a well-situated house."

"It is true, sir," Sarah said. "When my husband died, I was left penniless. I cannot impose on the Lockes any more than I already have."

"You have a good manner about you, Mrs. Carr. Your manner of speech is much more polished than that of most of the women I have heard speak in Cornwall."

Mary spoke up with a tilt of her head. "It is due to her upbringing and education, Mr. Sawyer."

Thankfully, he did not ask from where. A cruel, stout mistress ran the orphanage. One who gorged on the best food while the children ate gruel, stale bread, and stews whose ingredients could not be identified. Whippings were a daily occurrence, lice and fleas a way of life. The basics of reading and how to do figures were the extent of daily lessons. The only education Sarah knew she gained there was how to survive, how to endure. She recalled the books she managed to sneak and read by candlelight while the mistress snored in her bed.

She had never thought her way of speaking would aid her in finding work in a respectable home. But the look on Mr. Sawyer's face told her it was of the utmost importance to him.

"A refined voice is so much more agreeable than a coarse one, to be sure." He nodded to Mary, then looked back at Sarah. "May I call you Sarah?"

She nodded and smiled. "Of course. For it is my name."

Sawyer wiggled his head with a laugh. "Well, Sarah. I would like to engage you if you would agree to the terms of employment."

"I am listening, sir."

"Firstly, I must know your skills, your talents, and your strengths."

"I am good at caring for the sick."

"Well, that is something."

"And I am a good cook, baking mostly."

Mr. Sawyer's brows shot up. "I am exceedingly fond of blueberry cobbler."

"I can do any task required of me, sir, including making cobblers. I have run my own house, though a humble one."

"You would fit right in with my staff. My cook is in need of another pair of hands, and my wife is often sick with headaches and other maladies."

"Your wife, sir. She is poorly?"

"Every so often. Forgive me for asking, but does your abnormality hinder you in any way?"

She lowered her eyes. "Oh, that. It does not, sir. The only exception is if I attempt to run. And I have had little need to." She gave him a small smile.

Mary stepped in. "I am sure Sarah would be grateful for a position, Mr. Sawyer. Not many a house will take on a girl who has a leg like hers."

Sawyer paused, then said, "Is there anything else you should tell me?"

Sarah lowered her eyes thinking of what to say. She could not lie, nor conceal the truth. "I am carrying a child, sir. I will not give him up, if you were to ask me."

"Well, children are welcomed in my household. Please do not think me some pious person, Sarah, that I would reject you on that account. I am as much a sinner as anyone else and am called to good works. When I heard of your situation, my soul was convicted that I must help." He put his hand over his heart. "Are we not taught to take care of the widows and orphans . . . that this is true religion?"

The more Mr. Sawyer revealed himself, the more Sarah liked him. He seemed sincere. Why should she doubt him? He had to be a good man if he was willing to take on a widow with a baby. And she would be paid a wage. She scooted forward in her chair, her hands folded on her lap. "Where is your house, Mr. Sawyer?"

"Near Torquay. A fine area of the country. My wife was born there."

"Have you any children?"

"Unfortunately, we were not so blessed."

"Oh, that is a misfortune, sir." Sarah glanced at Mary, hoping she had heard clearly Mr. Sawyer's use of the word *blessed*. Mary was not moved.

"Indeed it is. However, my dear wife's charity keeps her maternal longings fulfilled. She is one of several benefactors for the needy children in our parish. It gives her great joy."

"Mrs. Sawyer must be a kind and good-natured lady. Unlike those who turn a blind eye to the poor, or think them too inconvenient to give any aid to."

She did not care that Mary coughed and Lem's face stiffened with offense. Sarah hoped perhaps now they would think of how they had treated her. Mr. Sawyer made no immediate reply, but rather shifted in his seat.

"Well, there are many who cannot afford to help. It would cause them to suffer if they did," Mr. Sawyer said. "Your in-laws for example. They haven't the means to support you and a child. I, on the other hand, by giving you a position, am helping myself, and my wife. You need a wage and we need the help."

Sarah frowned in thought. "But who shall look after my child when I am working, sir?"

"Oh, you needn't worry about that. We shall place you in the kitchen. There you can keep an eye on the child."

"Forgive me for being so bold, Mr. Sawyer. But it sounds too good to be true."

"Ours is a Christian household, Sarah. You should expect no less."

"Will I be required to work on Sundays?"

"Certainly not. You may attend church with the other servants. However, I am told some may be going to a field meeting next week to hear Mr. Wesley preach. He is controversial, but I hear his oratory is moving."

A thrill rose in Sarah. "I should like that, sir. Last year, I was saved by Mr. Wesley's teaching and should be happy to hear him preach again."

Lem huffed. "Well, you shan't get that kind of religion around here, Sarah. You had best accept Mr. Sawyer's offer."

Sarah met Sawyer's eager eyes and nodded. "I would be pleased to be in your employ, sir."

Sawyer slapped his hands on his knees. "Well then, it is settled. Pack your belongings, Sarah. I head for home tonight."

She stood and walked over to Mary, who sat quiet and accepting. "Mary? Do you think I should go?"

"We certainly cannot provide what Mr. and Mrs. Sawyer can," said Mary.

A worrisome feeling swept through Sarah. She hoped she was making the right decision. Leaving, traveling south with a perfect stranger, alone in his carriage, caused her some uneasiness. But what choice did she have? Lem had made his will clear. She could not stay.

Saddened that her late husband's family had rejected her, Sarah headed upstairs to gather her meager belongings. As she folded her spare dress and tucked it inside her bag, she felt some relief that the Sawyers would provide her with new clothes. And with the way Mr. Sawyer described his household, perhaps she would find a new family among the staff. She had heard that was the way among people who worked and worshiped together. She would find unity and kindness in Torquay.

As she cinched the sack closed, she smiled and thought of her unborn child. "Thank you, Lord God, for providing for us. My child shall live in a fine house and shall never go hungry."

Downstairs, she leaned over to kiss Mary's cheek, but her sister-in-law remained rigid and cold, showing no emotion at all. Mary stood, placed her hands on Sarah's shoulders, and turned her toward the front door.

"I shall write to you, Mary." Sarah stepped out into the misty gloom where the moon rode high in the night sky.

Mr. Sawyer held out his hand. "We head for the harbor, Sarah, where we shall take a ship 'round the coast. It is much faster than going overland, and easier on the body."

A bundle of nerves, Sarah climbed in. She could not determine whether what she felt came from fear or excitement. But her hopes were high that this opportunity meant redemption. Once seated with her bundle on her lap, she looked out the window and saw the Lockes' front door close. They were glad to be rid of her, Sarah knew, and she wished never to see them again.

She drew her shoulders back against the seat. "I am most grateful to you, Mr. Sawyer. If it were not for you and your wife, I would be destitute."

He set his tricorn hat on the seat next to him. "That is easy to tell."

"I promise I shall work hard for you and Mrs. Sawyer. And my baby shall be no problem to either of you."

"Do not worry about that. As I expressed before, we value children. More often than not, they are worth their weight in gold."

He leaned his head back and closed his eyes. Sarah felt happy as she gazed out the window at the moon.

4

A blustery wind beat over the cliffs and across the moors as the carriage traveled the last few miles to Hayle Harbor. The horses struggled against the gusts. Their manes whipped back and they neighed. Mr. Sawyer snored, while Sarah kept her eyes on the scene outside the window. A blackened landscape passed by swiftly. Patches of moonlight streamed down from the night clouds and illumined the gorse grass and fields.

She could not help but recall the times she and Jamie lay in each other's arms and stared up at a starry sky. Her heart ached thinking of him, regretting he had not loved her with the passion she had longed for. But his care of her had made up for that in numerous ways. He was gone now, and she was about to step into a new season in her life. Her hopes were high, and the burden of poverty lifted from her shoulders.

The rattle of the carriage, the wheels spinning over the sandy road, seemed endless, until the horses slowed and drew to a halt, and the din of the sea overtook the quiet. The carriage door swung open.

"Mr. Sawyer, sir." She leaned toward him. "We are here."

He stirred. His eyes opened and he picked up his hat and jammed it on his head. Out he climbed, and then called to her to follow. When she stepped out, the first thing Sarah saw was the moonlight dancing over the water, turning the golden sand amber. Out in the sea stood a ship. Brass lanterns blinked from its decks and the gentle peal of a bell marked the hour.

She drew her cloak closer against the chill of the wind. Now six months into her time, she felt her baby move and laid her hand over her belly, feeling through her clothes the imprint of a tiny foot. She smiled, and love swelled inside her. Life would be good for her little one.

Bobbing over the waves a skiff drew away from the merchantman's hull. "The *Reef Raider* is sure to be full of passengers tonight, Sarah," Sawyer remarked. "You are not afraid to sleep among servants, are you?"

"As long as I am placed with women only, sir."

"And so you shall be. There is a boat to take us over." He stepped away, trudging across the sand to the surf where the skiff slid in. The sailors all pulled off their caps and greeted them warmly.

Helped aboard, Sarah sat in the rear. She clutched her bundle and glanced back at the misty shore. Mr. Sawyer sat forward, and the sailors pushed the skiff into the waves, jumped in, and grabbed the oars. The vessel shot off like a dolphin cutting through the waves and Sarah shivered with the excitement it gave her. She scanned the shoreline and moved her eyes up to the heights of the bluffs. A lonely feeling filled her as she let herself imagine she would never see this part of England again, or her village, or ever visit Jamie's grave. She was going away for good.

Coming alongside in the skiff, she gazed up at the ship and felt swallowed by its massive size and the dark shadow it cast. On deck, seamen rushed about, making ready to sail. Canvas tumbled down and swelled in the sea wind. Mr. Sawyer walked ahead and stopped a sailor. He leaned nearer, spoke to him, and looked back at Sarah. The sailor nodded, stepped away from Sawyer, and approached her.

"Welcome aboard the *Reef Raider*, miss." He bowed short. "I'll take you down to your accommodations, if you would follow me."

She looked over at Mr. Sawyer and caught his eyes. "It is fine, Sarah," he said. "Go with him."

And so, desiring to please her employer, she hastened away with a lift of her skirts. She looked back over her shoulder as they approached the sterncastle door. Sawyer had disappeared. She followed the sailor down a set of stairs. He took out a large ring of keys and unlocked a door, pushed it open, and motioned for her to enter.

A polished brass lantern swung from the ceiling and dimly lit the room. All of her hopes sank when her eyes fastened on a wretched group of women huddled together in a corner. Each face glistened with sweat; their eyes were hollow and frightened. A chill ran up Sarah's spine and the hairs on the back of her neck stiffened. A cold sweat broke out over her body and she turned to see the sailor shut the door. Then, even more chilling, the key turned in the lock. She rushed to the door, tried the handle, and then pounded on it with her fist.

"It will do you no good." From the darkened corner, a woman moved forward and spoke to Sarah in a low, hoarse voice. Her hair hung about her face in thin, greasy strands, and her gaze was one of hopelessness.

"He locked us in. Why would he do that?" Sarah's voice trembled with panic. "Are we in some kind of danger and need to be protected? Please tell me that is what it is." She pressed her hand against her pounding heart, and with the other gripped her bag tight.

The woman stood, her knees buckling beneath her. "Danger, yes—because we've been kidnapped. Don't you see?"

Fearing it to be true, Sarah shook her head. "No, that cannot be. I am Mr. Sawyer's servant. We are sailing to Torquay. I have not been kidnapped."

The woman looked at her with pity. "I did not think so either."

"I do not belong here. There's been a mistake."

At that point, all the women stood, and the first put her hand on Sarah's arm. "You have been lied to. We are headed for the Colonies—maybe Barbados, the Carolinas, or the Chesapeake."

Sarah turned toward the door. "I will speak to the captain and demand he let us go. Who spirited you away? Do you know his name?"

"Sawyer. He's the one."

"Sawyer!" Shock coursed through Sarah's mind. How could he have lied to her, deceived her? Could it be true she had been hoodwinked? Had Lem and Mary known Sawyer's true identity? Had they schemed with him to get rid of her? She could believe it about Lem, but not Mary. No. She would never stoop to so heartless a crime. But then, she did not know her sister-in-law well enough to be certain.

Again, she pounded on the door until the key finally turned and it opened. "What is the problem, miss? Stop that noise at once," growled the guard. "You'll give the captain a headache and then he'll be angry as a typhoon."

She stomped her foot. "I demand to see him."

"He's busy and won't waste his time."

"Either bring Mr. Sawyer here immediately, or take me to him. Perhaps then the captain will see fit to involve himself. It is a horrible thing Mr. Sawyer has done to these women."

"Oh, is that what they told you?"

"Yes. I am his servant. He will speak to me."

The sailor stared at her a moment, then burst into laughter. "Well then, go on up. Find Mr. Sawyer. This should entertain the men."

Tossing back her hair, Sarah set her bag down, squeezed past the seaman, and hurried topside. Her eyes darted among the crew for a glimpse of Sawyer, and when he was nowhere to be seen, she hurried to the side of the ship and looked out into the water. Her heart plunged to the depths to see the skiff cutting away with Mr. Sawyer in it. She gripped the rail and a moan clawed up her throat. "Come back!" she shouted.

He turned to see her, grinned, and lifted his tricorn hat in farewell. Hands pulled her away. "He has no reason to come back, lass."

"But he is to take me to Torquay. I am to serve him and his wife on his estate." She realized how naive she sounded, but she could not accept she had been spirited away. She had only heard of such horrors, where men, women, and children are dragged from their homes, from the streets, and held captive in caves along the coast. Then they are taken aboard ships that carried them off to be indentured in the Colonies.

"Was he called back? Am I to go on to Torquay without him?" she asked, hungry for an answer. She stared at the men who gathered around her, watched in dismay as their mouths lifted into grins and their eyes flashed with amusement.

The seaman-guard laughed. "Torquay? His story gets better and better."

Then the jests began. "That red hair of hers is a sure sign of trouble. Better get her below in a hurry."

"Aye, and I pity the landowner that buys her. She's got a temper."

"Get back, lads. She's likely to scratch your eyes out."

Then a sailor with leathery features and a pocked nose stepped forward. His hair hung to his shoulders, and he had a look of sympathy in his eyes as the lantern light fell over his face. "Pity the poor lass. Just look at her. Sawyer said she's with child, and can't walk too well. Hold your tongues—say nothing against her."

One man folded his arms and stared at her. "Hmm. They'll pay less for a wench like that—a cripple."

Sarah hung her head. "Please. I am not meant for the Colonies." Then she lifted her eyes. "Is there not a man among you who would take me back, and the other women too? Are you so without feeling that your hearts do not convict you?"

"No," said the sailor guarding her. "You're to sail to the Colonies like the rest of the gutter rats below."

She trembled as if a blast of artic wind had shoved her. Her eyes pooled. She looked at their faces, scarred and rough. "Please, take me ashore," she pleaded. "I was brought here against my will. That man Sawyer deceived me. I cannot make the journey. Have pity on my poor babe."

"Pity indeed, for your indenture will be longer than most for bringing a child into the world." The more compassionate sailor stepped forward and held his hand out to her to take. "Make it easy on yourself and do as you are told. We'll be sure you have good treatment. We aren't so heartless to neglect a woman with child."

"What is that woman doing on deck, Mr. Smith?" boomed a voice.

Her jailer jerked his head. "Just getting her below, Captain."

"See that you do. And do not let it happen again."

The wind blew Sarah's hair into her eyes. With her hand shaking, she pushed it back and looked up to see the captain standing on the quarterdeck. He looked to be a man in his forties—his face profoundly lined and tanned, his eyes piercing and cruel. Looking into them, she dared to speak up. "I have been taken against my will, Captain. Please, have your men take me back ashore."

"And what will you pay for this?"

Sarah hesitated, but kept her eyes upon him. "I have no money, sir."

He sneered down at her. Then turned away.

5

The cabin where the women were held captive contained canvas cots, blankets, one bucket for a chamber pot, and a clay pitcher for water.

"Count your blessings, ladies," Sarah's keeper had said. "We've set you apart 'cause you shouldn't be with the male cargo. With your good looks, they'd spoil you. And don't complain about your cots. At least you have something to sleep on other than the floor, unlike the poor souls kept below deck."

His words caused her to shiver. But she knew it was true—she sat among the fortunate few. They had stern windows and the brisk sea air blew through them. It brushed over her, and Sarah put her face in her hands and cried. No one spoke. But sympathetic eyes were locked upon her, and she could hear some of the women weeping along with her.

A pair of arms went around her shoulders, and she looked into the face of a woman several years her elder, the first to speak to her of her plight. "You have your cry. We will all stick by you," she said, her dirty brown hair falling over her neck. "My name is Jane Drey. This is Wenna, Genna, Ebrel, and Selma."

"Sarah Carr," she said, wiping her eyes dry.

She glanced over at Wenna curled up in a corner. Signs of trauma marred her youthful face. Her locks fell over her eyes, which were large and on the brink of tears. The other women were equally frightened. Not a word passed their lips, forced into silence by what had befallen them.

"We were tricked, like you," Jane said. "I was told I would be sailing to London to serve as a lady's maid in a lord's house. I was happy for it at my age. I thought I would never be hungry again. But I was too trusting."

Her hands shaking, Sarah looked at Jane. "I tried to make them set me ashore, but they would not listen. The captain turned his back on me."

"No words will convince them to do anything for us. It is money they want. Money none of us have. We are worth more to them sold than a clear conscience." Sarah noticed the dark rings beneath Jane's eyes, from hunger, from the tension of her torment.

Sarah set her teeth. "I will not accept that my destiny is in their vile hands."

"It never shall be, for it is in God's hands alone."

"He will help me, of this I am convinced. I do not believe this is His will."

"There's nothing you can do. Nothing any of us can do."

"I will resist. I have to."

"And how will you do that when your belly is aching with hunger and they abuse you?"

Sarah knit her brows. "Surely they will not treat us that way. We are women."

"It matters not who we are. We are nothing more than chattel."

Jane's dark words cut into Sarah, and she stood. The other women stared at her, stunned by the reality of their terrible ordeal and by her boldness. "When we reach the Colonies, I will tell the authorities we were kidnapped. I will demand they release us."

Looking as if they did not hear Sarah, the women turned their eyes away. Wenna stared hopelessly into the gloom. "When we stand on the slave docks, hundreds of men's eyes will roam over us," she said listlessly. "They will think how they can use us."

"Do not dwell on it, Wenna," Jane urged.

Wenna jerked her eyes back at Sarah. "The worse is to come when we are put to work in the fields and forced into our masters' beds. I have heard of what happens, how women are beaten and raped by the planters."

"Surly there are good people there," Sarah said. "Ministers and physicians who will do well by us, and genteel ladies who will be kind."

Wenna laughed. "Have you forgotten? People grow weak and sick in body and mind when mistreated, torn from their loved ones, their homeland. I am only sixteen and chaste. People do not last long as indentured servants, especially women."

Compassion moved within Sarah. In such a short time, Wenna had succumbed to despair. She went to her, and forgetting her own plight for the moment, she sat beside the poor girl. "They will free us and hang these men."

"I tried to fight back. That is how I acquired these." Wenna moved the edge of her tattered dress to reveal a row of bruises.

Sarah touched the girl's cheek. "How could they have treated you so cruelly?"

Wenna's eyes glistened with tears. "What would we do even if freed? Starve?"

Sarah knew what it felt like to be hungry. But to starve? That was something she had not known, and it frightened her to even imagine it. She needed food and clean water, not for herself alone, but for her babe. She felt him flutter inside her, and her heart swelled with worry for him. She would do all she could to protect the innocent life growing within her. How far her protection would go, she had no way of knowing.

She picked up Wenna's hand and squeezed it. "We would find a way home."

"How? We will be forced to indenture ourselves in order to come back to England. There is war there, and savages, and things we cannot imagine."

"Yes, there is a war. And we shall be able, no doubt, to tell an officer we are Englishwomen taken by force. Surely they will help us."

Jane drew next to the pair. "You are with child, Sarah. Life will be hard for him. I shall pray some benevolent person takes pity on you."

Had they not heard a single word she had spoken? They had given in to their situation as easily as birds caught in a snare and caged. "I will not need it," she said. "I will find a way to free myself and safeguard my child. With God's help, I will."

The window banged against the cabin wall, and gusts of endless wind rushed inside. Thunder rolled above the sea and flashes of lightning crossed the sky. Sarah threw her hand over the latch and pulled until the window closed. She stared out at the waves. They mounted with foam, whirled into depths unimaginable.

"Have we anything to eat?" She looked around the cabin.

"A little bread." Jane reached for it and handed it to Sarah.

She sat down on the floor and the others joined her. Wenna being the last crawled from her shadowy nook. They huddled close, their arms linking, their heads resting on one another's shoulders. Sarah broke the bread into six pieces and placed one into each palm. A jug of water sat beside them. Jane pulled the cork and set it in the center.

The ship heaved and thunder rattled the timbers. Frightened by the power of the storm and sea, they bowed their heads and wept together, each whispering a prayer. "Help us, Lord. Save us, Almighty God."

They ate their bread and drank from the jug. Lightning brightened the cabin, and Sarah saw their faces illumined, the lines of despair, the closed eyes and bent bodies, wherein lay broken hearts.

$\mathscr{L}$

They had been weeks at sea. Wind seeped through the lattice windows without a stop. Dry biscuits, water, and a mashed vegetable were given the women once a day, and Sarah grew weak and lost weight. She worried about her baby.

On the twentieth day out to sea, the sky thickened with slate-colored clouds and the wind blew bitterly cold. Rain fell and icy droplets tapped on the windows of the cabin. By nightfall the storm calmed, but the waves were still rough. Upon their cots, the women slept curled up in their blankets—all except Sarah. Her babe moved within her as restless as the sea, and she was unable to get warm.

"My poor babe. Have mercy, Lord," she whispered into the darkness, feeling lonely and hungry, shivering with cold. Her mouth grew so dry she could barely speak. Nausea gripped her empty belly.

As if a leviathan had swum beneath the ship and pushed it above the sea, the *Reef Raider* rose and pitched. Its timbers groaned, and the constant rise and fall worsened Sarah's sickness. She twisted on the cot, and then pains gripped her middle with such violence that she cried out. Jane hurried to her side.

"Hold on to me," she said, grasping Sarah's hand.

Sarah sat up. She felt something warm and wet gush from her body. She drew her clothes above her knees. Tears flooded her eyes when she looked down and saw water and blood. Waves of cramps followed and she pulled Jane's hand closer and squeezed her fingers as tightly as she could. She was dizzy with pain, and her heart pounded in rhythm with the beating of the waves that crashed against the ship's hull.

"You are losing your baby," Jane whispered. "You must not be afraid. I will help you."

As if stones had been piled against her chest, Sarah struggled to breathe. "I cannot lose my child. I cannot," she groaned. Her throat tightened as tears slipped down her cheeks.

"Sarah. There is a reason, and you have to let go."

"You will not leave my side, Jane?"

"Not for a moment."

Another wave of pain shook Sarah's body. "Oh, God . . . I pray you spare my babe. But if not, take this child into your arms, into your glory."

Jane brushed back Sarah's hair. Wenna sat in her corner, her legs drawn up to her chest, her head resting on her knees. The other women gathered beside the cot. Sarah knew they wanted to comfort her, but their despair enslaved their tongues and stilled their hands.

A moment later, Sarah's baby came into the world, small and still—without a sound, without a whimper.

"Do not look, Sarah. It should not be the memory you carry all your life." Jane tore a bit of her petticoat and wrapped the child in it. "'Twas a boy."

"A son," Sarah sighed, and laid her head back. "My poor boy."

"He will not suffer in this life," Jane said. "He is with God."

Jane's words did not comfort Sarah. She knew he was gone, but she questioned why. Brokenhearted, she watched Jane trudge to the window. "No, Jane. Let me hold him."

Jane shook her head. "If you do, your heart will only break the more and you will not want to let go of him." She went to the window, opened it, and let the bundle drop into the sea. "Forgive me, Sarah. 'Tis harsh, I know. But it had to be done."

Jane helped Sarah wash the grime from her legs, then wrapped her in a blanket. Sarah cried a long while, quietly with opened eyes.

"I am sorry for you, Sarah," Jane told her.

"Have you children?"

"Eight in all. I lost three like this, and two as babes."

"Where are the others?"

"My son left home at fifteen and joined the King's Navy. That was many years ago. He never returned. Two daughters went into service. My husband died five years ago, and I have been poor ever since. So you can see why I wanted to believe Mr. Sawyer. He gave me hope."

"False hope. And now he has caused me to lose my child."

"That you cannot be certain of. But there is hope beyond this life that justice will be done."

"You said before my babe's life would be hard in the Colonies. There is no more worry for that now." Sarah breathed heavily between her sobs. "At least I know he will not have suffered. He is with his father, Jamie." She turned to Jane. "Still I shall give him a name, so he will not be forgotten."

"What name is that Sarah?"

"Bartholomew."

"Your father's name?"

"I had no father. I heard a minister once say in Bible times the name 'Bartholomew' meant *a son who suspends the waters*."

Yet, this did not console Sarah for long. She turned her face to the wall and wept silently.

My child is gone.

By midnight, the clouds broke away as the ship plunged through choppy waves. A full moon conquered the night sky. Sarah woke and brushed aside her hair. Her body felt empty. She had no other ailments, no fever, no bleeding, and thanked God. He had enabled her to get through the miscarriage. But she pleaded for him to soothe her grief.

Blue moonlight slipped through the windows and she watched it play with the shadows. Wenna stepped onto the beams, her feet bare. She moved toward the windows and gathered her dress in her hands. Then she knelt upon the coarse wooden window seat, released the latch, and pushed the window open. Cold wind rushed inside and smelled of brine.

Lifting her dress above her knees, Wenna climbed the seat and braced her hands against the window jamb—her hair whipping back, her face vacant and bathed in gray moonlight.

"Wenna, come away," Sarah called, worried at what she might do. "Jane, Jane! Look! Wenna!"

Jane scrambled from her cot and tried to reach the girl. But before her hands could pull her back, Wenna flung herself from the window and fell headlong into the sea.

Horror raced over Sarah. She crawled from the cot, staggered to the window, and stood beside Jane. She leaned out. Shocked, she gasped for air. "Wenna!" The wind pushed her back. The icy spray of the ocean hit the hull and smacked her face. Wenna was nowhere to be seen among the dark waves. She hurried to the door and pounded on it. "Help! Open up!"

The key rattled in the lock. "What is it, woman? It's the middle of the night."

Sarah pointed to the window. "One of us has . . ."

The seaman looked past her as the others gathered around. "She jumped, did she? Ah, that's too bad." He went to close the door.

Sarah snatched his sleeve. "You must tell the captain. Turn the ship around and look for her."

"Yes, look for her before it is too late," cried Jane.

He shrugged. "Those waves swallowed her and she's gone. She made her choice. You all best try to put her out of your mind."

"She might have slipped over," said Genna, her voice stern.

Ebrel wrung her hands. "And may still be out there."

Selma burst into tears. "Oh, poor Wenna."

He rolled his eyes. "That is extremely unlikely. But I'll tell the captain." As he closed the door, Sarah heard him mutter, "What a loss. Fifty pounds gone just like that."

The clatter of the key in the lock rattled Sarah to her bones. She turned to the others, their eyes wide and teary as they huddled together. She pressed her fist against her heart, and staring at the floor murmured, "God help us. Fifty. . . . Fifty pounds."

6

*L*ate November in 1778 was a bitter prelude to the first harsh days of winter. As the sorry cargo of captives approached the Atlantic shores of America, blue skies ruled the day with frigid temperatures. The season of Advent had arrived and the sky had turned white as frost, with a low wind blowing, and by twilight snow began to fall. It caked the stern windows of the cabin, and with nothing but their clothes and a blanket, the women knotted together to stay warm.

Sarah drew her cloak tight. She felt the heave of the ship. Her breath escaped her lips in a vapor. The familiar sound of the key unlocking the door did not stir her, but she stared at it just the same and watched the door drift inward. They named the sailor who had been assigned to them Footman John, for he was in every sense their servant and their jailer. He brought in the day's meal, a jug of fresh water, and five apples he had snuck from the ship's larder.

"'Tis Advent, ladies. My gift to ya," he said, handing them out.

Sarah bit into hers. It tasted sweeter than honey, the juice filling her mouth. "Where are we now, Footman John?" she asked, swallowing down the chewed bits.

"Near the mouth of the Chesapeake. We'll sail in at nightfall, so as not to be seen. There'll be no ship's lanterns burning tonight."

"You have been here before?"

"A dozen times."

Sarah pushed her dirty hair back from her forehead. "Why is the captain waiting until nightfall? Why doesn't he take us in now and be done with us? Isn't he anxious to sell his cargo and fill his purse with gold?"

Footman John shook his head. "Aye, I suppose he is. And the men are anxious to set ashore. We don't want any trouble with rebels or even the King's Navy. So we'll wait. And we don't want any trouble with landlubbers either, like those Quaker folk, over the selling of persons. 'Tis best to make the sale in secret and in the dark."

Sarah could not conceive this manner of thinking. "It is clear the captain is a coward."

A corner of Footman John's mouth curved. "Did you not say at the start of this voyage you'd tell an officer you'd been taken against your will? Our captain knows what you said and is cunning enough to outsmart a woman." He set the water jug on the floor.

Sarah raised her chin. "I suppose we should say good-bye, then."

Footman John shrugged. "I suppose. Good-bye, ladies."

Before he closed the door, he looked back at Sarah. After all this time a glimmer of sympathy surfaced in his eyes. "I wish you well, miss. I wish all you ladies good fortune."

After Footman John had gone, Sarah made her way to the window seat. She watched the light die from the rim of the sea and the waters deepen to murky green. Soon the sky turned black as ink, studded with countless stars that in the night so frigid they seemed like droplets of ice. A bright half-moon hung along the horizon where, across the bay, a thin line of land appeared black and ominous.

When led out of the cabin for the first time since leaving England, Sarah stood next to Jane and the others under an open sky. She missed Jamie, and thought of her baby, and how life could have been if Jamie had lived. She shivered and drew the fresh air deep into her lungs. Gazing up at the stars she felt her heart tremble. Awestruck, she traced their patterns with her eyes.

She felt small looking up at the night sky. God named each star, each constellation. The name *Sarah* had been given to her by the patrons of the orphanage. It meant "princess," and she laughed inwardly at the irony. A princess dressed in rags, her hair and body unwashed, with one leg a bit shorter than the other—to be auctioned off, indentured, and owned.

Each woman was lowered down to a boat of two oarsmen. Sarah was last. The women were warned to be still and silent as the skiff pulled away. The air here smelled different, a mix of sea and fresh water, marsh, and forest. She tried to make out the shoreline. A deeper black than the night, a seam emerged along the horizon, and a lantern brightened then waned upon it.

She lowered her hand over the side and let the water ripple over her fingers. It felt icy and numbed her skin. She thought of Wenna and how sad it was she gave in to despair, that the sea must have felt even colder than the Chesapeake, deeper and more solitary.

Shaking free the image and the sorrow it brought to her, she snatched in a breath and squared her shoulders. She would bravely face whatever lay ahead, and stand up to the hardship of it all, the debasement, and the shame. Somehow, she would rise out of this situation and be free again.

The skiff came to an easy halt and the women were handed out. The gray, weather-beaten wharf scratched at the thin soles of Sarah's shoes as she struggled to walk and regain her land legs. Her gait, hampered by her impediment and the long voyage, slowed. A sailor clapped his hand over her shoulder from behind and grunted.

"Too slow. Move quicker." And he shoved her forward.

A man carrying a torch guided the women over a path of sand and dirt. As they drew closer to what appeared to be a barn, Sarah made out the horses and wagons hitched outside it. She lowered her eyes so not to catch the stares of the men hanging about the entrance. As she stepped through, a pungent odor struck her. Thick bundles of golden tobacco leaves hung along rafters and below them lanterns on pegs were fastened to beams.

She and her companions clung to each other. Genna, Ebrel, and Selma silently wept, but Sarah and Jane fought back their tears. Heads turned in unison to study them—eyes roved over their faces and bodies as if they were examining cattle or thoroughbreds. Whispers and jeers scored Sarah's ears, and when one man reached out and stroked her arm, she quickly shrunk back.

Over on the far side behind a platform, men in ragged, dirty clothes were led out a rear door. These were the *cargo* kept belowdecks.

"They kept us for last," she whispered to Jane.

Led to the platform, the women stood side by side and faced the bidders. Their cords were cut loose, and they were told to stand straight and lift their eyes. Gathering her courage, Sarah approached the auctioneer. "I demand to speak to one in authority. We were taken against our will."

"Is that so?" He smelled of tobacco and rum.

"It is." She set her hands on her hips.

"You have to work off your transport. Do you think you would have been fed for nothing?"

"I'll not pay a thing. Is there a constable or a British officer here?"

The auctioneer sneered. "Get back in line." He grabbed her arm and set her back. "Speak to the gentleman that buys you, girl. It will be up to him what to do with you."

Shocked by the man's harsh reply, his cruel eyes, and his violent tone, she fell back.

"Who will start the bidding? Fifty. Do I hear fifty pounds?" cried the auctioneer. "Fifty pounds, sold!" And Ebrel was taken away.

Selma—eyes lowered, her hair braided over her shoulder, stood forward when he grabbed her arm. "Fifty, gentlemen?"

"Forty."

"Fifty and no less, sir."

"She is very thin. She won't be much good in the fields."

"Then who will buy her to work in your lady's house? Forty-five? Do I hear forty-five? Sold!" Selma whimpered and her owner swung her down and led her away.

"Such a comely face, this one, gentlemen. And she is a little stouter than the others. She will also do well as a lady's maid or a cook. Can you cook and sew, girl?" Genna nodded and blinked her watery eyes. "Fifty-five for this one since she can cook and do your mending. Sold!"

Jane came next. She stepped forward with her chin held high, her arms at her side, but her hands in fists. "Fifty? Do I hear a bid of fifty?" No answer, for she was older than the rest. "She is strong, gentlemen." The auctioneer lifted her arm, and Jane drew it sharply away.

"Stronger than you," she said.

The crowd laughed and a man in a black tricorn hat and greatcoat stepped forward. He drew off his hat and paused to study her. He appeared to be of the same age, and his eyes looked upon her kindly. Sarah could not miss the look that shadowed Jane, as if a bond sparked between her and the man.

"I'll take her for fifty. I have no wife and certainly could use one." With a sweep of his hat across his chest and a low bow, he said, "That is, if you will have me, madam."

Jane crossed her arms and stared hard. "Have I any choice?"

"You can reject me and have another bid for you. But I like your look, and I have a good farm and money in my pocket. You will not be a slave to me, but a helpmeet."

"Children?"

"Grown."

Someone in the crowd shouted, "Why not the younger, Samuel?"

Samuel turned. "And deal with the temperament of youth? No, this lady is of an age where she is wiser and settled."

"And more experienced, too." Laughter whipped around the room.

The auctioneer stepped to the edge of the platform. "This isn't a matchmaking holiday, sir, but an auction for slaves."

"What difference does it make to you," Samuel balked, "as long as I have the money to pay?"

"Accept him, Jane," Sarah whispered behind her. She believed the man to be sincere. Jane turned to look back at her, and they spoke their good-byes with their eyes. The man held out his hand and Jane took it. Strange as it seemed, a few in the crowd cheered. Then came her turn. She wondered if some man would want her for a wife, instead of a workhorse.

The auctioneer took Sarah by the arm and moved her to the edge of the platform. "Now, gentlemen. I have saved her for last, for she is the prettiest of the lot. Just look at this slender figure and these bright eyes. She is well worth sixty pounds. Do I hear sixty?"

"Sixty is outrageous for a woman," a man cried from the middle of the throng.

"Not if she is a willing female," one shouted. The men laughed once again.

"She will make a fine house servant."

"A beauty yes, but crippled. I wager she cannot walk a straight line."

The auctioneer leaned close to her ear. "Walk, girl. And be sure it is straight or I will have your hide for it."

Sarah narrowed her eyes and pressed her lips together hard. She would show him. She would show them all. Lifting her skirts just above her feet, she walked about the platform, slowly and carefully planting one foot in front of the other. She wished she could have jumped from the platform and sprinted down the aisle.

"There you see, gentlemen. A slight limp, but that is nothing. She is very fit, and pretty too. Just look at this hair. Does it not make up for her little flaw?"

She cringed as he lifted a few tendrils between his fingers and moved them in front of her shoulder. Her hair had been her pride, long russet twists that were soft as silk threads. Jamie had loved her locks and it had only been his hands that had moved through them. The auctioneer's fingers were dirty, coarse, and she turned her head to the side hoping he would stop.

"She would do well as a lady's maid—or a wife or mistress."

She took a step back. "I shall be no man's mistress."

"Be quiet," the auctioneer said.

Sarah felt her cheeks burn. The auctioneer's suggestions caused the men to rivet their eyes upon her. They knew nothing of her—that she had been a wife and a hopeful mother-to-be. She lost her husband, then her unborn child. They had no idea, nor did they care, about the depth of grief that pounded in her heart and the utter humiliation she felt standing before them. Was there not one godly man among them to pity her?

Then a round of bids began as if a dam had broken loose. Through the smoky haze stepped an older man in a flop hat and gray greatcoat. Of medium height, he made his way forward and stood at the base of the platform looking up at her. Their eyes met, and he stared into hers as if he were trying to sort her out. His bushy brows arched and he nodded his head to the auctioneer.

"I will pay sixty pounds for the girl—a lady's maid for my wife, Mrs. Temperance Woodhouse."

Silence followed, and then the gavel fell and she was led from the platform and placed in front of the man. He looked her over and she felt the heat deepen in her cheeks. "You look half-starved, and sadly in need of a bath. What's your name, girl?"

"Sarah Carr, sir."

"Well, Sarah. When we reach my house, my wife will insist you wash first. Then you may eat, and put some weight on those bones. Those rags will have to be burned."

"But . . . I have nothing else," she told him meekly.

"Not to worry. Temperance shall give you one of her old dresses."

Sarah opened her mouth to say more, but the words did not come. She followed Mr. Woodhouse through the crowd, and after he had signed for her and accepted his bill of sale, she found herself seated in a small boat beneath a starry sky, headed across the mouth of the Potomac toward Virginia.

Part 2

The LORD is nigh unto them that are of a broken heart;
and saveth such as be of a contrite spirit.

Psalm 34:18

7

Winter 1779

"Sarah, I have need of you," Temperance Woodhouse called from across the hall. Whenever she summoned Sarah, her voice rang out in the most urgent tone possible. Sarah had grown accustomed to it, knowing not a day would go by without her mistress fretting over something or other.

She had neglected her work for a moment's pause at the large French windows in the spare bedroom. The breeze blew inland from the Chesapeake, up the Potomac, and across the lush fields dotted with trees. She leaned against the jamb, her green eyes fixed on the sunlit fields beyond. Her hair hung loose without a ribbon or pin and tumbled down the back of her homespun dress. Her breath came fast as she longed to walk free through the grass. That time could not come fast enough for her.

Mrs. Woodhouse had been kind to Sarah. Mr. Woodhouse for the most part avoided her. She had caught him staring at her on more than one occasion, but each time he quickly shifted his eyes away.

The Revolution had not touched their little place in the world, but it saddened Sarah when she heard the Iroquois had massacred forty people in Cherry Valley, New York, in November. By the end of December, the British occupied Savannah, and she wondered if they would come this far. If they did, would they believe her story? Would they free her?

"Sarah, did you hear me?" called Temperance.

"Coming, ma'am." She moved aside the stack of linen she had finished folding, and stepped into Temperance's room. Bright with sunshine, the yellow walls paled, and the empty glass vase beneath the window sparkled. A full-length mirror stood next to it, and Sarah saw her reflection in it. Her cheeks were full, her waist slim. The food supplied to her filled her out and her health was vigorous.

With a light smile, Temperance glanced up from her writing the moment Sarah stepped inside the room. Upon the mahogany desk sat an inkwell made of blue glass and a blotter. At the windowsill, she kept her small lady's Bible, a book of hymns, and the Book of Common Prayer, in a neat stack.

Everything in the sparse room had its proper place, and when Sarah noticed the hymnal was crooked on the stack, she adjusted it with a pat of her hands. The Bible, which Mr. Woodhouse had given to his wife years ago on her thirtieth birthday, a milestone for most women, sat atop it. The hymnal had frayed edges from daily use, for Temperance loved to sing at eventide.

Sarah picked up the Book of Common Prayer, recalling it from her childhood, when the orphans would walk to service, rain or shine, and sit in the cold stone chapel. She flipped the cover open and read the line at the top of the page. *The Calendar, with the Table of Lessons*. Such restrictions, such rules, made Sarah wonder where the heart could strike the true chord of worship.

Temperance tapped the tip of her goose quill on the lip of the inkwell. "Sarah, never mind that. You can straighten up later."

She turned. "The stack was out of order, ma'am."

"Oh, was it? Thank you." With a sigh, Temperance leaned back in her chair. "I am writing a letter to Mr. Patrick Henry. Although there is naught he may do, seeing indentured servants are a commodity in Virginia, I wish to bring the plight of women such as yourself to his attention."

"What is it you wish me to do, Mrs. Woodhouse?" Sarah asked.

"That you read it. I want you to tell me what you think. Is it well written? Do I make my point forcefully enough?"

"I shall be happy to read it, but you may not like my opinion."

"You must put me to the test. I am as open-minded about people's opinions as the next person. Mr. Woodhouse said so. I draw the line when it comes to issues contrary to how our Lord would have us treat others though." She handed the page to Sarah. "Careful. Paper is so precious these days. Do not ruin it."

"I promise I shall take extra care, ma'am. May I sit down?"

Temperance motioned to the chair with a sweep of her hand. She fixed her eyes expectantly upon Sarah, and twirled the quill between her fingers. "Well? What do you think?"

Sarah skimmed over the page. The handwriting was difficult to read, and the content vague. But she could discern her mistress's heart behind the words. "It is a good letter, but I doubt he will concern himself with this subject. There are other important matters at hand, such as the Revolution."

Temperance shrugged. "I shall send it anyway. He cannot justify kidnapping."

"No, he certainly cannot." Sarah handed the letter back. "I admire you for speaking out against it, ma'am."

Temperance tapped her chin with the quill. "Perhaps I should write to King George and chastise him for turning a blind eye to these kidnappings." Again she sighed. "I hope you are happy Mr. Woodhouse rescued you, Sarah."

"I am, ma'am." Sarah wished the Woodhouses would go a step further and free her. She would stay with them if they did, for they were kind to her, and she had no place else to go. But she could not bring herself to broach the issue.

"Good. Now I must write another letter. I am a woman, and a woman's view is not always welcomed, but I do it just the same." Temperance took the letter from Sarah's hand. "I think Mr. Woodhouse would disapprove that I write to men of influence on any topic. So let us keep this to ourselves."

Sarah nodded. "Mr. Woodhouse said he would be home late tonight. Should I tell Celia to delay supper?"

"Yes, I want to hear what he has to say when he returns, and I do not like dining alone. No doubt there are issues about our liberty involved. I am so very proud of my husband." Temperance smiled. "He is a member of the Committee of Safety and dislikes Lord Dunmore very much."

Sarah cocked her head to the left. "I have heard you say before how little you think of his lordship. Was he not a good governor?"

"Oh, the very worst. I am glad he is gone." Temperance shook her head. "Poor Mr. Henry. I seriously doubt he has been to any social gatherings worth mentioning. I sent him an invitation last week that he should come dine with us, but I have yet to receive a reply. Perhaps the cold weather has kept him away."

Sarah looked at Temperance with sympathy stirring. Her eccentricities were mounting daily. "That may be," she said in a kind way. "But he may be delayed by the war. It may occupy his mind and time more than dinner parties. I am sure he regrets it at times. Perhaps when the war is over you shall see him at your table often."

"You may be right, Sarah. Why did I not think of that before?"

"I am sure you did, ma'am."

Temperance looked contemplatively out the window. "It is most sad that a war should douse all pleasure. Seems as though all the world has stood stock-still for it."

"I think all the world is watching."

"Well, I cannot dwell on it for long. It will depress me." Temperance pulled out another sheet of paper and scribbled over it. "Just some thoughts I am jotting down, Sarah. Would you like to hear them?"

"Certainly, if you would like to read them to me." Sarah scooted forward in her chair.

"I am to ask Mr. Woodhouse, Simon, to free you and our cook, Celia, when the war is over." Temperance lifted her quill with a little smile and a tilt of her head. "Celia would never leave me. She has been our cook since the day we first settled here. But, even though you would want to go, it would be best you stay with me. Here you are safe. Out there, you would face many dangers. Starvation for a start."

Then Temperance frowned and worry shone in her eyes. "You would not leave me and go back to Cornwall, would you?"

It was not her place to do so, but Sarah touched Temperance's hand. "This is my home now. I will not go. Not until God sends me away."

"He'd not do that."

"I have no reason to leave. There is no family in England to worry for me. I did have a friend in Bassets Cove long ago, but she has probably forgotten about me by now."

"Out of sight, out of mind." Temperance dipped the tip of the quill into the inkwell and finished writing Patrick Henry's address. Then she sealed the letter and handed it back to Sarah.

"Now, take this to Mr. Pippins and have him post this immediately. Take Celia with you. The fresh air will do you both well."

Sarah stood to leave. "I will go tell Celia."

"You will not have to take your time with Celia. She is very strong for her age and will not hinder your journey," Temperance said.

"How old is Celia, ma'am? I asked her but she would not tell me."

"'Tis a woman's prerogative, Sarah. I would not tell you my age either. All I know is she was born in the backwoods of Virginia fifteen years before the French and Indian War. You may sum it up."

Temperance handed a coin to Sarah. "If there is any money left, bring me back a little gift. I do not care what it is. But something sweet would be nice."

Sarah gave her mistress a little curtsey and left. She had come to love Mrs. Woodhouse, who at the age of sixty had grown wistful. Sarah knew Patrick Henry would not give much attention to a letter so poorly written, a jumble of thoughts and misguided advice. But she could not bring herself to tell Mrs. Woodhouse the truth. It was best to humor her.

Sarah drew her cloak closer as she headed out with Celia. The cold air blushed her cheeks. It had rained the day before. Puddles pitted the dirt and she and Celia took care to step around them. She looked up through the trees at the crisp cobalt sky and thought about Cornwall—the blue skies and restless sea, wintry heavens and violent storms. She would never go back to a place that held so many sad memories.

Currioman Bay had iced over near the shoreline, beneath yellow bluffs. Few ships sailed into the Potomac that winter. Sarah heard stories of the Great Falls upriver, and imagined if she could see them, they would reflect all that tumbled and churned in her heart. It would be a turbulent place, and she dreamed of standing on the cliffs and looking down at the rapids flowing over the rocks.

She walked along thoughtfully, listened to the birds—chickadees and nuthatches. She wished Mrs. Woodhouse had given her leave for the whole day. If it were not for the letter, she would take the long walk to Currioman Bay and sit at the top of a bluff until the sun came near to setting.

"How can there be a war and Indian massacres, when the world is so beautiful here, Celia?"

"Only the good Lord knows," Celia replied.

Upon reaching the little trading post situated at the side of the road, she went inside and handed Temperance's letter to Mr. Pippins. He sighed, brushed back the gray tufts of hair along the sides of his head, and then put on his spectacles. He looked at the front and shook his head. "Another letter from Mrs. Woodhouse to Mr. Henry."

"She enjoys letter writing," Sarah told him.

"Apparently." He pulled out a stack and set the new letter atop it. "It will be a long delay before any of Mrs. Woodhouse's letters are sent. I haven't seen a soul in weeks, except for you, Sarah. Did you hear the news?"

She drew her hood back and warmed her hands in front of the fire he had going. "No. What has happened?"

"The Iroquois massacred forty in New York."

"Yes, I heard. It is so terrifying."

"And there's been reports of more massacres along the Blue Ridge, as close as the Catoctins, so I have heard."

Sarah frowned. "I am saddened for the lives lost. You do not think they will come this far, do you?"

"Indians? I doubt it. Too many towns and soldiers for them to risk it."

"I hope you are right, Mr. Pippins."

"Who knows? It's a turned-upside-down world, Sarah. Seems the whole human race is declaring war. France, Spain, Britain, the Indians, and then there is our *Glorious Cause*."

She grasped the edges of her hood and drew it over her hair. "I hope it all ends soon."

Pippins adjusted his spectacles. "I do not doubt Mr. Adams will negotiate terms of peace by autumn."

Warmer, she headed toward the door. "Hmm. Let us hope he does, and that he also fights for the freedom of all indentured servants and slaves."

Pippins shrugged. "I doubt that he'd be successful, not with the Southern gentry in agreement to keep the business alive."

"Yes, and for their own selfish, godless reasons."

"You are opinionated for a young woman," Pippins said as she opened the door. "I think you'd be able to debate politics with any man in Virginia, Sarah, and win."

With the cold air caressing her cheeks, she gave him a quick smile and left, her errand done. What if she could sit with a group of gentlemen and plead her cause? Would they be persuaded or affronted? She tried to picture it in her mind, but all she envisioned were stern faces and the platform where she had been sold.

A carriage rumbled down the road and halted out front. Two finely dressed women were handed down, and, lifting their skirts above their ankles, moved toward the door with a servant tagging along behind them. Sarah and Celia stepped aside. Brows were raised, along with pointy chins, and the older woman placed a scented handkerchief to her nose.

"Why must they stare," Celia whispered. "We ain't got two heads."

"They believe they are above us."

"It is not their place to judge."

"That is true. Nor is it ours."

"Keep your head high, Sarah."

"I have no reason to act proud, Celia."

"Hmm. I think you do."

"It is best we do not linger. It grows colder and Mrs. Woodhouse will wonder why we are gone so long."

"She'll not complain when she sees the pot of honey you got for her. She'll want it with her tea and cornbread." She then placed the ceramic jar in her basket and headed down the steps.

They walked on. Sarah glanced back at the large carriage and horses. She wondered who the women were, for it was a rarity to see anyone of their station out and about without a gentleman. But then, most of the men were away fighting. No doubt they were Virginia gentry from a nearby plantation.

"Does your leg ache from the journey?" Celia asked.

"It always does when I have a long way to walk." Sarah paused to sit on a large rock. "You go on ahead of me. I will catch up."

"Are you sure? I can wait."

"I am sure. I just need to rest a moment. Just listen to the way the breeze is sighing through the trees. It's so soothing."

"Soothing? It's cold, that's what it is."

"Maybe. But here, I am just Sarah. I am not a servant or a slave. I am God's child in God's garden."

Celia curled her lips and gave Sarah a sidelong glance. "You are an odd one, Sarah Carr." Then with her basket balanced on her hip she walked off.

The wind strengthened and crows cackled in the trees. The clean scent of snow descended, and she knew it would fall soon, and she needed to get home to gather the eggs in the chicken coop in case it would come deep.

After a moment's pause, she stood and then strode down the road that led back to the Woodhouses. But as she rounded a bend, she met a man on horseback. His horse blew out a fog from its nostrils and shook its shaggy mane. She stepped to the edge of the road and did not look at the gentleman. She would have walked on, if it were not for the fact he spoke to her.

"Miss," he said, bringing his horse to a halt. "Can you tell me which way I am to turn? I am going to Benjamin Hutton's house. I have been there once before, years ago, but cannot recall which direction I took. There was another person walking down this road ahead of you and she could not answer me. I think I frightened her."

Briefly Sarah met his eyes, and thought him chatty—and handsome. "Well, you are a stranger, sir, and you ride a large horse. He looks frightful."

The man patted his mount's neck. "Charger? No, he is as gentle as a foal."

His dark blond hair had been cut at his shoulders, and he wore no queue. But oh, how beautiful were his eyes—the deepest brown she had ever seen, unlike Jamie's, which were icy blue.

Realizing she had been staring, she felt a flush rise in her cheeks. "I do not know the place, sir. You might ask Mr. Pippins at the trading post just down the road."

"Thank you." He inclined his head and looked at her curiously. "I will take your advice. Thank you."

He wore no regimental uniform of either an American or British soldier, but instead a black coat, bronze waistcoat, and black breeches. His riding boots were worn, without sheen, black as the mane of his horse. He gave the appearance of wealth. But that meant nothing. Anyone could buy a good suit of clothes and fine boots if they had something to barter.

He paused a moment, dragging the reins through his gloved hand. His gaze made her feel uncomfortable.

"Is there anything else, sir?"

He shook his head slightly. "No. Forgive me. I was just thinking I had forgotten how beautiful this part of Virginia is, especially the Potomac at the mouth of the bay. Do you agree?"

"I have no great opinion of it." Annoyed at the way he looked at her, she raised her chin. "I am from Cornwall where the sea . . ."

"Cornwall? My parents were born there."

This time, she looked away, trying to be unimpressed. "Are you always this friendly with strangers, sir? I should not be talking to you."

She went to leave, but he said, "What brought you to Virginia?" and it made her turn around, hands on hips.

"If you really want to know, I was brought here against my will."

A look of surprise shone on his face. "Kidnapped?"

"Yes. I was put on a rat-infested ship, and auctioned off like a piece of merchandise." She pointed back in the direction of the river. "Right across the Potomac they do that kind of business. I must pay off my passage in servitude for many years before I can return home . . . if I want to return home."

He frowned. "Well, don't you?"

"It depends."

"On what, may I ask?"

"Well, I do not know. Circumstances, I suppose."

"I am sorry for your situation."

"You have no reason to be."

"I apologize for asking. Perhaps after we win this war, our new government will end all that."

She narrowed her eyes directly at him. "Hmm. King Solomon said we should not put our trust in princes. He was a king and wrote that. I trust no one—not anymore." And with a swish of her skirts she turned her back on him and walked on. She could feel him watching her, most likely appalled by her impediment.

"Does that hurt you?" he called to her. He stepped his horse toward her and walked him alongside her. "Your leg. Does it hurt?"

"You are bold to ask, sir."

"It is not unusual for a physician. I am only concerned. I would like to help you if I can."

After taking a moment to think whether or not she should answer, she decided there would be no harm in it. "Sometimes, when I have walked a great deal my muscles ache. But that is all. I was born this way, and have accepted it as my lot in life."

"I see. What is your name?"

"Sarah Carr, sir."

"And where do you live, Sarah Carr?"

"At the Woodhouse farm. It is just down this road to the left."

"I know I am forward for asking. But are you wedded?"

"I am a widow."

His brow creased. "You are so young to be."

She looked past him, down the road. "You bring no wife with you, sir?"

"I have yet to find my life's partner, Miss Carr," he replied. "I will pay the Woodhouses a visit as soon as I can." He then tipped the corner of his tricorn hat to her. "I am Dr. Alex Hutton. I bid you good day."

He turned Charger, jabbed the horses ribs with his boot heels, and galloped off. Dry leaves whirled beneath the horse's hooves. Sarah stood in the middle of the road watching him fade into the distance. A wonderful sensation bubbled up inside her, similar to the first time she saw Jamie leaning on the fence rail watching her. It made her heart race. Only this time the man had intrigued her. A physician. A healer. What was his life like, ministering to the sick and wounded?

She headed back down a narrow path that led to the farm-house and thought of his eyes. They were noble, with life sparkling warmly within them. But she was a poor, crippled servant, pitied by her owners, in submission to laws that prom-ised harsh punishment if she tried to flee. He'd never look on her as anything but lowly.

He had a handsome face, too, and for a moment, she com-pared it to Jamie's plain looks. Then she shook her head, dis-mayed she would judge him against her deceased husband. Ashamed, she tried to forget Dr. Alex Hutton and his large, frightful horse.

The fields lay barren where corn had once been. It made her think of those days when she helped with the wheat har-vest, when she first met Jamie. Tears swelled in her eye and she dashed them away. It would do no good to cry now.

She followed a brickbat walk that led to the garden Temperance kept. A grapevine arbor served as an entrance. Trim boxwood hedges enclosed the sanctuary, a place of soli-tude and escape. She went to a spot in the north corner and sat at the base of a pear tree. She lifted her hair over her shoul-der, and then raised her skirts to the middle of her calves with her legs stretched straight out in front of her. She placed her feet together, ankle to ankle, and studied them. Such a slight difference—but it was enough to mark her.

If it were in the Almighty's plan to make her whole, then she would rejoice. But if not, she willingly accepted her burden, and tried to comfort her aching heart. It proved hard, and she shoved her gown down as far as it would go, and put her face within her hands and wept.

8

Alex had been reluctant to leave his group of ragtag patriots fighting in the backwoods when he received a letter from his sister-in-law. It had been dated three months earlier, for getting a letter deep in the wilderness took extra time. He bid them farewell when cold mountain mists ribboned down from the Blue Ridge into the valleys and plains, and the rivers and streams caked over with ice.

From atop his horse, he saw farms and plantations spread out across a vast plateau. His brother practiced law for the wealthy estate owners, and he wondered if it had been taken over. With so many men away fighting, he doubted it. He would have gone on, but a farmer, leading a bull by a lengthy rope attached to a ring through its nose, came toward him.

"Is that you, Dr. Hutton?" The farmer paused and set his hand on his bull's neck. The beast stood several hands taller than his horse.

"Do I know you, sir?"

"I'm Flenderson. I've got a farm next to your brother's place."

"Yes, I do remember. It has been a long time—years in fact."

"You have been out fighting the British?"

"I have been caring for the sick and wounded."

"A noble thing. Taking some leave are you?"

"For a time."

"I heard about Benjamin."

Knowing how his brother must have suffered caused a dull pain within him. If only he could have been there with him. "Typhoid, while camped near a swampy area in eastern Maryland. Those places are a breeding ground for disease."

Flenderson shook his head. "I'm sorry for it, sir, especially for Emma and her girls. I brought them a basket of apples at Christmastime. Haven't seen them since."

"Was my sister-in-law well, and my nieces, when you visited them?"

"Emma was thin as a reed. Her mourning made her that way, I suppose. She told me her serving girl ran off."

Alex's worry for Emma and his nieces rose. "She has been alone all this time without any help?"

"That's right. I've done all I could, but I've a family to look after too. Emma told me she didn't need help and that I should not come back 'cause there is no man there and it wasn't proper I should show up."

Indeed, he knew grief would take its toll, yet Alex hoped it wasn't something more. And the fact that her servant abandoned her and the children gave him reason to believe life had been made much harder for Emma. The last time he saw her, she seemed incapable of hard work. He recalled a conversation at his brother's table on fetching eggs beneath the hens and how mortified Emma acted. She explained she would not know what to do, and feared being pecked. Perhaps all that had changed and she had learned to do the chores in order to survive.

"Well, I hope to help in any way I can," Alex said. "I owe it to my brother. He paid for my medical training in Philadelphia at the university there."

"Aye, Benjamin was a good man."

"But it is not only for that reason. Emma and the girls are my family. I'll not turn my back on them for anything in the world."

"I wish you well, Dr. Hutton." Flenderson tipped his hat and proceeded to leave. He looked up at Alex as he was passing by and smiled. "Lily and Rose are a pair of sprites if you do not mind me saying."

"No, I do not mind. I am anxious to see them."

He clicked his tongue and urged Charger forward, worried what he might find when stepping through his brother's door. He knew from what Flenderson told him that he'd find a grief-stricken woman. But would he find hungry children, too? The thought of his five-year-old nieces suffering cut him to the quick and caused him to urge Charger into a canter.

Moving on, he thought of the girl he met on the road. Sarah was it? She had kind eyes, and spirit. If he needed help, would the Woodhouses allow it until his aunt's arrival? He had sent a letter to his aunt, asking her to come, but he expected she might decline, it being winter and she being at such an age that the cold and a long coach ride would cause her a great deal of discomfort.

The road forked and he turned to the right and traveled a quarter-mile until he saw the house his brother had built, situated in a small vale surrounded with trees. Stone hedges enclosed the yard. Frost glazed the windows of the colonial saltbox. No smoke blew from the center chimney. They had to be cold without a fire, hungry without a hot meal. He headed down the lane and dismounted near the door. Before he reached for the latch, snow had begun to fall in enormous flakes.

"Emma." She did not answer, and so he removed his hat and stepped inside.

A gloomy light pervaded the house. The floorboards creaked under his footsteps as he stepped into the room on the left and saw Emma and the two children huddled together under a mound of quilts on a settee. The room smelled of hearth fires and unwashed bodies. The girls looked over at him with wide, frightened eyes.

He touched his sister-in-law's cheek, then her forehead. She moaned. Fever. "Emma, can you hear me? It is Alex. I have come to help." She looked up at him with glassy eyes and a blank stare.

He spoke softly to the girls, drew venison jerky from his pocket. They were so hungry. "Do not be afraid, Lily, Rose. I am your Uncle Alex."

Above the fireplace hung a musket and powder horn, and on the flagstones next to it a cart of wood and a basket of twigs. He grabbed the iron poker and stirred the ashes. A few red cinders appeared. He threw sticks across them and they caught fire. Then he stacked a few logs over them. Soon the room simmered with heat.

"Come here, girls." He gestured to them with his hands. "Sit here by the fire where it is warm."

They crawled out of the quilts and hurried to him without speaking. He saw they had no shoes or stockings on. When they sat down, he took turns chafing each child's feet. He'd find wool leggings, hopefully, in an upstairs bedroom.

Rose held out her arms to him, and he drew her in. She cried, and his heart broke. "You are hungry, aren't you?" She drew back, nodded, and put her finger in her mouth.

"Do not worry," he said, brushing back her curly hair. "I will find something more than jerky for you and your sister to eat. But I must help your mama before I do."

Emma twisted beneath the quilt she gripped. Alex ran his fingers through his hair and thought what to do. *Take her upstairs and put her in bed, bank a fire . . . water, food, Peruvian bark.*

He had to isolate her from the children, and prayed the fever raging through her body had not infected them and that she would recover. He lifted Emma in his arms and carried her up the staircase where cobwebs quivered between the slats. She felt like no more than a child in his arms. Pushing a door in with his shoulder, he brought her into the room that she had shared with his brother and laid her in bed. He drew off the sweat-soaked clothes she wore. They were filthy and foul-smelling. He tossed them aside. Her skin had turned a ghastly shade of yellow along her arms and throat.

"It is as I thought, Emma. You have yellow fever."

He tucked her beneath the bedding and spoke softly to her, hoping not to alarm her delicate spirit. But it could not be helped, for she opened her eyes and looked up at him afraid.

"So hot. I thirst."

With no water in the bedroom pitcher, he opened the window and scooped up snow from the sill and brought it to her lips.

"Am I going to die?"

"I will do all I can to help you, but you must fight, Emma."

"Lily? Rose?"

"I am going to take care of the girls and will be back when I am finished. I pray God you have food in your larder. They look half-starved."

As he was going through the door, she held out her hand. "Take care . . . of my dear girls . . ."

He looked back at her. "I will, Emma. But I must keep them from you until you recover. Rest now."

Downstairs, the girls were waiting in the doorway of the sitting room and followed him out to the kitchen. On the oak table sat a basket of apple cores. Water in the bucket had frozen solid. The only things in the larder were a bit of cornmeal, sugar, a bit of salt, and dried beef. What he could do with such meager provisions he did not know, but he would make something edible.

He broke the ice with a mallet from the drawer, and set it in a black kettle. Then he built a fire and the ice slowly began to melt. He threw in the beef and salt, and made a mush out of the cornmeal. That night Lily and Rose ate their fill and slept side by side, covered in the down quilts their mother had made, warmed by the hearth fire that crackled in their room.

And while they slept, Alex washed Emma and spooned broth into her mouth. So little she took, until she slipped into a deep stupor. As the wind seeped through the walls of the house, Alex lit the logs in the bedroom fireplace and burned Emma's clothes. By midnight, the snowfall had ended, and a bright full moon shone through the windows.

At least his nieces were safe. But he feared for Emma.

9

*D*awn came, and snow sparkled over the fields. Soon a clear blue sky greeted the world, misty and soft like the down of a dove's wing. Sarah, warm in her heavy wool cloak, headed toward the well over grass that crackled beneath the soles of her shoes. She looked down into the yawning dark cavern and could not tell if the water had frozen during the night. Hopeful, she lowered her bucket, felt it sink, and hauled it back up.

Having done most of her chores before the sun peeked over the horizon, she trudged back to the house and filled her mistress's pitcher and emptied the rest into the cask near the door. Temperance washed each morning at the strike of nine, and told Sarah it was next to godliness to be clean. But Sarah already knew that, being of that habit herself.

She glanced at the miniature clock on the mantle, and seeing she had a quarter hour before Temperance would call for her, she heated water in the kettle until it warmed. Then she poured it over her hair and rubbed it dry with her apron in front of the fire.

"You have pretty hair, Sarah," said Celia. "But Mistress Temperance says you wash it too much."

"I know. Back home I was ridiculed for washing it so often, instead of keeping it hidden beneath a mobcap. I never cared what the mockers would say. I cannot be convinced of letting my hair go for weeks, even months, like other women."

"I have heard ladies have found mice nesting in their hair."

"Well, I do not know about that. But it would be awful."

Celia tied her apron string into a bow. "It sure would be."

Sarah remembered how much Jamie loved the silky feeling of her locks and the way they smelled. For a second, she wondered if Dr. Hutton would like the way her hair felt—if he were to touch it.

She dipped her fingers into the water. It felt freezing cold, and not only shocked her when she splashed it over her face, but dashed her thoughts of Dr. Hutton ever doing anything of the sort.

Celia stood back, large wooden spoon in hand. "I imagine the water from the well is freezing cold, Sarah."

"Very. You want some?"

"I will need some for tea. Fill the kettle and put it on."

Upstairs, Temperance stirred. Sarah did as Celia asked, then lifted the pitcher in her arms. "I used to dream my mother was a woman like Mrs. Woodhouse—one who took care of her looks, but not one lifted up with conceit."

"There ain't a proud bone in Mrs. Woodhouse's body. But her mind is none too good, is it?"

"I like to think she has a vivid imagination."

"It's vivid alright. She told me yesterday that I would have to cook a four-course meal because Mr. Patrick Henry and other gentlemen would be coming here to dine."

Sarah smiled. It would be nice for Temperance to have company. "I am sure that is not so. Mr. Woodhouse would have told you, and Mr. Henry is away, like most of the gentlemen."

"I did not argue. . . . She gave me a menu. Look here." Celia drew a slip of paper from her apron pocket. "A green salad." She looked at Sarah with wide eyes. "Now where would I get greens for a salad this time of year?"

Celia smacked the page with her finger. "And then corn chowder. We have no corn, and it has to be fresh off the stalk to make good chowder. A haunch of roast venison, and molasses dumplings for dessert."

Sarah smiled. "It sounds delicious. You should save it, just in case Mrs. Woodhouse should ever have dinner guests."

While Celia returned the menu to her pocket, Sarah stepped out into the hallway and headed for the staircase. Outside a horse neighed, and she hurried over to the window next to the front door and looked out. To her surprise it was Dr. Hutton, and seated in front of him were two little girls.

"Who is that?" Mr. Woodhouse strode from his library, cinching the sash to his robe tighter.

"It is Dr. Hutton, sir." That drawn-to-him feeling overtook her as she watched him dismount. He reached up to the girls, lifted them down, and carried them toward the door.

"Something has happened." She turned to Mr. Woodhouse. "I met Dr. Hutton on the road yesterday. He was going to his brother's house to help his widow and daughters." She looked back out the window. "But she is not with him."

"I will go dress. Let him in."

Mr. Woodhouse took the pitcher from her and proceeded upstairs. Sarah drew back the latch on the door and opened it. Alex anxiously met her eyes.

"Miss Carr? We met yesterday . . . on the road."

She made a short curtsey. "I remember, sir. Please, come inside. It is too cold for little children to be out of doors."

"These are my nieces. Lily and Rose." He ushered them inside, and Sarah shut the door against the chilly air.

The rosy-cheeked girls looked at Sarah with their large brown eyes, and her heart was immediately taken. If custom allowed, she would have lowered herself to their level and embraced them. The gleam in their eyes was forlorn, and if only she could comfort them, she would. A smile would have to do, and a kind greeting.

"I am Sarah," she said.

"Can you not say hello to the lady?" Alex said, setting the girls down.

"Oh, no, sir. The children need not speak to me. I am but a servant."

"Politeness has no class boundaries, Sarah," he said. "But you are right. They are young, and their world has been turned upside down."

She took his hat. Their fingertips briefly touched, and she drew back. "Forgive me for being so bold, sir, but where is their mother?"

He swallowed, his brow furrowed. "She . . ."

Instantly Sarah understood and her lips parted. "I am sorry. How?"

"Fever. Starvation. They are now alone in the world except for me. That is why I have come to speak to Mr. Woodhouse. Is he at home?"

"I am, sir." And Mr. Woodhouse came down the staircase.

Alex walked up to him, held out his hand, and gave his name. The two men shook hands as Sarah watched. She wondered what the good doctor had in mind as far as Mr. Woodhouse was concerned. What could he do for two small, orphaned girls? She gazed at them a moment, noticing how thin they were. She wished she could take care of them and keep them safe. She hoped Mr. Woodhouse would at least allow Celia to feed them a huge breakfast.

"Forgive me for disturbing you so early in the day, Mr. Woodhouse."

"Not at all, Dr. Hutton. And who are these fine children?"

"My nieces, Rose and Lily Hutton." Alex brought them forward. "May I have a word with you?"

"Certainly. We can speak in the dining room. I am about to break my fast. Have you and the girls had your breakfast?"

Alex glanced up and said sheepishly, "I did my best with a little cornmeal."

Mr. Woodhouse looked at the girls, then at Sarah. "Temperance has sat down to write letters."

Sarah fixed her eyes on Mr. Woodhouse. "Then she does not want to be disturbed, sir?"

"Not this morning. You may watch these children. Take them to the kitchen and have Celia feed them. And bring an extra plate for Dr. Hutton."

Alex started to object to being served, but Mr. Woodhouse held up his hand. "You are a guest, sir. No one goes without something to eat in my house."

Pleased Mr. Woodhouse would be so generous, Sarah glanced at Alex and smiled. Gratitude showed in his eyes. "Thank you, Mr. Woodhouse," he said. "They ate the mush I made without complaint. But I can assure you it was foul."

And then, his gaze grew into something more as he looked back at Sarah. It dropped along her face, and then back to her eyes, the kind of look Jamie had given her when they first met. But this time it seemed forged by a deeper emotion that she could not quite understand. Why would he have feelings for someone as lowborn as she?

Mr. Woodhouse stepped away and went through the dining room door. A warm fire burned in the hearth, and a spray of amber light crossed the floor. Alex touched the tops of the girls' heads and followed. The door shut, and Sarah leaned down to remove Lily and Rose's cloaks. How slight they seemed, like the children she had known in the orphanage in England.

"Both of you are chilled to the bone, you poor dears," she cooed. "Come with me and you will have something good to eat."

Rose's eyes lit up and Lily clapped her hands. "I am hungry, Sarah," said Rose.

"Yes, we shall remedy that, dear one."

Lily placed the palms of her hands on Sarah's cheeks. Her hands were small and soft like lamb's fleece. Her eyes bright like her sister's, she murmured, "Gingerbread."

Sarah's heart warmed at hearing their voices and seeing the excitement in their eyes. She grasped the twins' hands and hurried with them back to the kitchen. Celia turned from her kettle and lifted her brows in surprise. "Oh, who may these little ones be?"

With gentle hands, Sarah moved them in front of her. "This is Rose and Lily Hutton, Celia. And they are hungry. Mr. Woodhouse says we must feed them."

"Well, set them at the table, Sarah." Celia piled bright yellow eggs and slices of crisp bacon onto two pewter plates and set them in front of the twins. Neither dove in, but waited with their eyes fixed on Sarah.

With no time to make gingerbread, she mixed sugar with ground ginger and cinnamon. Then, after adding the spices to butter, she sliced hunks of bread from the loaf on the table and slathered it across them. "Shall we thank the Lord for his bounty?"

As the children ate, kicking their legs back and forth beneath the table, Sarah prepared the serving dishes. She was careful to arrange them on the tray and thought how good it felt to feed a man. She carried it out to the dining room and went in. The men were seated and ceased talking when she drew up to the table and placed a china plate in front of Alex, along with silverware and napkin. Feeling the closeness of him as she served, her heart pounded and she wished it would slow. She hoped what she felt did not show on her face.

"Sarah, Dr. Hutton and I have been discussing his situation." Mr. Woodhouse paused to taste his eggs. "He has made a request—unusual, but nonetheless made sincerely. What would you say to helping him with his nieces? It would only be for a short while until his aunt, a more suitable person to care for them, arrives."

I am not suitable? I already love them. How she wished she could say the words out loud, but she held her tongue. "I am your servant, Mr. Woodhouse, until I have paid all I owe. According to the rules of masters and servants, I have no say."

At first, he looked at her perplexed with his brows knit together. Then all of a sudden, a smile spread across his face. "She is bold as she is wise, wouldn't you say, Dr. Hutton? Do you really think you can handle such a wench?"

Alex set his fork down on the plate and sighed. "Oh, I would not call her that, sir. I do not know Sarah, but she seems too refined for her position."

"How refined can she be? She's from Cornwall."

"I hear Cornish women are forthright, and she has the lilt of a lady of quality."

"A little, yes." Mr. Woodhouse turned to Sarah with his brows pinched. "How did you come to have such a smooth way of speaking, Sarah? The few Cornish folk I have known have had rough speech."

She wiggled her head, not liking his comment. "They forced me to speak clearly and distinctly in good English, sir."

"They?"

"The teachers at the orphanage where I grew up."

Alex's eyes shifted to hers. "I trust you will understand the twins better than anyone."

"It is a sad thing to be without father or mother—unless they were cruel and neglectful." She picked up an empty covered dish and set it on the tray. "But I imagine, sir, your brother and sister-in-law were good parents. I can tell by the twins' manner. They are very sweet and polite for their age."

"But too young to understand they have lost both parents."

"At least they have you, sir."

He looked reflective. "I am no expert on the care of little girls, and I refuse to send them away, not with the war and the fact that those places are deplorable."

"You say you have an aunt. Are there no other relatives but she?"

"None at all. So you see the fix I am in until I hear from her. She may decline to come, being a much older person set in her ways."

She drew in her lower lip and thought. "If Mrs. Woodhouse can spare me, I shall do my best."

"Of course Temperance can spare you. Celia will take your place while you are gone. Have her fix a basket of food to take along."

"Yes, sir."

Mr. Woodhouse turned to face Alex. "I will loan Sarah out to you, sir, until your aunt arrives. If you will permit me, I know of a lady who will suit your particular set of circumstances perfectly. She is a very capable woman, having brought up twelve of her own children and helped with many more. I shall write to her right away and see if she is interested in . . . being employed by you."

"Mr. Woodhouse, I am grateful. But I must wait to hear from my aunt. God bless you for your kindness."

He wants me. Not anyone Mr. Woodhouse knows. Her heart warmed toward him all the more.

"'Tis bread upon the waters, sir." Mr. Woodhouse resumed his meal, and for a moment Sarah stared at the floor taking in the task she had been ordered to do. *Sold, bought, owned, loaned.* How she despised these words.

Turning out of the room, she walked back to the kitchen and told Celia to pack what the Woodhouses could spare in the way of food. Lily laid her head upon her folded arms on the table. Rose reached out to her and Sarah lifted her from the chair.

Like a songbird bursting from a tree, Temperance came downstairs singing loudly, then stood out in the hallway. She would not step foot in the kitchen, and so Sarah set Rose down and hurried to the dining room door before her mistress could reach it.

"I am looking for more writing paper, Sarah. Have you seen any?"

"Yes, it is in your writing desk drawer in your room. Shall I get it for you?"

Temperance had her eyes fixed on the column of sunlight coming through the window. "That is not necessary. Oh, I do wish for spring, for then I can go out and sit in the garden. Where is Mr. Woodhouse this morning?"

"In the dining room, ma'am."

Temperance went through, pulling Sarah behind her. Her husband introduced Alex, who stood upon her entrance. "Do you know Mr. Patrick Henry, sir?"

"I am afraid I do not, madam."

Temperance screwed up her face. "Oh, that is a pity. I was hoping you would."

Mr. Woodhouse came around the table and took her hand. "Temperance, my dear. Dr. Hutton is in a desperate situation.

I am sending Sarah with him to help with his small nieces until his aunt arrives. Celia will serve you until Sarah returns."

With a look most anxious, Temperance turned and threw her arm across Sarah's shoulders and drew her close. "This is your will, my husband, that you send Sarah away from me?"

"Only for a short time. Dr. Hutton will see her back to us safe and sound."

"Indeed I shall, Mrs. Woodhouse." Alex's eyes moved to the doorway. "There, behind you, are Rose and Lily now."

Temperance turned and when she laid eyes on the curly moppets, she sighed with a thrill of delight. "They are precious! I should like to adopt them. May we, husband?"

"They have their uncle, my dear, and a great aunt."

"Oh, well, if he should ever change his mind . . ." She leaned down and kissed the tops of the twin's heads, and then swept from the room. Sarah felt a bit embarrassed by the way Temperance behaved. Instead of acting like a well-bred lady, she acted childlike and impetuous, on the border of insanity. But her husband adored her, and Sarah loved her as well with a compassionate heart.

Dismissed from the room, Sarah fetched a change of clothes, stuffed them in a sack, and hurried back downstairs. As her feet reached the last step, the awareness she was about to leave washed over her. Her nerves grew taut, and her hands trembled a bit as she tied the tassel of her cloak. After she put the girl's cloaks on them, she met Alex by his horse.

"I shall walk. You ride with the girls." And without delay, he placed his hands around her waist and lifted her onto the back of his mount. It had been a long time since a man had touched her.

10

$\mathscr{S}$arah had never been this far inland from the Potomac before. The road they traveled narrowed and grew overshadowed by rows of elms and oaks. Even though the branches were stripped bare of leaves, bark blackened by wintry weather, beauty lingered about the woodlands and struck her deeply. It spoke of hearth fires and heavy quilts, warm stews and hot cider. Spears of hazy sunlight pierced through the trees, and bird song echoed from near and far.

She shook back her hood, wanting to feel the breeze ripple through her hair and the northern frost to brush across her cheeks. Banked on each side of the road lay heaps of autumn leaves—reds and golds, blotched and curled, mingled with patches of snow. As the clouds thickened above, she reflected on the beauty and diversity of the Lord's creation—how each thing had a purpose, and how the seasons moved from one to the other year after year.

The loud jeers of jays echoed in the forest. Alex drew Charger to the side of the road and raised his hand to Sarah and the girls to be silent. Again the same cries, followed by clicks and *toolool* and *wheedlee*. Captivated by the ruckus the birds made, Sarah looked up into the trees to see them flit among the branches. Flashes of blue and grey, they flew from limb to limb, and then the woods grew silent.

Sarah's blood turned to ice and she drew the children closer, and when she saw Alex draw his pistol from inside his greatcoat, her hands trembled as she grasped the girls tighter. Her breath held, she was scared at the sight of Indians passing between the trees, dressed in their winter hunting clothes of deerskin and bear fur, bows and quivers strapped over their shoulders. Were they there to hunt this far south of the tribal villages, or were they scouting for the British?

Alex cocked the hammer of his flintlock and bent his arm so that the weapon would be ready to fire. A twig snapped and Sarah jerked her head to the left to see four other Indians stalking toward them. Outnumbered, Alex lifted the children and Sarah down from Charger and put them between his body and the gelding's.

"Do not cry out," he said, as the Indians walked closer and surrounded them.

Fear rippled through Sarah. "I am afraid. The children . . ." she whispered.

He warned her quietly yet firmly, "Be quiet."

Rose and Lily buried their faces in the folds of Sarah's cloak. The Indian leader, a strongly built warrior, wore the mask of the wolf across his eyes, and turkey feathers dressed his sleek black hair. He was a fearsome sight to behold, one that struck terror into her heart. Sarah kept the girls from seeing him.

"British?" he grunted.

"No," Alex replied. "Americans. I am a doctor."

The Indian quickly glanced at Sarah and the girls. "Your woman, children?"

"They are. And I will protect them." She knew he said it to guard her and the twins. And for a fraction of a moment she thought how wonderful it would be if it were true. The Indian cocked his head and looked down at the girls.

"I have daughter. We will not harm yours." He placed his hand over his heart. Sarah stared at him, and marveled at the fatherly pride in his dark eyes at the mention of his child.

"Our wives and children are sick," the Indian continued.

Alex nodded. "We, too, have had sickness, and death has visited our houses."

"The British do not help us. The deer run from their guns and we have left the redcoat devils to starve."

"You do not fight with them?"

The Indian's lip curled. "We are done with them. We are going back to our village beyond the mountains."

"I have jerky in my saddlebag and medicine. The medicine will help your women and children."

The warrior stepped up to Alex's horse, opened the saddle-bag, and took out a fistfull of venison jerky and two bottles of a powdery substance. He turned the bottles upside down, looking carefully into them.

"Peruvian bark. Good for fevers." Alex cupped his hand and made a circle in his palm. "This much, with water. Do you understand?"

The Indian nodded and walked off with the rest of his braves into the woods.

Quickly, Alex set the girls back on Charger. Sarah, her nerves trembling, walked alongside him. She admired him for his compassion and bravery. "They could have killed you, and taken the children and me captive."

"I gave them medicine. It is powerful to them. Now they consider themselves indebted to me, and will not harm us. They will go back to their village, which is far to the west, past the headwaters."

Her fears still unabated, she looked back over her shoulder where the warriors had been. "They will not come back?"

"No," he said, but even he had a quiver in his voice. "Come we have to hurry. It grows colder."

"You lied to them," she said.

He shook his head. "God forgive me, but what else could I do? I thought it would make a difference to say you are my woman and the girls mine, in case they were hostile." He paused and put his hands about her waist then lifted her up behind the twins. "It is easier this way," he said.

Layers of gray clouds darkened the path, and a threat of more snow scented the air. The cold deepened and Sarah felt it creep through her wool cloak. She shivered, keeping her eyes on the forest, watchful and fearful the warriors might return.

When she saw the saltbox house, a sense of relief filled her, not for herself alone but for Rose and Lily. Still, she tightened her hold on the girls, wanting to protect them from any further unhappiness.

Alex took the twins down from his horse, but before he could help Sarah, she slid off the gelding's back, gathered the twin's hands, and proceeded toward the door. He stepped ahead and opened it. By the state of things, the dust and disorder, much work had to be done, and Sarah was prepared to do it with all her being.

She glanced over her shoulder and saw Alex hesitate in the doorway. Wintry air blew inside and rustled a few dried leaves over the threshold. "Stay inside with the children," he told her. "There is something I must do and I do not want their eyes to see."

She understood his meaning and nodded. "Yes, sir. The children are in sorry need of a bath. Is there water and soap in the house, wood for a fire?"

"The cask in the kitchen is full. There is plenty of soap on a shelf in the larder, and wood stacked near the hearth."

Catching a glimpse of a worn Bible on the table near the door, Sarah picked it up and handed it to him before he stepped back outside. "The war has called our ministers away, sir. But that does not mean you cannot speak some words yourself."

He took the Bible that had belonged to his brother from her. "Yes, of course."

"Psalm twenty and three, perhaps?"

"Yes, though I walk through the valley of the shadow of death—I shall fear no evil—for thou art with me."

A sad hint of a smile lifted Sarah's wistful mouth. "I think of those words often. I am determined to walk beyond the valley and find a new life one day—until my Shepherd calls me home. . . . At least that is my prayer."

"It is a good one, Sarah. I hope God grants it." Soberly he went up the staircase, to the room where the body of Emma Hutton lay in repose.

It was dreadful listening to Alex's footsteps descend the stairs, the weight of what he carried causing the steps to creak beneath the soles of his boots. The front door opened. Then she heard the click of the latch as he went outside, and she pictured in her mind the burden that was slumped over his shoulder.

She did not watch from the window to see which direction he had gone, but led the children to the kitchen to wash the grime off their bodies and the grease from their hair. Setting them each in a chair, she started a fire in the large stone hearth and heated water in a cast-iron kettle. A wooden bathing tub sat in a corner near the fire, and after finding soap, Sarah filled the tub and gave the girls a good washing.

They shared a room upstairs, and there she found sets of clean clothes for each, warm woolen stockings and caps. Once they were dressed, she put them on her lap and brushed their hair until dry, speaking to them softly as a mother would have. She found wooden blocks, rag dolls, and small wooden animals in a chest against the wall. Sarah set the girls on the floor to play, kissed the tops of their heads, and stepped out of the room when she saw how content they were. She smiled at the way they spoke to each other, giggled, and playacted with their dolls.

Back downstairs, Sarah stood in the doorway to the kitchen and thought about what she must do next. Check the larder and add to it from the basket Celia had filled. A backdoor led out to a garden. The old plants were withered and brown, encrusted with mold. Perhaps the plot at the far end was a potato patch.

Throwing her cloak over her shoulders, she grabbed the empty basket and went out into the chilly air. She got on her knees and dug through the earth with her hands. There she found sweet potatoes and a few carrots that had not gone to rot. When she sat back, a hand reached down and she looked up to see Alex standing over her, dirt upon his clothes and boots.

"I would not have thought of that." He spoke softly, she knew, because of what he had just done. "I am glad you did, Sarah."

"All country houses have gardens, sir." She brushed off a carrot and set it in the basket. "Even in the cold of winter, we may find a small bounty."

He drew his hand away when she did not take it. "Do you like sweet potatoes?"

"It does not matter whether I do or not. I will bake some and put butter on them for the children."

"And none for me?" he jested.

"Of course, for you, too, sir," she answered with a smile.

"They are not as brightly orange as the color of your hair."

This time she caught the more serious tone in his voice. He complimented her in a way that made her feel admired. Again he held his hand out to her. She grasped it and he lifted her to her feet.

"I have never been very fond of my red hair," she told him. "Makes people think I have a bad temper."

"That is an old wives' tale, Sarah. I daresay some women must envy such beauty. Haven't you ever stopped to see how it looks when the sun shines through it?"

"No, that would be vain." She picked up the basket, and they headed toward the house.

"Then *I* shall tell you what I see."

Her heart pounded and she lowered her eyes. "Why?"

"Because life is short. The world would be a sadder place if a woman did not hear such words from a man."

Befuddled, she wondered if she had interpreted his comment in the wrong way. She knew he would think her naive, but asked, "Are you speaking to me as a physician? Is there something I should know?"

He gave her a little laugh. "Just be proud of what you have been blessed with. Do not discount it."

When he stepped back inside the house, he ran a weary hand over his face and dragged off his coat. Sarah took it from him and set it over the back of a chair. They could hear the twins chatting away upstairs in play.

"I am glad to hear that," Alex said. "And I have you to thank for it, Sarah."

Sarah set the basket on the table. "All they needed to make them happy was some good food, a good washing, and their dolls."

"They have lost their father—and their mother. They need love above all else."

Saddened, Sarah set out to clean the vegetables. How different a man Alex Hutton seemed. She had not known any as compassionate and understanding as he. For him to have left the patriots and traveled to Virginia to help his grieving sister-in-law and twin nieces was not something she thought a man in the throes of war would so readily, or willingly, do.

"Thank God they have you to love them, sir. Some would have abandoned the girls to an orphanage."

He looked at her. "I could never do that to Rose and Lily. They are my flesh and blood."

"And very sweet, I might add." She grabbed a cast iron pot from a hook in the wall, placed the sweet potatoes within it, and secured the cover.

Alex banked the fire in the hearth and sighed. "What I just did, I never thought I would have to do, and hope I never shall again." He placed another log on the fire, and then dusted off his hands. "But at least Emma is at rest."

Sarah could see how it tore at his heart to have buried Emma. "God only knows how it would have turned out if you had not arrived when you did." She set the pot on the hook and swung it over the coals he had shoved to one side. "You might have had three to bury instead of one. It is a thought too terrible to think of."

"Yes, I hate to think that might have been the outcome." He picked up a carrot and brushed off a speck of dirt she had missed. "I have no appetite. I'm sorry."

She smiled lightly. "Oh, but you must eat, sir. I will prepare a good supper for you and the girls, if you would give me an hour."

He nodded and set the carrot down. "An hour it is. And later, when it has grown dark and the girls are abed, come sit with me by the fire in the sitting room. I will grow lonely without conversation."

He turned and left her to her task, not realizing that within her heart feelings for him were growing.

11

*C*edar logs flamed and seethed and brought cheerful warmth back to the house. Rose and Lily were sound asleep upstairs, rag dolls cradled in their arms, snuggled in a heavy quilt upon a down-filled mattress. The day she arrived, Sarah had swept the room clean and put fresh sheets from the hall cupboard over the beds. Alex slept in his brother's master bedroom, which faced north toward the river. The windows in it received the best air—air that had lost its brackish fragrance.

Snow flurried in a soft winter breeze for several days. Tonight a candle burned in the socket of a brass holder and hurricane dome in the sitting room where Sarah waited for Alex to come home. He'd been called away to a neighboring farm, to a family whose children were suffering with the croup. Here, too, she had swept and cleaned away the soot and dust that clung to every stick of furniture, to the floorboards, and to the mantelpiece.

The room smelled of cedar and the pungent cinnamon she had tossed into the fire. Gone were the scents of sickness and privation. She glanced up at the clock on the mantle. Eight. Tonight they had not met at their usual time of seven, to sit and talk by the fireside. She so enjoyed their conversations and found herself missing him.

Darkness fell deep, and a full moon hung in the sky with Venus beside it. At least he would find his way home easily, if he were to come home tonight. Perhaps he would not be too weary to sit and tell her about his day. Sarah determined she would listen intently and hang on to every word.

Upon the table, beside the high-backed chair close to the fire, she set a glass of wine, a pewter dish, a bone pipe she had found on the mantle, and a tin of tobacco. The rich burgundy liquid in the goblet shimmered over the polished wood of the table. Sarah's heart leapt when she heard the clop of a horse. She dashed to the window and watched him lead Charger away. A few minutes later, he stepped into the room with a look of surprise.

"I do not know what to say, Sarah." He glanced around the room and smiled. "You have worked miracles since coming here. Ah, a warm fire. Lord knows I am in need of it." He drew off his gloves and held his hands close to the heat.

"No miracles, sir. Just ordinary housekeeping that is all." She averted her eyes, for when she looked into his it seemed everything inside her suddenly seized up.

"Is that wine on the table?"

"Yes, sir. It is Celia's best raspberry wine. I had forgotten it. But tonight is a good night for it after you have had a long day. It is not strong like most, but sweet to the tongue."

"And nourishing, I wager." He picked up the pipe. "My brother's." Then he set it down on the plate. "I do not smoke, Sarah. Some of my colleagues disagree, but I find it bad for the lungs. Why put something into them other than what God intended?"

He slumped into the chair, one foot crossing the other, his legs outstretched.

"How is the family you visited?" she asked. "Are the children out of danger?"

Alex shut his eyes. "They are, thank God. It was a long ride back. I am weary."

"Shall I bring you some food?"

He glanced at her. "I'll not refuse. You are as excellent a cook as you are a housekeeper. Did I tell you that before?"

Several times, but Sarah enjoyed hearing his praise again. "You did, sir. Shall I bring in your dinner?"

"A little later. I am not hungry at the moment. My boots. Help me remove them."

Without delay, she knelt in front of him, clasped her hands around the heel of the first and slid it off, then did the same with the other. "You must eat something. We cannot have you falling sick. What would the girls do?"

She felt his gaze upon her, kept her eyes from looking up at him. Scooting closer to the fire, she began to buff his boots with the hem of her apron.

"Your hands are not made for such work," he said.

She waited a moment to speak, swallowing down the tight feeling in her throat. "I polish Mr. Woodhouse's boots and shoes all the time," she finally said. "He has never complained. Not once."

"Nor told you what I just said, I am sure."

Quietly he sipped the wine, and they did not speak for a full minute. After he set the empty glass down, he leaned forward and said, "When we first met, you told me you were kidnapped and then sold to the Woodhouses. How did this awful thing happen to you? You are too good a person for so ill a fate."

"Good? I have many shortcomings."

"Do not we all?"

"I have not yet figured it out, but God must have had a reason for this to happen to me. I hope I understand someday. At present, I do not."

"For you to have suffered as you have is no blessing, Sarah."

"I suppose not. I do not blame the Lord. I blame the men who deceived me, out of their own free will." She paused and sat back. "Why do you want to know anything about me? I am a servant and lowborn."

A corner of his mouth lifted a moment as he gazed into her eyes. "You are a human being. Perhaps it would help to talk about it. Tell me how it all began."

Tears hazed her vision, and she blinked them back. "It began with Jamie."

"Who is he?"

"My late husband."

"Yes, you told me you were a widow. He must have been a good man."

"He was. He did not care I was orphaned, poor, and crippled. We lived in a small fishing village on the coast. When there is a shipwreck, the people scavenge for what they can find. Some go out into the water, even in a storm. Jamie drowned—left me alone. I went to his sister and her husband, and that is where I met Sawyer."

"Was he the man who kidnapped you?"

"Yes. He deceived me into believing I would work as a servant in his house." She went on, telling her sorry tale and all that had befallen her. "I lost my baby—a few months before he was due to be born into this world. It broke my heart."

"I am sorry, Sarah. Have you felt well since?"

"I have, sir."

"No pains of any kind?"

"None. I think living with the Woodhouses has helped. They have given me good food and a secure roof over my head. I have never been hungry or cold."

"I have seen many women lose a baby. I will not deny I have had to steel myself against their suffering and grief. But I cannot with you."

Their eyes met and held. Sarah went back to polishing the boots.

"Why have you not married, sir?"

"I have not found the right woman. Perhaps my expectations have been too high, or I have looked in the wrong places." He stood and ran his hand through his hair. "It is late. Go to bed. And don't worry. I will go to the kitchen and fix myself something to eat."

She smiled at him, setting the boots aside. Then she got up from the floor and picked up the glass to take it away. "May I sleep in the girls' room tonight? They were weeping for their mother when I tucked them in."

By the look on his face she knew this distressed him. "Yes—of course. You know they love you, don't you, Sarah?"

She nodded and left him standing alone in front of the fire.

❧

The next morning, Alex called Sarah into the study that faced the front of the house. When she came in, she could not help but notice the papers he had spread out over the desk. Handling the details of his brother's estate could not be so easy a task, she thought. She waited for him to look up and speak to her.

"I have something for you, Sarah. But first you must stand with your back against the wall and assume your normal posture."

Baffled, she did as he asked. "Like this, sir?"

"Yes, but do not try to straighten up. Stand as you normally would." He drew up beside her and then took some measurements.

"I do not understand," she said.

"I think I know the reason for your impediment. A birth injury, such as a dislocated hip sustained during delivery, may have been the cause."

"And how would this knowledge help me or make things any better?"

"Here, I will show you." He handed her a half-inch pad of felt. "Place this inside your shoe. Let us see how you do with that."

She slipped off her shoe, added the felt, and then put her shoe back on. Then she looked at him. "What now?"

"Walk. Let me see how you do."

She crossed the room taking slow steps at first. Then she picked up her pace and realized she no longer limped. "It feels strange. I am even!"

"You should never limp again as long as you keep padding in your shoe. Does it make you happy? Do you feel comfortable with it?"

Tears sprang into her eyes and she laughed with joy. "This is marvelous! You have saved me, Dr. Hutton."

She hurried to him, and without thinking she threw her arms around his chest and embraced him. A breath escaped her lips, slow and silent. She had taken a liberty she should not have. Mortified, she felt her cheeks heat with embarrassment, and she glanced up into his face, as his hands slipped down her arms.

"Forgive me, sir. I did not mean . . ." She dropped her hands.

"For what should I forgive you? To see you happy gives me joy. Why should you not express it?"

"It is improper of me."

"Nonsense. Dance about the room if you wish."

"Oh, I cannot dance. I never learned. I could not learn."

"But you are happy?"

"I am. Thank you. How can I repay what you have done for me?"

Without an answer, Alex pulled her close, and then brought his lips near hers. "You owe me nothing. Do not ever think you do. I am indebted to you, you who have been a godsend. You've made me happy, Sarah." He then touched his lips to hers, with so little pressure, yet so pleasant.

Shaken, Sarah stood back. "That mustn't happen again. I am not meant for you."

Alex leaned on the windowsill. "You think I should have been more constrained—thought of my station and yours?"

"I should not have dared to embrace you, sir."

"You were happy. I do not blame you."

"But I am at least partially to blame."

He drew away from the window. "I should apologize for my lack of willpower. But you are so exquisitely pretty, kind, and good."

Sarah frowned. "What am I to say to that, Dr. Hutton?"

"Nothing. It is obvious you did not like it. But I meant every word."

He was wrong. She did like it. Sarah lowered her eyes and felt as if she were going to crumble to the floor. This emotion that stirred within her was new. She had not felt the same way with Jamie. This caused her heart to tremble, her hands to grab hold of her dress and twist it, her mind to whirl. She had to fight it. Be controlled and remember who and what she was.

Left with not knowing what to say, she opened the door. "Thank you, Dr. Hutton, for helping me. I shall never for-get—your kindness."

He stared at the floor. "Any good doctor would have done the same."

"I have known a few in my past and none ever showed con-cern for me." She walked out, and then turned back, trying to smile. "If you are hungry, I have breakfast ready. Do you like apple dumplings?"

He shook his head and laughed lightly. "Oh, Sarah. You have no idea."

12

Sunshine crept through the windows in the hallway and heightened the happiness that fell over Sarah. Nothing would come from the kiss, but to know he admired her, thought her worthy of his affection, pleased her deeply. But now that this had happened, she knew she could not stay in the house alone with him. She hoped his aunt would show up soon, for she could not just up and leave. How would she explain?

Looking down at the floor in front of the door, she set her hands on her hips and frowned. There were tracks of mud from his boots. He needed a boot-scraper out on the porch. She removed the one outside the back kitchen door and set it out front. Then she filled a bucket with soapy water and, with brush in hand, got down on her hands and knees and scrubbed the floor with verve.

While she dried it with a rag, someone knocked on the door jarring her concentration. She stood, pulled back the bolt, and opened it. Out on the brick walk stood a woman in a dark russet cloak and broad straw hat. In her hand she held a valise. A coach waited out on the road at the end of the drive.

"Good day. Is Dr. Hutton at home?"

"He is." Sarah brushed back the loose twists of hair that had fallen over her eyes. "May I ask who is calling?"

"Moria Burnsetter. I was sent for."

Before Sarah could invite her in, Mrs. Burnsetter waved the coach on and stepped through the door. With a sigh that spoke of satisfaction, she set her bag down. "Ah, 'tis a fine house and exactly as Alex described it in his letter. It has a good kitchen with a large hearth, and a comfortable sitting room, has it?"

"Yes, ma'am, and the bedrooms are also a good size."

"And a kitchen garden for planting vegetables?"

"Yes, Mrs.—"

"Burnsetter." She tossed off her cloak, then handed Sarah her hat, an antique with frayed edges decorated with a faded ribbon and flower.

She made a nervous gesture with her hands, as if patting something invisible. "Take care, please, not to crush the silk rose on my *Bergere*. Hats like these are so costly, you know. I have had this one for years and it is quite dear to me."

"I will be very careful, Mrs. Burnsetter, and treat it as if it were my own. Please, let me lay your cloak aside, and then I will call Dr. Hutton." After setting the hat gently upon the table near the door and the cloak over the back of the chair beside it, Sarah stepped away.

Mrs. Burnsetter folded her hands. "How many rooms for servants?"

Sarah turned. "I believe only one. I am currently occupying it."

"'Tis hard not to sleep in the bed you have grown accustomed to. You will be pleased to know, Mrs. Woodhouse wishes you to return to her house and resume your duties there. I met a messenger on the road. His horse was in the way and the driver stopped. When I told him who I was and where I was headed, he gave me a note to give to Alex. And to you, of course."

Sarah could not smile. "I cannot say I am pleased."

"Why not? Mrs. Woodhouse is your mistress after all, and their home is very fine from what I could see of it in the distance."

"That is true. It's just that I have grown attached to the girls, and I shall hate to leave them." She had also grown attached to Alex, and the thought of parting from him caused her spirits to sink.

Mrs. Burnsetter looked sympathetic. "I can understand. But you do realize it is unseemly for you to stay longer, if you should have been here at all. Alex is a bachelor, and you the only woman in the house. Where are the children?"

Then she snapped her head upward and looked toward the top of the staircase. "Ah, those must be the little angels. Hello, children. Come and greet your auntie."

With a great toothy smile, Mrs. Burnsetter spread her arms wide. But being shy, Rose and Lily leaned on the railing. Mrs. Burnsetter swiveled on her heels to Sarah. "Why do they not come down?"

"You must excuse them. They are a little bashful." She went up the steps and took the girls by the hands and brought them down. Standing in front of the newcomer, the girls stared, wide-eyed.

"Say hello to your great aunt, Rose, Lily."

Mrs. Burnsetter threw her arms about them, practically smothering them in her ample bosom. "They are indeed precious. But so thin?"

"Until Dr. Hutton arrived, they had had little to eat."

Mrs. Burnsetter wiggled her head. "Poor dears. And to lose their mother shortly after their father is unfortunate indeed. Where is their uncle? Why have you not called him?"

"I was about to when you stopped me."

Sorry she would have to return to the Woodhouses, Sarah headed for the study. Alex opened the door before she could knock, and stopped short upon sight of the generously proportioned woman standing in the hallway with his nieces.

"Ah, at last." Mrs. Burnsetter wiggled her head again and held out her arms. "I barely recognize you, Alex. It has been so long."

"Aunt Moria!" He smiled and kissed her cheek. "I am so pleased to see you."

"And I you, Alex. You look so well, and so handsome."

"I have grown older and war-weary. How was your journey?"

"Tolerable."

"Please come and sit down." He turned to Sarah. "Bring the girls in with us, Sarah."

Aunt Moria followed him into the sitting room. Sarah and the girls trailed behind. The fire had burned low and Alex banked it with a fresh log. Sarah led the girls to the opposite settee and fluffed the pillows on Aunt Moria's chair.

"Have you a blanket, dear?" she asked, sitting down. "My limbs are chilled to the bone from riding in that creaky old coach."

Sarah drew one from the back of the settee and laid it over Aunt Moria's knees with the same kind of gentle care she showed to Temperance.

With a sigh, Aunt Moria settled back. "I was so grieved to learn Benjamin died, Alex, and then that his wife had followed him. When I read your letter, I got down on my knees and thanked the Lord you had arrived when you did. What would have happened to these children if you had not?"

Alex leaned forward in his chair. "The girls are doing much better since Sarah has been here. My cooking is poor and she has made up for that."

"Well, they needed a woman to care for them. She has done a good deed."

"Yes, she has been a godsend."

Sarah did not meet his eyes when he spoke of her. A gentle smile lifted her mouth ever so slightly, and she hoped he would realize the blessing that had been born out of tragedy.

"Oh, before I forget, Mrs. Woodhouse has sent you this. I met her messenger on the way here, as he was out on the road but a short distance away. I hope you do not mind." Aunt Moria handed Alex the note. After he read it, he placed it in his waistcoat pocket and stared at the fire. Sarah could tell the news disappointed him by the lingering sadness in his eyes.

"Mr. Woodhouse wishes you to return home, Sarah," he said, a hint of regret in his voice.

But I want my home to be with you—and the twins. "Yes, I know."

"He says his wife has been whiling away for you and he is worried."

Sarah lowered her eyes. "Indeed I am sure that is true. She has delicate emotions."

When she saw Rose blink her eyes and watched the frown on Lily's face deepen, she could bear it no longer. It seemed the air had been sucked out of the room, that the sunlight that streamed through the windows had suddenly clouded over. She turned and walked out, then went upstairs to gather her meager belongings.

13

Frost coated the corners of the window. Sarah shivered and stepped away after she saw Alex ride up on Charger. He had been gone not quite an hour and looked harried as he dismounted and guided his horse to the small barn at the rear of the house. Her window faced the barn, and the fields of grass that met a border of pines. She thought perhaps he had gone to check on the family with the sick children, and was unconcerned about her.

She delayed packing her things. They were piled together on the bed next to her bag. Instead, she had stood by the window all this time, praying Mr. Woodhouse would change his mind. But she knew it was not meant to be. In a few moments, she would be out on the lane headed back to her master's house, possibly never to see Alex again. She did not like the ache this thought brought to her heart. Tears pooled in her eyes and she let them fall, and then wiped them away with a stroke of her hand.

"I do not want to go back." She whispered the words. "I do not want to leave him and the girls, Lord. I want to stay, even if it means I would be indentured to him. If he cannot love me as his wife, let him have me as his servant."

Then she turned away from the window. She heard his boots stump up the stairs and come down the hall. A shadow fell near. She could feel him close to her—sense the beating of his heart and his eyes upon her.

"You are ready to leave?" he asked softly.

She lowered her head. "Yes, I suppose I am."

"You know I have no right to keep you with me, Sarah."

She folded her spare dress and tucked it into her sack. "It is the law I obey, Mr. Woodhouse, until I am free."

"Try not to worry about Rose and Lily."

"Your aunt will take good care of them. So why should I be concerned? She is so experienced, and is family." Her horsehair brush sat on top of the dresser. She grabbed it and packed it.

He stepped closer. "My brother and Emma would have wanted it that way. But I will miss seeing your face every day and our conversations in the evenings."

She swallowed the tight feeling in her throat. "As I will, too. And I shall miss the twins. Their smiles always brightened my mood."

"You should know, I rode over and asked Mr. Woodhouse to allow you to stay longer. He said he could not oblige me, and saw no reason for you to stay on."

Sarah smoothed the spread that lay over the bed. "If Mrs. Woodhouse is throwing fits over me, and I do not go to her, she will fall sick. I have seen it happen before. She panics."

"She is ill already. I will try to help her."

"Then you will come to the farm?"

"Yes, but only a few times. I do not think it will take long for her to recover. Mr. Woodhouse said she has a cold."

"Oh, I see." She closed the doors to the mahogany armoire, now empty of her scant possessions.

"I wish you would be still, Sarah. There are things I wish to say."

Sarah lifted her sack and turned. "It is best you do not. Why give me hope where there is none?"

Stepping to the door, he moved aside, but stopped her with a touch of his hand on hers. "We have feelings for each other, have we not?"

She pinched her brows together and lowered her gaze. "I cannot admit what I feel. It would not be right."

"Yet, I see it in your eyes every time you look at me. You can say you love me without words, Sarah."

She fought the rise of emotion bubbling inside her. "You must not speak these things to me."

"Why not? Give me a reason."

"I am indentured, poor, and lowborn. You are not."

"Those are your circumstances, Sarah. Not who you are."

"You are wrong. They have made me what I am. I will carry a stigma for the rest of my life. I am not for you. You deserve a woman higher than I."

Frustrated, he shook his head. "I want you. Can you not see?" He put his hands on her shoulders. "I will pay off your debt and free you. Mr. Woodhouse will welcome the money. He will let you go."

He spoke with passion, and Sarah fought back the tears that pooled in her eyes. Still she could not throw herself upon his mercy, and for what reason she could not explain either to him or herself.

She gripped the sack as hard as she could, as if to choke it.

"And be indentured to you? Again, I am to be bargained for." She shoved past him. "I shall work and pay my own debt. No man shall ever buy me again if I can help it."

Knowing what she had just asked God, that, if not a wife then let her be a servant to the man she loved, would only make her heart break. For if she were his property, and he were to find a wife, how could she live in the same house, under the same roof, still loving him? Without another word, she hurried down the stairs to the front door, grabbed her cloak from the peg, and rushed out. The cold smacked her full force. Alex followed her.

"I will not have you walking there alone."

"I do not need protection." And she stormed on, angry that she had to leave him.

"None at all? You have forgotten the Indians we met before?"

"They will not harm me," she said over her shoulder. "You said so."

"There are no guarantees of that."

"They went away, back to their villages."

He moved in front of her and she stopped. "As long as you are with me, you are my responsibility. You will go on horseback, not walk. Understand?"

Stunned, she looked up at him. What he told her seemed fair and true, and she had no reason to treat him so rudely. None of this was his fault.

He snatched her bag out of her hand. "Now, go back inside and kiss the girls good-bye. They will be disappointed if you do not. I will be waiting outside with Charger."

14

Alex turned his horse onto a narrow path, and they emerged in a place where the land opened out. He drew rein at the edge of a cliff that overlooked the mouth of the Potomac as it flowed peacefully into the Chesapeake Bay. Seabirds swooped above, and the water shimmered as the sun briefly broke through the clouds.

The feel of him behind her, his knees holding her in place, made Sarah feel safer than she had ever felt. She gazed at the scene before her until her eyes smarted and the wind brought tears to them. Her hair lifted back and she filled her lungs with the scent of land and river.

"Not a ship in sight," Alex said. "But beyond that point where the land juts into the water, the British are warring against us. And across the river, see that strip of yellow? That is the road I took before crossing here—where I found you." He spoke the words into her ear, and a sad smile quivered over her lips.

"Was it a long journey?" she asked.

"Yes, and it is not over."

She glanced over her shoulder. "What do you mean?"

He ignored her question. "I wish we could stay, but those clouds to the east mean snow within the hour."

He turned Charger and went down the road toward the Woodhouse farm. Soon small flakes of snow whirled about them, as clouds drifted overhead in sheets of gray and white. Sarah drew her hood over her head and as they rode on, she watched the snow coat the ground and glaze the trees. Smoke curled from the chimney of the house, and she suddenly felt the icy air seep through her woolen cloak. Alex dismounted, reached up, and helped her down.

"Be sure the girls keep their woolen stockings on," she said. "And tell your aunt to put the warming pan under the covers before she puts them to bed."

"I will." He shoved his boot into the stirrup and remounted. She watched him ride away, wondering when, or if, she would see him again.

Shutting the door against the wind and whirling snow, Sarah leaned her back against it and shut her eyes. She heard Temperance upstairs whining to Celia. After a moment's hesitation, she climbed the staircase and made her return known. Relief sprang over Temperance's face when Sarah stepped through the door. She let out a little cry and waved her handkerchief for Sarah to come further into the room.

"Oh, thank the Lord you are back, Sarah." She held the handkerchief to her nose and sniffed. "My life has been in tatters while you have been gone."

Sarah pulled off her cloak and laid it over the back of a chair. "I am sorry to hear that, ma'am. Has something happened?"

Looking as if ready to burst into tears, Temperance slapped her hand on the arm of the high-backed chair she lounged in. "Everything has gone wrong. Mr. Woodhouse has left on business, so he claims. I do not know when he will return. He left me here with only Celia as company. She is none too good at it."

"He has gone before and has always come back. You have nothing to fear, for Mr. Woodhouse loves you." Sarah straightened the rumpled bedcover and then laid a wrap over Temperance's shoulders.

With a gasp, Temperance snatched Sarah's hand and squeezed it. "I fear something is about to happen that shall make me very unhappy."

"God is the only one who knows our future, mistress. Besides, what you might be feeling may not be fear at all. Perhaps you are mistaking it for anticipation. Perhaps something good is about to happen."

Temperance blinked her eyes. "Like what?"

Sarah sat on the footstool in front of Temperance's chair. "Well, maybe Mr. Woodhouse will return with a special gift."

Enlightened, Temperance's eyes widened. "I had not thought of that. My birthday is in a few weeks. He may bring me a present he had to collect. I wonder what it could be? Thank you, Sarah. I am glad he commanded you home."

Command. Demand. How she wished to be free, to make her own choices again.

"Yes, but I shall miss the twins," she said, standing and closing a few books that lay on the table. "They have become dear to me."

"Children do that. But you mustn't be attached. They are not yours to love." Squinting her eyes, Temperance studied Sarah. "What is this? You are walking so normal. Has a miracle occurred?"

"A miracle by way of Dr. Hutton." Sarah slipped off her shoe and showed Temperance the padding within it. "He made this for me."

"Well, he is a very good physician indeed. But I think my husband took a risk in allowing you to help Dr. Hutton."

"Hmm. I think him too wise to take undue risk, ma'am," Sarah said. "I'm sure he thought Dr. Hutton's request over thoroughly."

"I know. He is shrewd when making a decision. But Dr. Hutton is single and very handsome. And you are pretty and young. Did you feel an attraction toward him?"

Caught off guard, Sarah had no idea what to say. If she said she had, they might forbid her to speak to him whenever he was called to attend to someone's ailment at the farm. If she said she did not, she would be lying.

"How did you feel when you met him, ma'am? Did you think well of him?"

Temperance nodded. "I thought him excellent—a fine man."

"That is how I felt as well."

"Well, I doubt there is a woman alive, young or old, that would not feel some sort of attraction to him. But it is not a feeling an indentured servant should entertain. You understand, do you not?"

Sarah struggled to deny what thrived in her heart. But she could not tell Temperance the truth. "I do. You have no reason to worry."

Temperance clasped her hands together. "Oh, Sarah. You have no idea how relieved that makes me feel. I was so afraid you would fall in love with him and that he would take you from me. But I shall have you always, for you care too much about me to allow that to happen."

15

*H*ungry sparrows chirped outside Sarah's slit of a window, lusty chatter that awakened her from a dream world. She tossed back the quilt she had patched together from scraps. The morning air smelled of cold and frost. With haste she dressed and laced on her leather shoes.

A glaze of ice lay atop the water in her washing bowl and when she tapped it with her fingers, it broke open. Shivering, she washed her face and dried it with a towel. She gripped her arms and looked out the window at the misty landscape. Out in the barn their cow lowed in between intervals of the cock's crowing. The old girl needed milking.

Frost coated the grass, and when she went outside, it crunched beneath her soles as she headed to the barn. She smiled at her even gait. How good of Alex to fashion a cure for her shorter leg. How considerate of him to concern himself with her problem.

When she pictured his face and when she recalled the touch of his lips against hers, a swell of emotion flooded her being. Every time a horse galloped down the road, her heart soared in hopes it was he.

After Sarah finished milking the cow, she gathered the pail and carried the steamy milk toward the kitchen door. Porridge had to be made and she stepped across the yard feeling hungry.

When she heard a horse pound down the hard earth, she looked up with a start. Alex brought his mount to a halt a few yards from where she stood, and dismounted. Charger bobbed his broad neck and Alex patted him. Alex's eyes smiled and he drew off his hat.

"Good morning, Sarah. It's a brisk day."

"Indeed, and I prefer the fireside to the cold." She shifted the pail to her other hand, and he glanced at it. "Come in and warm yourself, Dr. Hutton. Celia has a good fire going in the kitchen."

"Here, allow me. It looks heavy." He stepped forward to take the pail from her hand, but she moved back.

"No, Dr. Hutton. This is not your kind of work to do. Rather, a servant's."

"That is absurd," he said, holding out his hand. "Let me have it, dear girl."

With a coy look, she moved the pail a little way out of his reach. "Such an improper name for you to call me by."

"What would you have me call you?" He stepped closer. "It is no lie you are dear to me."

"You know you should call me by my first name. The Woodhouses would disapprove of anything else, especially if it is an endearment."

A wry grin lifted one corner of his mouth. "You suppose so?" He leaned down closer to her until his lips were a mere inch from hers. "I will have that pail of milk, Sarah Carr, and if some is spilled, it will be your fault."

Sarah raised her chin. "Then I surrender." And she brought the pail forward.

"I would prefer you surrender your heart." He took the pail from her hand, his fingers brushing hers. "Now, you will rebuke me for that, I suppose."

"Indeed I should."

"Can you surrender?"

She lowered her eyes. "I could—if I were free. But I cannot forget my place." She lifted her gaze. "So, the answer is no."

"It is true some would agree with you, but not I."

"Then you welcome my reproof?"

"A woman has a way of keeping a man in check. Where my bold tongue has come from, God only knows. But I have been too free with it since meeting you."

She laughed. "You cannot blame me for your lack of discipline, sir."

He shook his head. "No, I cannot."

The breeze tossed Sarah's hair, and she pushed it back. She glanced at the pail and said, "Celia will be needing that milk to make our porridge."

Turning away, Sarah smiled, both delighted and confused they could speak as freely as they did. But it could only be when they were alone, and never in front of others. Reaching the door, she gripped the handle hard and pushed it open.

The course of her life bewildered her. God turned a bad thing into good, gave her beauty for ashes, joy for tears. For now, loving him sufficed. She never would have met him if she had not suffered kidnapping and slavery. She would still be in Cornwall, poor and alone, seeking work to care for her baby. *Oh, but my little one might have lived if I had been wiser, had not believed Lem and Sawyer.* This brought on a feeling of guilt that she had been unable to defeat.

Red coals smoldered in the fireplace. From an iron hook the kettle puffed out steam. Alex set the pail on the table and

Sarah poured the milk into a ceramic jug, then into a smaller one that had a lid.

She looked over at him. "For the girls."

He came around the table. "This is kind of you, Sarah. Thank you."

"Thank Mr. Woodhouse. He told me to give you some when you visit."

"But you would have done it just the same even if he had not."

He was close to her now, and she glanced up into his eyes. They were warm for her. "How are Lily and Rose?" she asked, feeling shy under his gaze. "Are they adjusting to your aunt?"

"They are both very well. Aunt Moria is firm but loving, and more like a grandmother than a great-aunt."

Sarah set a tray on the table. "I am glad everything is going so well."

"The girls miss you, though. They ask about you."

"I miss them too." A blue willow bowl slipped in her hand as she placed it on the tray along with a silver spoon and a napkin embroidered with the initials T W. "I will ask my mistress if I may visit sometime."

He frowned, and she wondered what she had said to cause it. "How I hate the word *mistress*," he said. His mouth twisted over the syllables. "You should never have to call anyone that. You should not have to work from sunup to sundown at the whim of an idle person."

His words smote her heart, and Sarah lowered her eyes again. "It is the will of Almighty God, sir."

He huffed. "Is it? Maybe. But not forever—not for you."

"As long as I keep myself in good health, you are right. In a few years I'll be free." She paused, looking back into his eyes, marveling at the compassion that swam in them. "Why are you here?"

"I was asked to call on Mrs. Woodhouse. She sent Celia yesterday with a note."

Sarah ran her finger along the edge of the table. "And not I."

"She could not spare you, I suppose."

"I know. She did not like me gone for so long, and has clung to me ever since."

"I can understand why."

"I feel sorry for her. She is so sad some days."

He leaned an elbow on the table. "What if I told you I am sad without you? What if I said I need you? Would you feel sorry for me?"

Her heart pounded. "I would feel sorry for us both," she whispered.

He touched her cheek. "Twice I have asked Mr. Woodhouse to release you. Twice he has turned me down. I will keep asking until he accepts my offer."

"And then, I would be your servant?"

"Servant, never. Wife, yes." He leaned down, his lips brushing over hers. How wonderful it felt, for his words, his touch, his gaze, were bathed in love. "Do you believe I love you, that whether you are a servant or a lady, all that matters to me is you?"

"Yes, I believe you."

His smile brightened. "God will show us a way, but only if you tell me you will be my wife one day. I am sorry I'm asking you in a kitchen and not in a garden full of roses, or on a starry summer night with a full moon. That is how it should be. I should like to see the moonlight in your hair."

Her mouth fell open and she stared at him. Before she could answer, the kitchen door banged open and in stepped Celia. She stood stock-still, as they parted. "Dr. Hutton? I did not hear you arrive, sir."

"I came through the back, Celia, when I saw Sarah carrying a heavy load."

Celia glared at Sarah. "Heavy, indeed. You best get busy with your chores, Sarah." It was not Celia's place to order Sarah about, but because she was a much older woman, and had been with the Woodhouses more years than Sarah, she did not argue. But she could look defiant.

"I have Mrs. Woodhouse's tray ready." She moved it to the edge of the table. "Just the way she likes it. With only her china and her napkin." Temperance would not eat from any dishes others used.

"Good," said Celia. "She's up and calling for you. Tell her I will have her coffee ready shortly."

Swallowing down embarrassment, Sarah stepped around the table and moved toward the kitchen door.

"Coffee, Dr. Hutton?" Celia's tone smacked of knowing. "Had your breakfast? I will make a mess of eggs for you. I do not serve guests porridge. 'Tis too lowly."

"I am not hungry, thank you just the same," he said. Sarah looked back, saw him pick up his hat and head toward her.

Out in the hall, he followed her up the staircase.

"Will you give me an answer?" he said.

"They will hear you." She moved a little quicker.

"I do not care if they do. Will you marry me?"

"You are making fun of me, Dr. Hutton. You know I cannot promise that." She reached the upper floor, and he walked alongside her down the hall.

"Very well. Then I shall make a promise to you. I swear one day to clear your indenture and make you my wife. I will do everything in my power to make you happy."

She paused at Temperance's door. "You are in earnest?"

"I am serious, Sarah, and a man of my word."

"I cannot believe what my ears have heard." They turned and saw Celia standing near. She had brought Temperance's coffee with her. "You should be ashamed of yourself, Dr. Hutton, leading Sarah on like that. Mr. Woodhouse would not like this. No, he'd not like it at all." And she hurried to open Temperance's door.

Temperance yawned and stretched out her arms. "What would he not like, Celia?"

Celia set the coffee on the bedside table. "Dr. Hutton wants to marry our Sarah, ma'am." She shook her head with a chuckle. "Can you imagine that?"

"Oh, no Sarah. I forbid it."

Sarah set the breakfast tray across Temperance's lap. She was furious at Celia.

Dr. Hutton stepped forward and said, "Mrs. Woodhouse, what I wish to do is none of Celia's business. Please tell her to hold her tongue."

Temperance pursed her lips a moment, and then gave Celia a look of reprimand. "Dr. Hutton is correct, Celia. You are not to meddle in his affairs. This is how rumors start and then people have their feelings hurt. Still, Dr. Hutton. I pray what Celia says is not true."

"Why, ma'am? What is wrong with me wanting to marry Sarah?"

"Well, for one she is below your station."

"That does not matter in the least."

"And she's been wedded before."

"That is not uncommon."

"But you cannot take her away from me, Dr. Hutton."

"Surely you will be able to find another servant."

"Not like Sarah. My husband will not free her—not yet."

"Then I shall continue to offer to clear her indenture or wait until her time is over."

A blush rose on Temperance's cheeks. "Oh, that says you care immensely for my Sarah. Oh, but I feel so faint today."

He picked up Temperance's wrist and timed her pulse. "You must eat more, Mrs. Woodhouse, and take walks in the fresh air."

She widened her eyes. "Alone?"

"No. Sarah will go with you, or your husband."

"And why must I do this?"

"The air and exercise will do you good. It is unhealthy for you to sit in your room all day with your windows shut and the curtains drawn."

Temperance screwed up her face. "I do not like the sunshine in my eyes when I wake."

"No doubt you don't." He tucked his watch into his waistcoat and walked out the door.

When he left, Sarah drew back the curtains and the room flooded with morning light. From the window she watched him climb back into the saddle and turn his horse. It felt as if a part of her left with him, and the loneliness she felt caused her to heave an unsteady breath. She believed that what he said to her was from his heart. Mixed with the feelings of missing him, joy filled her. Dr. Hutton loved her.

"Is something the matter, Sarah?" said Temperance. "You look so sad today."

"I shall be fine, ma'am." She turned. "You will listen to Dr. Hutton's advice, won't you?"

"I will. I suppose a walk after breakfast will be alright. I have a letter to give Mr. Pippins. Hopefully, Mr. Henry will answer this one." With a sigh, Temperance leaned her head back against the pillows.

Sarah closed the door behind her.

16

We are ruined! How could you have let this happen to us?"

Sarah looked up at the top of the staircase where her mistress was making her way down.

"Be calm, Temperance." Mr. Woodhouse followed close on his wife's heels.

Temperance pressed a handkerchief against her mouth when she reached the first landing. Then she threw her arms down with fists tight. "What shall we do? You have ruined us! And all this time without me knowing."

"No. The King has ruined us with his unreasonable demands on the people, and Dunmore was no help. We've been taxed into oblivion."

Temperance whirled around to meet Mr. Woodhouse nose-to-nose. "Oh, blame it on someone such as the King. Mr. Henry will hear of this, and when he does . . ."

Mr. Woodhouse spread out his hands. "He will do what?"

"Well, I do not know. He will advise us, I suppose. This revolution is about thwarting the tyrant in London, is it not?"

"Partially, yes. But, my dear, we will rally. You will see." Mr. Woodhouse placed his hands tenderly on his wife's arms. "I have to sell in order to pay my debts. All will be well."

"No it will not." Weeping, Temperance started down the staircase. Sarah had never seen her in such a panic before and feared she would fall.

"I promise you it will. We will have a new start in Jamaica."

Jamaica! An icy chill rippled over Sarah's skin, passed straight to her bones and into her core. Her knees weakened. *He cannot make me go. He cannot force me away from Alex!*

Temperance's eyes shot wide open and she stood stock-still. Her flushed face turned white. "What? Jamaica, you say?"

"Yes. You know my brother has a sugar plantation there and has become rich. He has written to me and invited us to come stay with him. He wishes for me to go into business with him. We shall be very wealthy one day."

Temperance flopped down on a step. "And hot, I wager, and prone to all kinds of tropical fevers and pirates raiding every bit of it!"

"It is a paradise there, with orchids and flowers you cannot imagine. You will not have to endure cold winters."

"The flowers shall make me sneeze, every last one of them." She wiped her eyes, stood, and came all the way down the stairs. Disturbed by the news she was overhearing, Sarah tried to slip away unseen, but Temperance saw her and called out. "Oh, Sarah. Oh, thank the Lord, you are with me."

"Let me bring you some tea, ma'am." She did not know what to do.

Sobbing, Temperance threw her arms around Sarah's shoulders. "I dearly missed you when you were away. We shan't be parted ever again."

Mr. Woodhouse drew Temperance back. "Control yourself, my dear."

"How can I when you are determined to uproot me?"

"Go sit down and rest a moment."

"I want Sarah with me." She took Sarah by the arm and strode into the sitting room. "Oh, it is a very bad day." After two quick intakes of breath, Temperance wiped her nose. "Did you hear what Mr. Woodhouse plans to do, Sarah?"

"Yes. And forgive me, for I did not intend to."

"So you heard he wants to sell all that we own and drag me off to some heathen island in the *Carri-be-no*? Oh, but at least I shall have you and Celia to comfort me. And when we are rich, we can return to Virginia." She looked back at her husband for assurance on that fact.

Mr. Woodhouse shrugged. "I suppose we might, my dear."

"And by that time, Sarah's indenture will be over. Oh, but she will want to stay with us, won't you, Sarah?"

"She cannot go with us, Temperance." Mr. Woodhouse spoke as if his wife were a frail piece of crystal that could shatter if his voice went any higher. All at once, Temperance's face turned as red as the ruby choker about her throat. In spite of her mistress' distress, Sarah could not help but smile. It could only mean one thing. Mr. Woodhouse intended to give her to Alex. She'd be free to become his wife.

"On this, I demand." She shook her fists. "You will not deny me Sarah."

"I have to. I have to sell everything. We are in that poor a state. If I do not, I will go to prison."

The dam burst, and Temperance fell apart. She collapsed on the floor weeping and wailing, flinging her arms across her face and kicking her legs. Sarah had not a moment to let the plans for her sink in. Only the words *she cannot go with us* echoed in her mind.

Sarah crouched down and put her arms around Temperance. "Do not cry, mistress." Then she helped Mr. Woodhouse gather his poor wife up and help her to the settee.

"I will hurry and get Dr. Hutton," she said.

Temperance refused. "I do not want him knowing why I am so utterly devastated. All because my husband could not manage his affairs." She gasped between sobs. "I do not want anyone to know. I am so ashamed."

Mr. Woodhouse looked worried. "I am sorry, Temperance. It will prove a hard day for you no doubt."

Temperance looked at him. "Do not tell me there is more."

"Creditors are arriving this afternoon with a buyer."

Sarah frowned and looked over at Celia when she walked into the room. She seemed impassive to what was happening. "As long as I can stay with Mrs. Woodhouse," she said to Mr. Woodhouse, "I will be content. But sell me off and I shall pine away to nothing and die within a year."

Mr. Woodhouse held up his hand. "Not to worry, Celia. You have been with us for many years and will come with us."

Temperance blew her nose into her handkerchief. "And what about you, Sarah? You stand there not saying a word. Persuade Mr. Woodhouse to bring you, too."

Sarah did not want to persuade him to do anything, especially to change his mind. She swallowed. "I . . ."

"There is nothing to say," said Mr. Woodhouse. "It would be prudent to have Sarah pack some of your favorite things— clothing particularly."

Shock fell over Temperance. She stared forward with a blank expression on her face. Sarah felt sorry for her mistress, and the thought of separating from her now pained her. But not as much as being separated from Alex and the twins.

She followed Mr. Woodhouse out into the hallway, and stood in front of him. "Dr. Hutton will settle my indenture, Mr. Woodhouse. You have only to send him word."

"I am sorry, Sarah. But I have already taken care of this. Mr. Thrasher is arriving within the hour. No one said your life would be easy. I can tell how upset you are. I hope you can forgive me."

She dared to grab his arms and shake him. "Please. Do not sell me to this man. I'm begging you. Let Dr. Hutton have me."

"No! It will be best for you this way. I know how attached he grew to you. I would not want you used in that way, and then he marry and have a wife, and you be a mistress to him. I cannot be a party to that."

Tears welled in her eyes. "Who is Mr. Thrasher? A plantation owner? A gentleman? Is he an American soldier?"

"He is a wealthy landowner, though he explained he lives a humble existence. Whatever that may mean." Mr. Woodhouse squared his shoulders. "Not that you have a say, or can ask me such questions, Sarah."

She lifted her chin. "I think I should have some right to know to whom I will be enslaved, sir."

"Now, do not speak to me in that harsh tone, Sarah. I did what I felt best for you. You will go with Mr. Thrasher when he arrives, and say nothing more to me about it."

"Please." She fell on her knees weeping. "Please undo it."

Mr. Woodhouse looked aghast. "Good lord. You are in love with the man. Do not deny it, Sarah. I know what I see. Dr. Hutton is above you, and it would be inappropriate for him to have you under his roof with the feelings you have for him."

She stood back, head down. A gruff voice, carried on the breeze outside, ended their exchange as the sound of a horse and wagon drew up to the house.

"Hi, ho! Mr. Woodhouse. I have come for my property."

Panic prickled over Sarah's skin and she broke out into a cold sweat. *Please, God. Have I not suffered enough? Do not let this man take me away. Bring Alex back.*

"Bring the lass out and let me have a good look at her. I bought her sight unseen, but believe what you say. Bring her out, Mr. Woodhouse. I am waiting."

The man's voice, the way his words tripped over his tongue, cut into Sarah like the edge of a razor—slowly, slowly, grating against her skin.

Mr. Woodhouse ordered his wife to dry her tears. "Behave like a lady, Temperance."

She smoothed her hair and followed Mr. Woodhouse to the door. Sarah and Celia went to the window and looked out. Upon sight of the man, Sarah's blood ran cold.

"Oh, Lord Almighty," whispered Celia. "Take this cup from Sarah."

Sarah turned into Celia's arms and wept against her shoulder.

17

Sarah's hopes were dashed to begin with, but the instant she laid eyes on Jebediah Thrasher they were crushed. He was a middle-aged man, barrel-chested, and practically bald save for a few wisps of wiry hair around his forehead. How Mr. Woodhouse could have chosen a grubby backwoodsman over Dr. Hutton confounded her. Apparently she did not know her former master as well as she had thought.

Thrasher tapped her on the shoulder. "You call me Mr. Thrasher, Sarah. Other folks call me Jebediah T, 'cause I have a brother by the same last name. Just so you won't be confused if some stop by my place."

"I cannot think of calling you anything else, Mr. Thrasher." She kept her sad eyes fixed ahead and glanced at him when he let out a high-pitched chuckle. His teeth were as brown as the tobacco he chewed, and he smelled as gamey as the animals he hunted.

"Oh, I imagine you could dream up any number of names for me, Sarah girl."

Growing annoyed, she scooted as far away from him as possible on the wagon seat. "I am not that kind of person. I will keep other names for you to myself."

Again he laughed, this time a little lower. "Did you know I've made a good living as a trapper? I'm a wealthy man, though you'd not know it to look at me."

"Mr. Woodhouse did not share your occupation with me, no."

"Furs, you know, are a lucrative trade," he told Sarah as he drove his horse and wagon down the river road above the Great Falls. "I'll teach you how to skin and tan. I might even let you keep a bear fur for a coat."

She crossed her arms and glared. "I am better as a cook and housekeeper. You should hire a man to do that."

Thrasher shook his head. "You're a sassy one. Cooking and housekeeping is what I got you for really, so don't worry about learning anything else unless you want to. But I warn you. First time you run your hand over a bear fur, you're gonna want that coat."

"Are there other people where you live?"

"Miles apart maybe. Anyway, as I was saying earlier, I had my fill fighting in the last war against the French and Indians. The patriots can fight their revolution with men younger than me. I prefer otters, muskrats, and beavers for my killing."

Feeling as if she would go mad, Sarah shut her eyes. She wondered if Mr. Woodhouse realized the fate he had consigned her to. She had loved him and his wife, but now resentment replaced the affection she once felt.

Thrasher pulled to a stop. He jumped from his seat and walked into the woods. Sarah was alone. She knew he'd gone off to relieve himself and this might be a good time to run away. Whatever the consequences, she would accept them over a life with him.

She drew her cloak around her knees and turned to jump down. But he stepped out of the woods, noiseless as an Indian.

"You need a womanly moment, Sarah? I'd have to stand near to be sure you don't run off."

"No."

"Have you stopped weeping?"

"I stopped miles ago."

"You'll grow accustomed to me. I ain't so bad. Under this rough hide is a gentleman. I'll do right by you. Be kind, and not lay a hand upon you. So don't worry."

"I cannot help it. I have been deceived before."

His tough looks suddenly softened with a furrowed brow. Perhaps he meant what he said. "I'm no different than Mr. Woodhouse. I just don't have a big house like him—hmm, like he had. Do you know how to cook deer liver?"

Sarah cringed. "I do not."

"It's what I like most." A pause followed. Thrasher glanced at her with a contemplative expression. "Were you thinking of running away when I went into the woods?" He climbed back into his seat and picked up the reins. "'Cause if you did, you'd regret it. I'd not hurt you, but there are other things in this wilderness that would."

She made no reply. Melancholy sealed her tongue and she shut her eyes.

"I'm not kidding when I tell you there are dangers. Venomous snakes. Cougars and bears. Come across one of them, and you'll meet your end."

"I do not care anymore."

"Oh, don't say that. Life is a gift from God."

She frowned. "Even a hard one? How can it be a gift?"

"Well, I don't really know. But it is just the same. Move on there, Bernie." He snapped the reins, and then turned to Sarah. "Want to know why I call my mare a boy's name?"

"Not really." She looked at the aging gray horse. "But I suppose you will anyway."

"I had a sweetheart when I was a young man and Bernie was her pet name. She was Bernice McGreevy—prettiest girl for miles around. Want to know what happened to her?"

"I have no other choice but to . . ."

"She ran off with an officer. That red coat and gold braid won her over. Not my buckskins and wilderness living."

"I cannot say I blame her, Mr. Thrasher. Most women would choose a comfortable life in a town to an isolated one fraught with hardship."

"Smart you are, Sarah. But you'd be surprised."

With a sigh, she glanced through the woods from her side of the wagon. She had no reason to care about his love life, or hear anything more about the wilderness existence he was leading her to. But it made her think of Alex. What she felt for him intensified with each passing mile. She had not forgotten Jamie, only realized what she felt for him was a friendly love—far from being in love, the longing and missing.

What made her despair even worse? Alex would forget her. Lily and Rose, too. Still she wondered if he had heard the news that the Woodhouses were selling everything and leaving Virginia and that she had been sold to the first man who offered good money. If he had, how did he feel now that Mr. Woodhouse sent her away with a middle-aged back-woodsman?

Thrasher nudged her on the arm. "Did you hear what I said, Sarah? I ain't interested in you in no wifely way. Don't fear on that account. I just want someone to cook and keep house for me. My porridge is like paste and my meat like leather."

What am I doing? I could jump down this minute and walk off. I can run faster now, more than he could with his short bowlegs.

Her hand gripped the edge of her seat and she felt the rough wood scrape against her skin. She thought of what Thrasher had said about dangerous animals, and that when it grew dark and cold, she could die from exposure.

She then decided to tell him her story. Perhaps he would feel sympathy for her and let her go. Maybe he would turn the wagon around and head for the Hutton House and bargain with Alex.

Quietly, Thrasher listened to her woeful tale. He paused at times to scratch his head. "Oh, that is sad, Sarah."

"Will you have pity on me and send me back? Dr. Hutton will pay you well for me. You spoke of love. You must know how it feels to be apart from the one who holds your heart. He and I love each other, and I grieve thinking I might not ever see him again. He does not know where I have gone."

"Where's this doctor?"

"He lives near the Woodhouse farm."

"Hmm, well, we are close to home now and it's too late to turn around. I'll think about it. Maybe when I've got to go back to sell my furs, I'll consider paying him a visit. He'll have to make me a very good offer, 'cause I'll have to go back across the river and get someone new."

"You mean it, sir?"

He shrugged. "Sure, why not?"

Though slight, a smile finally made its way across Sarah's mouth. She had the urge to throw her arms around him and give him a hug, but he smelled too bad for that, and he might get the wrong idea. "Thank you, Mr. Thrasher. God will bless you if you do this good deed."

"Well, I hope so, Sarah. Just let me think on it."

Above the river rose great hills clad in thick forests and limestone cliffs. Soon, across the span of water, she saw a gristmill along a creek in the blue haze. The sun set, and Sarah gathered her cloak tighter about her shivering frame as darkness fell.

"Climb to the back, Sarah," Thrasher said. "You'll find a blanket there among my stuff to keep you warm. There'll be a full moon tonight as big as an October pumpkin. We won't reach the cabin for a while, so go to sleep."

The hoot of an owl startled Sarah. She looked up into the trees. Black tentacles reached out across a spangled night sky. The moon, large and brilliant, illuminated all around her. No wind, not even the slightest breeze, blew. But the winter's air seeped through her cloak in a chilling frost.

Another hoot echoed through the woods, and she saw Mr. Thrasher sit straight up and draw his musket across his lap. Then he lifted a jug to his lips and drank. She could smell its woody scent, the ale within it, on his breath. She had seen what a few mugs could do to a man—inflame his emotions and bring out the beast in him, or cause him to retreat into giddy laughter and fall asleep.

Brave to confront him, she said, "You are not drunk, are you?"

"No," he grunted back over his shoulder. "Just a nip to keep me warm." His eyes in the moonlight were glassy onyx. "Want some?"

"No, thank you. The Bible says it makes a man a fool to drink too much."

"Does it now? Well, I guess I am a fool, then. Go to sleep."

She crawled under the blanket and stared up at the moon and the stars that twinkled above. So cold and desolate they seemed against the inky sky. Her heart trembled within her breast, and she flung her arms across her eyes in an attempt to sleep. But the sway of the wagon and the crunch of the wagon wheels made her restless.

In the woods, a dark shape stole among the trees, and fear rushed over her as if the wind had passed through her body. Bernie whinnied and Sarah looked up with a start. The horse halted, pawed the ground, and snorted. Thrasher shook the reins and urged her on, but she would not move. Through the moonlight shambled a mountain cat. Its fur bristled across its back as it growled and slunk forward.

"Gad, it's a big 'un," whispered Thrasher over his shoulder to Sarah. The cat stopped directly in front of Bernie and snarled.

Thrasher held the reins tighter. "Stay still, Sarah. He'll not spring at us unless maddened. Most of the time they are cowardly creatures."

"He looks mad already. Do something," she said, peeking over the back of the seat.

The cat whipped its tail from side to side, and slowly paced. Sarah widened her eyes and fixed them on the cougar.

Thrasher cocked his musket. "He's got a nice pelt on him."

With a ferocious cry, the cougar sprang before Thrasher could fire. His horse plunged back and forth to avoid the razor-sharp claws and flesh-tearing fangs. Thrasher struggled to hold onto the reins with one hand, while balancing his musket with the other.

Although frightened out of her wits, Sarah snatched the musket out of Thrasher's hand and raised it to her shoulder. And just as the cat pounced up to the wagon to attack Thrasher, she fired before it could sink its claws into him. The blast echoed through the forest. The cougar screamed, twisted, and fell to the ground near the front wheel. From its throat came a low, prolonged cry. If only it had avoided them and gone off into the woods, it would have lived to hunt another day.

"On my life, you killed it, Sarah!" Thrasher slapped his thighs with delight. "You sure are a good shot in the dark. You saved my life. I'll make you a cap out of the pelt."

"I do not want it." She handed him back his musket.

Thrasher tumbled out of his seat and drew out his hunting knife. "You'll change your mind when you feel how soft it is."

Sarah turned away as he cut into the pelt.

18

When dawn broke, Sarah looked over the edge of the wagon and found they were traveling through a narrow pass above the Potomac. Here the river flowed placidly. Great rocks jutted skyward through the water. Cranes perched upon the shore, and trees ready for spring bent over with morning frost. Veils of mist moved here and there, and she heard deer running through the forest.

She rubbed her eyes in the morning light, and her stomach ached with hunger. Mr. Thrasher handed her back a strip of venison jerky and she ate it. She wondered how many miles they had gone—how far was she from Alex? She missed him so much. He'd be rising now, shaving and preparing for breakfast. She hoped Mrs. Burnsetter would make his eggs the way he liked them, and his coffee strong. Weary in body and mind, Sarah laid her head in her arms, forcing back the urge to cry, and wondered if the girls were happy. Did they miss her?

Thrasher turned his weary horse up a slope and stopped before a log cabin. Smoke spewed from a stone chimney. A dog barked and ran to greet his master.

"This here is Ben, Sarah. I would've brought him with me, but he's no good for protection. He's too old and would have drove me crazy wantin' to run off into the woods and sniff everything. More than likely he would've run into a skunk and then I would've been done with him."

Sarah stroked the dog's ears and it rubbed its nose against her palm. Her hand began to shake when she thought of going inside the cabin where she'd be alone with Thrasher. He seemed harmless, and true to his word. But Sarah had trusted before and vowed she never would again.

Before she could set foot upon the first step of the cabin, the door swung open and out stepped an old woman in a deer hide frock. Wiry steel-gray hair fell to her waist and over her eyes. Her feet were bare and dirty. She threw her hands over her hips and glared at Sarah.

"It's alright, Sally. No reason to get your feathers all ruffled." Thrasher dragged his musket and a leather bag off the seat of the wagon. "This is Sarah. I brought her here so you'd have less work to do, not that you do much of it anyway, you lazy ol' coot."

Sally grunted, threw up her fist, and swung it at Thrasher.

"She ain't got a tongue to speak, Sarah. The Indians cut it out." Bounding up the steps, Thrasher leaned close to the unfortunate woman. "Didn't they, Sal? They cut it right out to keep you from screaming, or was it 'cause you talked too much?"

Sally slapped her palm over her mouth. Sarah stared at her, thinking what a terrible ordeal the woman had been through, and wondering about the reasons Mr. Thrasher had Sally living in his cabin. What was she to him? "Who is she, Mr. Thrasher? Your wife?"

"She's too old to be my wife, Sarah. Sally's been my helper for many a year, until she got sickly with rheumatism. Took pity on her up at Fort Frederick during the war. She'd been captured by Indians, escaped, and took refuge at the fort. No one wanted anything to do with her when they saw she'd been spoiled and her tongue cut out."

Compassion and pity stirred in Sarah. Sally's lot in life seemed so much harsher than her own. "I believed my story to be the worst thing a woman could face. But I was wrong." Then she stepped up to Sally. "Hello." She held out her hand. Sally stared at it. She touched Sarah's fingertips, and then snatched her hand back.

After a restless night's sleep, Sarah woke at the break of dawn and set to work. She shoved back her hair as she stacked logs next to the fireplace, forcing back the sorrow that stirred in her chest. If only there were a way for her to go home to Alex.

Sally gripped her arms together and twisted. Sarah knew the cold made the old woman's bones ache. "I cannot set a fire in the hearth, Sally, until I clear away all this ash. When was the last time it was cleaned?"

Sally shrugged and shook her head from side to side.

"A long time obviously," Sarah said. "Well, as soon as I am finished the cabin will be warm with a fire. Mr. Thrasher should have done this before he set out this morning. But since I am his servant, I suppose he expects me to do it."

She got down on her hands and knees and shoveled gray cinders and bits of burned wood into a large copper pot. Her hand gripped the handle hard and a lump grew in her throat the more she dwelled on her fate. A fog of ash blew into her eyes when the wind swept down the chimney. Her eyes stung

and watered. She wiped her apron over her face with the want
to cry.

She stood, wiped her hands across her apron, and turned
to Sally. "The floors need sweeping. I suppose you are unable
to help?"

Sally clapped her hands over Sarah's shoulders and moved
her toward the door. Then she handed her the broom that
sat next to it. Sarah handed it back and gripped Sally's hand
around it. "You do it."

Sally shoved the broom back and frowned.

"We are both hungry. Every pot and dish needs scrubbing.
I can't make porridge until I do."

With a grunt, Sally set the broom back in its place.

"Very well." Sarah stepped away. "You think I am your servant, don't you?"

Sally narrowed her eyes and nodded.

Sarah found it hard to be angry, and so she moved Sally to
the rocker and sat her down. She banked a fire and it warmed
the cabin with an amber glow. Soon she had breakfast bubbling in a skillet. She spooned the porridge into a wooden
trencher and handed it to Sally.

Mr. Thrasher had gone down to the river to check his
traps. Snow fell, and she heard him whistling on his return
home. She looked out the window. He had a string of pelts
in one hand, his leather bag in the other, and his dog trotting
alongside him.

Snow tumbling from an evergreen and blowing into a vapor
caught Sarah's eye. Through the woods something drifted,
tawny like the color of deer. Eagle feathers and beads stood out
against the white frost and bare trees. The hair on the back of
Sarah's neck bristled and sweat broke out on her palms.

Sally smoked a clay pipe in her rocking chair by the fire. Sarah swallowed hard. "Sally, get up! I saw Indians in the woods following Mr. Thrasher. Hurry! We must hide."

Sally blew smoke into the air, stood, and walked over to where she slept at night. She drew a blanket around her bony frame and sat down. It seemed she knew what was coming and had resigned herself to it.

Sarah hurried to her, clasped her hands. "Sally, please. Can you not crawl under the bed?"

Sally shook her head no.

Sarah hurried back to the window. She could not see Mr. Thrasher, and went to bar the door. "Dearest Jesus, help us. Protect us."

A long, chilling war-whoop struck fear into her heart. Then she heard Thrasher's blood-curdling scream. His dog yelped. Cold fear raced through her body. She turned to lower the bar across the door. But before she could secure it, it crashed in.

In the hazy sunlight stood a warrior, dressed in deer hide and a mantle of bear fur. He stood aside. Another warrior rushed in. He raised his tomahawk and plunged it into Sally's chest. Then he turned on Sarah. He grabbed her hair. She struggled and cried out. He set his tomahawk into his belt and pulled out a knife. He jerked her head back and placed it at her scalp. Her body went limp with terror. Tears blurred her sight.

The first warrior shouted. The Indian drew his knife away. Released, she scrambled back against the wall. "Lord Jesus, save me." The words came from her in a whispered prayer. The warrior squinted his eyes as if he understood. He reached his hand down to her.

"Come. You not die," he said.

Trembling, she got to her feet. She braced herself against the wall, afraid to move. Her wrists were tied with a leather thong, and the warrior led her from the cabin. On the porch lay the bodies of Mr. Thrasher and his dog. Two arrows protruded from in his back, and the attackers had taken his scalp. Shocked into silence, she looked away from the blood and gore, from the lifeless eyes.

Sarah shivered in the cold, quaking from the horror around her. Her heart drummed in her breast and tears drifted down her face. "Though I walk through the shadow of the valley of death, I shall fear no evil." She spoke the verse in a low, trembling voice, her breath escaping into a soft mist.

Alex. Oh, Alex.

The Indians ransacked the cabin. They gathered pots and blankets and all the food. They took Thrasher's old mare. Then they set the cabin on fire. Sarah stared at the burning logs. Flames reached higher. Black smoke whirled. Too stunned to cry any longer, she covered her eyes and turned away.

And as the cabin and its dead burned, the Indians yelped their victory. The chief strode over to Sarah and hauled her up. He had let her live. Did this mean she now belonged to him? "You come. You ride."

He removed his bearskin mantle and threw it over Sarah. She did not know whether to thank him, whether it would make a difference in how she would be treated. His large hands grasped her about the waist and set her on the horse.

Down to the river they rode. Ice encrusted the bank, and snow coated the bare limbs of the trees. The smell of burning flesh and wood sickened her. Smoke drifted above the trees, gray and translucent. She leaned to one side and vomited, wishing the Indian would give her water to wash the bitterness from her mouth. He ignored her.

She bowed her head, thought of all that had happened up to this moment—the loss of Jamie, her brother-in-law's betrayal, the women aboard the ship, the Woodhouses. And then Alex had come riding down the lane on Charger. She would never forget how he fitted her shoe so she would not limp, or forget the touch of his lips on hers.

19

*A*lex dressed in his best suit of clothes and saddled Charger. The girls stood in the window and waved good-bye. Aunt Moria stood behind them with loving hands on their shoulders, and drew them away as he turned his horse.

He had not seen Sarah in days and anticipated the sight of her opening the door, her hair flowing about her shoulders, her eyes warm and her smile bright for him. He'd made several calls in the area, and the more affluent patients paid him in coin. His purse plump with enough money to free her, he rode toward the Woodhouse farm with his heart galloping in time with his horse.

As he rode beneath the trees, he recited what he would say to Mr. Woodhouse—what his most convincing argument would be if the gentleman rejected his offer again. Alex would not wait for years to pass before her time of indenture was paid. It had to be now—today.

Another reason caused him to be anxious to have her. He had to do his duty and return to the sick and wounded patriots. He could not leave without marrying her. She, the twins, and Aunt Moria would be safer if he moved them to

Annapolis. His aunt owned a brick townhouse at the end of Market Street, where salty sea breezes blew in from the bay and where food was abundant in the waters. If he left them in the country, he knew they would not be immune from the hardships that crisscrossed Maryland and Virginia.

As he neared the Woodhouse farm and saw the house, it struck him how oddly silent it seemed. No lowing of a cow in need of milking. No rooster's crow, no chickens clucking and scratching about the yard.

He dismounted, stepped up to the door, and knocked expecting Sarah to answer. He waited and knocked again. Then he grew concerned, for there came Flenderson waving his hat and riding an old brown nag down the lane toward him.

"Good day, Dr. Hutton. Certainly is a brisk one."

"Good day, Flenderson. I have come to see Mr. Woodhouse."

"You'll not find anyone at home. They've gone, sir."

"When will they be back?"

"They won't."

A feeling of dread bristled Alex. "What do you mean? Has something terrible happened?"

Flenderson steadied his horse. "Mr. Woodhouse went into debt and sold everything, the land, the house—all of it. Don't know whom to, so there's no reason to ask me. Mr. Woodhouse sold me his bull and I am here to fetch it out of the field."

Alex felt the blood rush from his face, and grief rose in his heart. "Where is their maid, Sarah?"

"You mean the pretty one with a limp? I heard tell they sold her and took the other with them. Celia I believe was her name, their cook. Not too many folk would pass over a good cook for a housemaid."

Ice raced through Alex's veins. "Sold her?" The words slipped out in disbelief.

"Aye. It been a long time coming, and poor Mrs. Woodhouse hadn't an inkling of the trouble her husband was in. They have left for Jamaica, to join his brother who owns a sugar plantation. I do not envy them one bit, Dr. Hutton. Mr. Woodhouse said they would travel by carriage down to Cape Henry and board a ship, said he'd claim loyalty to the Crown with the wish to immigrate to the islands if he came across any British soldiers."

His hopes dashed, Alex stared at Flenderson. "I am amazed how much you know about the Woodhouses. But you know nothing about Sarah's whereabouts."

"Mr. Woodhouse did not say. I had no reason to make further inquiry about the girl. And even if I did know where she'd been taken, what could you do?"

"Find the place . . ."

"And face her new master? He might not be so willing to let her go."

"It is a chance I would gladly take." Alex mounted Charger in a fury.

"Dr. Hutton, you might have some luck finding her if you head south toward Port Henry and catch up with Mr. Woodhouse."

Alex nodded. His hands shook as he gathered up the reins and nudged his boot heels into his horse's sides. Long into the day he rode, until he reached the port. It looked eerie in the gray of the day, the water slate-colored and still. A lone fisherman sat on a dock mending a net. Alex questioned him about a gentleman and his lady traveling by carriage.

"They are of middle age, and have a female servant with them."

"Yes, I saw them, sir. They boarded a ship. They said nothing to me, and I don't know where they or the ship were headed, except it sailed out during the night, 'cause this morn it were gone."

Could things get any worse? He had lost the chance of finding Mr. Woodhouse and thus discovering where he had sent Sarah.

Remounting, he rode home. Complete darkness covered the land by the time he stepped inside the house. The girls were asleep. His aunt met him in the foyer in her robe, pistol in hand in case he were an intruder, candle in the other, her cap awry on her head. He told her what had happened.

"Oh, dear, Alex. This is a tragedy for sure. What will you do now?"

"I will continue my search. I am setting off in the morning. Hopefully I will return with her in a few days. I doubt she was taken far."

The doubtful look on Aunt Moria's candlelit face made him wonder if it were a lost cause he pursued. "I will pray you do," she said, and offered to make him a hot cup of tea and a plate of dinner. He thanked her and declined.

"Tomorrow pack the girls' clothes. It is best they live with you until I am settled. Winter is quickly descending, and they will be better off in town, where they will be kept warm and fed."

Moria laid her hand on his arm. "Indeed that is true. I have no idea how to build a fire on my own in the hearth, let alone live in the countryside in winter without a man to help. It is different in town. I have my housemaid Millie to help me."

He went upstairs to his room, drew off his waistcoat and boots, and tried to sleep. Drifting in and out, he dreamed of Sarah, longed for her. At sunrise, he dressed and saddled his horse. Eager to find Sarah, he rode on to the plantation houses and homes and made inquiry about a girl sold recently, with long red hair and green eyes. No one knew anything about her. No one recognized her name or description.

Each mile Alex traveled, his heart broke a little more. He gripped the reins more tightly, set his jaw more firmly, as his face contorted with anger. How could Mr. Woodhouse do this and not tell him beforehand? How could he do this to Sarah? Did anyone care how she came to be a servant, what terrible plans had been carried out to spirit her away against her will?

He had offered to purchase her for more than what Mr. Woodhouse had paid. But he was refused, and Mr. Woodhouse would never give an acceptable reason why. How could he have sold her to someone else, when he must have known how much they meant to each other? Perhaps this other man had given him more money than Alex could have come up with.

After making inquiry after inquiry with no success he returned home. Discovering her whereabouts seemed an insurmountable task. How he would ever find her, he did not know, but there was one in whom he trusted who knew.

Into the Almighty's hands he placed his goal and hoped God would guide him. But with no news in hand, he prepared to take his little charges to Annapolis. He would not forget Sarah, nor would he stop trying to find her even when revolution impeded his efforts. He had little time remaining on his leave, before he was expected back to the field where he was urgently needed.

On the way, they stopped at the trading post. Aunt Moria warmed her hands by the fire with the girls, while Alex spoke to Mr. Pippins.

"Have you any idea what happened to Mr. Woodhouse's servant Sarah Carr?" Alex asked, placing a coin on the counter.

"No, sir. But they sell souls on the other side of the river, along St. Clements Bay. Said to be a large tobacco barn."

Pippins leaned on his counter. "If you take enough coin with you, you may convince someone to tell you to whom Mr. Woodhouse sold the girl."

"You've sparked my memory," Alex said. "She told me they bought and sold persons across the Potomac. I had not remembered until you mentioned it. You have my thanks, sir." He walked out to his horse, mounted him, and turned him toward the river.

It was a clear day, with the sun shining, and the Potomac ran clear of ice. They crossed by ferry, and Alex secured a carriage at Coltons Point. From there they traveled north over rough roads, avoiding the main thoroughfares where British troops might linger. At each place he made inquiries as to the tobacco barn and the selling of slaves and indentured servants. Wary eyes looked back at him, without giving him an answer.

By the time they reached Annapolis, lanterns glowed along the streets, and a night watchman passed them with a tip of his hat. Alex settled his aunt, Rose, and Lily in the brick townhouse near the harbor. At dawn, he donned his cloak and hat. Aunt Moria met him in the foyer.

She leaned up and kissed his cheek. "Godspeed to you, Alex. I know you are disappointed by the turn of events. I shall keep you in my prayers."

He patted her hand. "Thank you, Aunt. I shall need them. You are sure you will be fine here with the girls?"

"Better here than the house in the countryside." She drew open the curtains over the window beside the door. "I have neighbors to turn to, and a few have children. The girls shall not lack for playmates, Alex. We shall do very well. When you can, write to us, for I shall worry."

"I will. I promise." He handed her a leather moneybag. "This should keep you and the twins well provided for until I return."

She looked shocked. "Money? I am set up very well. There is no need." When she handed it back, he gently moved her hand aside.

"I insist."

Rose and Lily hurried down the stairs into his arms. He kissed both of them. "Be good for Aunt Moria, my darlings."

"Yes, Uncle Alex," said Rose.

"We promise," said Lily, touching his cheek with her palm.

"I will come home as soon as I can."

"With Sarah?" Rose clapped her hands.

"Someday I hope I shall. Will you keep Sarah and me in your prayers?"

They nodded and threw their arms around him once more. Sorry to leave them, he closed the door and went to his horse. The morning broke clear with frigid winds that blew across the bay into the town. He turned Charger away from the hitching post. The horse made a low, throaty neigh.

With his hopes high, Alex headed south out of town, toward St. Clements Bay in search of the tobacco barn.

20

*A*t the brink of a hilltop, Alex looked down at the yawning mouth of the Potomac River. Along the shoreline, a whitewashed tavern stood on a grassy slope that leveled off to a sandy plain.

Less than a quarter mile from the tavern, a tobacco barn appeared to slate gray in the fog. Beyond it, a dock jutted out into the water, and alongside the weathered pilings a few boats were moored. It was a harrowing place, where suffering souls were bought and sold like livestock. It represented the evil and greed rooted in the hearts of the men who dealt in such a business. Sickened by it, Alex tightened his grip on Charger's reins and thought of Sarah. He pictured her shackled, led across the wharf, for all eyes to ogle. What had they bid for her? How much had Woodhouse paid? It grieved his heart to think of the humiliation and abuse she had suffered.

He moved his horse down the hill, rode beyond the tavern. He heard laughter within as he passed by. With the tobacco barn in full view, he waited to see if anyone would approach him, ask his business there, ask who he was.

All along the base of the structure, tall grass and weeds intertwined. Horses tethered to posts rippled their coats against the cold and snorted. He turned up the collar of his coat and rubbed his gloved hands to warm them. Then he nudged Charger on.

Close to the door he dismounted. He pushed it open and stood for a moment surveying those within. Torches and lanterns dazzled his eyes. On the far side, a man sat at a table, quill poised in his hand. He dipped the tip into an inkwell and scribbled across a sheet of parchment. The man before him handed coins to a treasurer. He plopped the pieces into a wooden coffer, shut the lid, and smiled.

Drawing off his hat, Alex strode toward them, his boot heels sinking slightly into the soft dirt floor covered with straw. He stopped in front of the table and the man writing glanced up.

"May we help you, sir? The bidding hasn't begun but we just accepted an early offer." The writer's bushy black brows shot up. "A patriot. I can see your uniform behind your coat, sir. You are far from the fighting today, and without a regiment?"

"I am a field surgeon on leave for a short time."

The man set the quill aside. "You are in need of laborers at your home?"

"A doctor has little need of slaves."

"Then perhaps you need a woman to follow you into the field and tend to your needs? Wait over there and you will see the best stock first. Wenches from England, and right under the British fleet's nose." The man chuckled.

He wished he could have said exactly what he thought, but he held his tongue. Wisdom in his choice of words was required if he were to discover anything about Sarah. "I am seeking neither. I need information regarding a recent sale for Mr. Simon Woodhouse of Virginia—a girl with red hair."

The man screwed up his face with a knowing look in his eyes. "Sales cannot be disclosed."

Reaching into his pocket, Alex tossed a gold piece onto the marred table. "Make an exception."

The treasurer picked up the coin and examined it through his spectacles. "What information do you require, sir?"

"The sale of Sarah Carr. Who bought her and where she was taken."

The writer turned to his fellow. "The book, lift it to the table."

From behind, the treasurer heaved a ledger as large as his chest, plopped it on the table, and flung it open. He muttered as he turned the pages and ran his finger down the page. "Here it is. Sarah Carr—indentured to Jebediah Thrasher—trapper, landowner, the Potomac. Formerly owned by Simon Woodhouse, also of Virginia."

Alex sighed with relief that he had not met with a dead-end. "Do you know where I can find this man?"

"All we know is what is written in the ledger. I do recall that girl from the first time she stood on the platform. Pretty, she was. She had a limp when Mr. Woodhouse bought her. I did not see it this time and have wondered why. You say you are a doctor. Did you have something to do with that?"

"I helped her, yes," Alex said, trying to control his impatience. "Trappers are more likely to be upriver, are they not?"

"I suppose so. But it is winter. Your search for this girl will not be easy."

"With God's help, it will not matter what time of year it is."

"Why would you care to find such a lowly person? Is there a legal matter regarding this indenture?"

"That is my business, sir." Slapping on his tricorn, he turned to leave, but a hand touched his chest and prevented him.

"I know that rascal Jebediah Thrasher. He owes me pelts."

Alex stepped back, his hand set over the pommel of his flintlock. His eyes met those of a backwoodsman dressed in deerskin, holding a long musket decorated with turkey feathers on the end of the barrel.

"And you are—?"

"Riddance." A shaggy coonskin cap sat cockeyed on his head of brown shoulder-length hair and at the end of his beard a thin braid hung. He dragged off the cap and slapped it on his thigh. A puff of dust rose and he sneezed.

"A unique name," Alex said. "What is your Christian name?"

"That's it. My ma gave it to me with no last name that I know of. She said to me before she passed on, 'Riddance, you delivered me from a childless life. I named you that way 'cause I said, "Good riddance to being a barren woman."'"

"You say you know Jebediah Thrasher?"

"I do. I can take you to his cabin if you're willing to pay."

Alex eyed him carefully. "How do I know I can trust you?"

The ledger writer spoke up. "I can vouch for Riddance, sir. He knows the river and everyone on it like the back of his hand. He is a tracker, you see."

Riddance drew back his shoulders and adjusted the powder horn slung over his shoulder. A large hunting knife with a bone handle hung from a belt at his side. "That's right," he said. "I can find anything and anyone. It's a gift."

"Jebediah Thrasher purchased an indentured woman that I am searching for."

Riddance scratched his beard and narrowed his eyes. "Hmm, he did? Well, he'll likely not give her up so easily. You'd have to give him more than what he paid. Most likely double." He dropped his hand. "It could be for nothing going there."

"I will take the chance," Alex said. "She's to be my wife."

"Wife? You're in love with the girl? Well, that'll make a man do things he ordinarily wouldn't."

"Riddance was in love once," said the money collector. "Weren't you, Riddance?"

Riddance nodded and a sentimental gleam shone in his brown eyes. "Aye, I was. But not anymore."

"Hear tell, she ran off with another man. A plantation owner wasn't it?"

"Aye, and if I ever see them again, I'll kill him and sell her to the Indians for betraying me."

The seated fellows gasped, but Riddance slapped his knees with a laugh. "But I am not the vengeful kind, you lily-livered fellows. I won't do it, being a Christian man and all. It would go against God's commandment. Only time I have taken a life was in battle."

"Redcoats and Indians," said the ledger writer.

"Aye. And I ain't going to boast. A man tries to forget those things."

"Name your fee, Riddance," said Alex. "I haven't any more time to waste."

Riddance threw his hands over his hips. "Five gold pieces."

"Four. I will give you two now and two when we return."

"And a horse."

"You do not own one?"

"Hmm, I do." Riddance guided Alex to the barn door and stepped out with him into the frigid dusk.

Walking ahead of the backwoodsman, Alex paused and turned. "Is that your horse?"

"Yes, that's the ole nag." The brown mare lifted her head. Riddance patted her rump and dust puffed from her bristle hairs. Alex wondered if grime layered everything Riddance owned.

With deft hands, Alex ran his hand down her broad neck to her shoulder. "She appears fit to me—strong. I will not buy you a new mount."

With a shrug, Riddance stroked his mare's muzzle. "I guess it was a foolish request on my part. Sorry."

"Are we agreed on your fee?" Alex held out his hand. Riddance stretched his forward and the two men shook.

"Agreed. We leave at first light." He set his hand on Alex's shoulder. "Now, let's go up to the *Grey Heron* and get to know each other better. I'm thirsty."

Riddance climbed onto his horse and headed toward the tavern. Alex grasped Charger's reins and looked back at the tobacco house. He hoped one day it would burn to the ground, bringing an end to its terrible purpose.

21

*T*he next day at sunrise, Alex and his guide rode up the river road, where the morning light turned the clay cliffs to gold. The sun flamed through the forests and warmed his body beneath his heavy greatcoat. As he followed Riddance's lead, he looked down and noticed the numerous tracks from horses and wagons that littered the path. After several miles, there were none to be seen.

When they reached the Great Falls, they tethered their horses and set camp to sleep under the stars in front of a blazing fire. With his knife, Alex sat down and scraped the mud from his boots. Somber thoughts filled his mind as he fell to sleep wrapped in a heavy wool blanket, listening to a hoot owl call from a distance to its mate.

When he woke in the morning, he smelled breakfast roasting over the fire. He wiped the sleep from his eyes. Riddance had a rabbit on a spit and sliced some of the greasy meat free. Settling back, he popped it into his mouth. Hungry, Alex leaned forward, speared a piece of meat with his own knife and ate it.

"How much farther is Thrasher's place?" he asked.

Riddance smacked his lips and tossed a bone into the brush. "Hours. But we'll get there. No signs of Indians or British so far, and I doubt there will be."

Alex drank from his canteen, then wiped his mouth with his sleeve. "How can you be certain?"

"No signs, like I said." Riddance stood and stretched. "Time to go. Winter is closing in, and I expect more snow." He kicked dirt and sand into the fire. The flames and coals died. Shoving his coonskin cap on his head, he pulled himself up onto his horse.

Alex lingered, and shut his eyes.

"What are you doing, Doc? Praying?" Riddance teased.

Alex turned and headed for his horse. "Yes. We will need it, don't you think?"

Riddance smiled. "Aye, we will. The Almighty knows these hills and this valley better than any man."

Charger snorted as Alex climbed into the saddle, his moneybag lighter under his coat after paying out several coins. He owed Riddance two more, and that left him four to offer Thrasher. If he would not accept them, he'd give him his flintlock pistol, his regimental coat, his tricorn hat—even his boots if it meant freeing the woman he loved.

He looked up at the bare and brown trees that towered above the forest floor. Mist flowed between them, and he felt God's presence here, in the wilderness, more than in any building made by man's hands. Yet, he did not feel peace or comfort here. Within him nagged anxious feelings. Was she lost to him?

Not wanting to give in to despair, he turned his eyes toward the path ahead. *I will find her with your help, God. I have so little time. Guide our path.*

After the sun peaked in the sky and dropped toward the ridges of the hills, Riddance halted in his horse near the mouth of Israel Creek.

"We cross the river here where it is shallow. Once we reach the other side, we haven't much farther to go before we reach Thrasher's cabin."

Alex glanced inland. "There's a mill farther up the creek. Perhaps we should stop and speak to the owner. Maybe he will know something."

Riddance looked up at the clouds moving slowly across the sky. "No time. We should go on."

Nudging their mounts on, they brought the horses down to the brink of the Potomac. In the misty light, Alex ran his eyes across the span of water, from shore to shore. There were no barriers of rock to impede their crossing, no deep pools whose waters would rise over their horses' heads.

Old Indian trails lined the slopes on the Virginia side. When they reached the heights above the river, they rode along them, through thick forest heavy with vines. Riddance bent over and studied the ground. "Moccasin prints. Four men. No horses."

"Then they have come this far," said Alex.

"Aye, weeks ago. They're probably long gone by now."

After riding three miles upriver, Riddance pointed out a grove of oaks and maples. Beyond it lay a green field dotted with patches of melting snow.

"Through there is Thrasher's place." Riddance sniffed the air. "Smell that? Ah, that is not good."

Stronger than that of a campfire, the scent of smoke wafted in the air. Alex frowned. "No it isn't. Something has been on fire."

With a *yah*, he urged Charger forward and hurried through the grove into the field. Coming over the crest of high ground, he looked down at the charred remains of a cabin, the yard littered and scorched. Dread washed over him. As if a fist had struck him in the gut, pain shot through his core and he bent forward.

The shadow of Riddance's horse came alongside him. Upon what had been the porch lay a charred body, the scalp gone. Bloody gore stood out against the blackened flesh of the skull. Arrows in the back were scorched and the fletching burned away.

With his heart in his throat, Alex dismounted. Riddance approached the body first and crouched down. "The arrows are badly burnt, but I'd say Shawnee."

Alex had seen death in countless ways, but never like this. He turned his eyes away from the gruesome sight, only to see a charred hand stretch upwards, the fingers crooked like the prongs of a claw hook.

"Dear, God. There is another," he said, his throat dry, fearing it was Sarah.

Riddance moved to the body and squatted down. He looked up at Alex, his brows pressed into one hard line. "A woman."

Every muscle in Alex's body tightened. His hands wanted to strike something. Teeth clenched, he kicked a timber out of his way.

"Wait," Riddance cried. He drew out his hunting knife and lifted away debris. "You said she had red hair. This woman was old. No teeth. And here is a bit of gray hair beneath her. The Indians took the rest."

Alex crouched next to Riddance to examine the body. "You are right. This cannot be Sarah." With care, he lifted away the remains of her deerskin frock. "Symptoms of scurvy. Porous bones. A fall would have been fatal."

"Poor old soul."

"Yes. Such a sad way to end one's life."

Sighing, Riddance stood and strode out into the grass. "Killed the dog, too." He yanked an arrow free. "Shawnee for certain. Guess these fellows don't like dogs. Looks like he was a good one."

He walked around. Stopped and stooped. "Took Thrasher's horse. Moccasins—a woman's footprints."

Alex crouched down and ran his finger across one small footprint. "She is alive. But God help her—they took her, Riddance."

He stood and saw the hopeless look on Riddance's face. Then he went for his horse. "Let's go. We've still some light."

Riddance dragged off his coonskin cap. "They're far from here—probably four or five ridges over the Blue Ridge by now. No telling exactly where."

"You're a tracker. You can find them."

Riddance looked up at the sky. "Snow will be coming down from the northwest pretty fast. In an hour, it will be too hard for us to go on. Paths will be covered in snow, making it difficult for the horses. I'm heading back."

Alex set his mouth hard. "I will go on without you, then."

"You're crazy. It's the middle of winter."

"I have endured worse."

Riddance huffed. "I know of no cabins between here and the headwaters that'll be welcoming to strangers."

"Get on your horse, Riddance. I hired you to help me find her."

"I have done all I can. If you go on, you'll starve, and freeze to death. It's hopeless at this point."

"To you, perhaps. But not to me."

"Even if you survive, it will take you months, maybe a year, before you ever find the camp they took her to. The Indians move around and it will be difficult to find her."

"I cannot accept that, Riddance."

"Didn't you say you have to report back for duty? You want to be shot as a deserter? You need to listen to your head, Doc, and not your heart. Wait for spring."

At this point, Alex could find no rebuttal. The man knew the woods and the ways of the Indians better than he. Still his heart ached and he felt he had failed Sarah. His ambition sank. "You are sure of what you say?"

"Hard as it may be, you have to accept they've taken her far into the Alleghenies, or beyond the river. I know what I'm talking about. I have seen this kind of thing before. You go now, and it will be a miracle if you find her. You'll die out there. I ain't going with you, Doc. I enjoy my life too much to risk it."

Alex turned on his heels, shoved his boot angrily into Charger's stirrup. The horse snorted when he settled into the saddle and drew the reins up in his hand. He knew Riddance was right. Without a guide, he would be lost and likely die from cold and starvation. He hated his duty. He hated winter. And he hated war.

Riddance's eyes pleaded with him. "Be smart. It won't do your woman any good if you don't make it."

Swallowing the advice like bitter water, Alex drew away from the ghastly ruins and the stench that caused his horse's nostrils to flare. Before nightfall, they crossed the river to Fort Frederick. Dense snow fell and the wind increased to gale force. He turned the collar of his coat up against his neck. Icy flakes smote his face. Evergreens bowed as the snow gathered on their needles. Trees swayed and limbs snapped. Charger's coat rippled from the cold and wind.

Riddance had been right, for it looked as though the storm would last long into the night, grow into a massive blizzard. Freezing cold and hungry, they trudged through the gate with their weary horses as it opened. Once inside, two soldiers with muskets shut the massive doors and drew down the iron bar.

"You made it just in time, sir," one shouted over the howling wind. "Looks like we'll be closed in from this storm."

"Can you stable my horse and the one belonging to my guide?"

An orderly nodded and moved off with the horses. Then, led by a soldier, they were ushered inside to a small room with two windows. The commanding officer looked up from his desk and Alex informed him who he was, and that he was reporting for duty.

From the mess came the aroma of rations cooking, and being taken there, each was handed a plate of fish, a hunk of cornbread, and a jack of ale. The food and drink warmed Alex's body, but his soul could find no comfort.

Part 3

Thou art my hiding place; thou shalt preserve me from trouble; thou shalt compass me about with songs of deliverance. Selah.

Psalm 32:7

22

Sarah shoved her sleeves above her elbows to keep them from catching on the blackberry thorns. Her dress was quite tattered, and her fingers were sore and stained. She had gone all this time without a proper washing, and used her fingers to comb out the tangles in her hair. Setting her basket down, she gathered it into a braid over her shoulder. The color fascinated the people of the village, who said their fire god had bestowed it upon her. Some believed it had healing powers and would cut a lock from the nape of her neck. Others thought it powerful magic and treated her kindly for fear if they did not, bad luck would befall them.

Many stones lighter than when she was taken, Sarah's clothes hung loose over her frame. Her hands were raw and red from hard work, and when she lifted the basket to her arm, the reeds scraped her skin. Each day, she gave thanks for her shoes and Alex's remedy for her limp. When she slipped them off and on again, she yearned for him, cried for him when alone, and whispered prayers that he would find her someday. But then, he might have forgotten her by now.

The basket grew heavy with the first berries of a warm spring. The other women walked ahead of her, talking to one another in a language she had difficulty understanding, save for a few essential words. She trailed behind with her eyes fastened upon them, watching to see if they noticed. Had they grown so accustomed to her that they did not think she would have it in her mind to escape the first chance she had?

Like tawny does, the women slipped over a hill and were soon out of sight. After waiting a moment in case one returned or called to her, Sarah set the basket beneath the bush and walked backward. Then she turned and stepped away. After several yards, she began to run. Her heart pounded like a drum. She held her shabby dress above her bare calves as she made her way over a fallen tree and through bramble.

Help me, God. I have to get away. Do not let them pursue me.

But her prayer had been too late. Tackled from behind, she fell to the ground with a great thud. She could not breathe. She gasped for air. Terror raked over her like the claws of a bear. Having fallen on her back, she stared horrified into Black Fox's face. He pressed her arms back, his hands fastened on her wrists in an iron grip. Anger stiffened his jaw and blazed in his dark piercing eyes. The lines in his face deepened and his mouth pressed together hard into one thin line as he straddled her.

"Please do not hurt me, Black Fox." She struggled to speak clearly but her throat constricted and she tripped over her words.

"No run away." He stood, grabbed her ankles, and unlaced her shoes. Then he yanked them off. "No shoes. No run."

"Oh, that is wicked. Give them back!" She scrambled to her feet. And when she reached for her shoes, he laughed at her and held them above his head. "Run again, I will trade you to another tribe—one far from here."

"I won't run. I promise." But she could walk and no promise would be broken.

"Your eyes lie. I am weary of this."

"If you take me down river there is a man who will trade good for me. He will give you whatever you want. And he has medicine."

"Maybe." And he shoved her forward toward the village. Twigs and stones pricked her soles and she winced.

"You see, Black Fox." She threw her hands out to him. "I cannot walk properly without my shoes. Please, give them back to me."

"Better this way," he grunted.

Sarah set her mouth firm. "You are a thief to take them."

He clenched his teeth and then drew out his knife. He tore the shoes apart and tossed the pieces into the underbrush. Tears sprang into Sarah's eyes. Black Fox stepped in front of her. She moved back. He moved closer. Then he lifted her hair between his fingers. She jerked away from his touch.

"My hair has no power," she said. "But the one who made it does. Let me go, and you will not feel his anger."

He stared into her face. "Fire god?"

"No, the one that created all things."

Black Fox lifted his chin. He did not speak and stood motionless before her. His eyes narrowed. He then took her by the arm and led her back to the village. The tribe gathered around, some of the women shamefaced that they had let her out of their sight. Black Fox tossed her toward the wigwam where she slept. She scrambled inside and huddled in a corner. She hugged her knees. And by quick degrees, her hopes sank within her.

A full moon rose high in the heavens that night. The others inside the wigwam slept soundly. Men snored and women with their children beside them sighed content in their slumber. Sarah lay on a mat and stared up at an opening in the earthy roof above her. She could see the moon with Venus below its rim. A multitude of stars filled the night sky. It felt as if stones weighed upon her chest, and in anguish she stretched her soul out to heaven.

She dare not speak her prayers aloud and risk awakening her captors. Instead, the silent plea for help echoed through the chambers of her heart. No longer could she bear to be the prisoner of the Shawnee. No longer could she endure another day under the menacing eye of Black Fox.

Slowly and steadily, she crawled from her sleeping place to the entrance. Careful to lift the mat that covered it, she slipped out into the darkness. Crouching low, she scanned the village and saw no sentry. A low fire burned in the center of the village as tree frogs murmured in the elms.

She scooted away and stood. The blue moon shot beams between the blackened tree trunks of the deep forest. Owls hooted one to another and the absence of a breeze forced Sarah to walk heel-to-toe as quietly as she could, barefoot. She clenched her teeth. One whimper could betray her.

She pressed her back against a tree and searched the woodland. Which way to go? Below the hill she had climbed she could see the village. Smoke rose from their campfire. A dog barked. Then she moved on, and an unexplained peace fell over her as she walked away. Somehow she would make her way downriver and back to Alex.

In a short time, the soles of her feet grew sore from the twigs and stones that pricked her tender skin. She hurried on, her feet now scored and bleeding. She sat beneath a pine, tore the hem of her dress and wrapped her feet with the cloth. The muscles in her legs ached. But she would bear it.

Slowly and with care she reached an Indian path above the Potomac. For a moment she listened to the river murmuring over the rocks below. Through the trees she could see the moonlit water and regretted she had no time to pause and enjoy its beauty.

The moon descended, and an hour into her flight she sat down on the crest of a slope to catch her breath. She lingered there in the quiet solitude, praying for strength. Wolves howled and yipped on the other side of the river. She knew if they smelled prey, they would find a place to cross. And so she huddled against a tree, gathered fistfuls of leaves, moss, and dirt to rub into her clothes and bare skin thinking it would mask her scent.

At sunrise, she woke. Chickadees hopped along a limb and called. *Dee-dee-dee.* She rubbed her eyes and brushed back her hair, then watched them flutter to another tree. She stood, raised her face to meet the morning light, and felt the breath of morning dew on her cheeks. Her empty stomach gurgled, but, bearing it, she continued her journey until she found a blackberry bush heavy with fruit. She gathered a handful and kept moving, even though the pain in her feet caused her eyes to tear.

Soon the sun rose above the treetops. The cry of a crow startled her. So long and frightening, it caused her skin to prickle and dread spread through her body. She never had learned the difference between the cry of an animal and its imitation by an Indian.

With her eyes wide, she stepped off the path into thicker brush. Thorns and sharp twigs snatched at her dress and scratched her arms. She moved as quickly as her bruised and bleeding feet could carry her. She could feel Black Fox near. She had to go faster, smarter, hide if she must.

Two days later, she reached a creek that spilled into the Potomac. She unbound her feet and stepped into the water. The silky creek bottom soothed her, but she knew she could not stay long.

Refreshed, she gathered up her rags and bandaged her feet again. Above the creek, she found a deer trail that led inland through deep forest. Old sycamores of enormous girth loomed over her.

The woods grew sparse, and as she approached a meadow laced with thistle, she saw in the distance Black Fox and another Indian dressed in loincloths and moccasins. Shivering with fear, Sarah sank back out of view and waited for them to pass. In the far distance, a house stood upon a patch of green. A broad porch stretched across the front, and large windows were flanked with shutters.

If she could have, Sarah would have run across the field to the door and pounded on it for help. But when she spotted Black Fox standing on a knoll, she crouched down into the bramble. Afraid he might see her, she lay on the ground and drew her legs up against her chest.

Sarah heard a cow lowing. Peeking out from the bushes, she saw Black Fox stride toward the woods with a woman captive. Her hands were tied at the wrist, her face lowered, covered by dark hair. Sarah's heart reached out to her. Had she a husband, children that she had been taken from? Had they been killed right in front of her eyes?

Well hidden, and not daring to move a muscle, she watched Black Fox lead the woman to a stream and push her down. The woman remained on her knees, trembled like a leaf. Her hair had tumbled forward, her torn dress revealed her shoulder. Sobbing, the woman leaned forward, dipped her bound hands into the tepid water and brought it to her lips.

Black Fox grabbed the woman's hair and grunted. Sarah moved her lips in silent entreaty that he'd not draw out his knife and take it. The woman whimpered and tried to rise. Black Fox hauled her to her feet and pressed her against him. Sarah knew Black Fox's look all too well. Savage hatred boiled in his stare. His companion stood by watching, a grin upon his painted face, eyes filled with sordid pleasure. How could they take joy in seeing a woman suffer?

Now that she had slipped out of his cruel grasp, he had found another to replace her, and a sense of guilt washed over Sarah. If she had not escaped, Black Fox would not have pursued her, and this woman would not be in this dire situation.

Minutes seemed like hours as Sarah tried to remain still in her hiding place. She watched Black Fox sit on the ground, eat the jerky from his pouch and hand a piece to his companion. The woman captive sat on her haunches, head down, her hair covering her face.

If only I could help her. If I give myself away, he might treat her with less cruelty.

She gripped her hands, and struggled to gather the strength to do it. Still she held back in fear. As she watched, the wind blew down from the pine trees overhead and the needles fell all around her.

The woman's pleas went ignored by Black Fox. It smote Sarah's heart, and she clenched her teeth and tightened her fists. She looked up through the tangled bramble and tried to rally her courage. A small amount seemed enough and made her inch forward, ready to rise and face Black Fox.

Then a musket snapped and Black Fox jerked. Birds shot off from behind their covers. Black Fox's eyes rolled back in his head. He swayed. Blood fanned across his chest and he fell to the ground dead.

Eyes wide, the woman fled behind a tree. The other Indian rushed toward her with his tomahawk raised. He was cut down in an instant as a bullet entered his heart.

Stunned, Sarah's stomach heaved at the sight of Black Fox's lifeless eyes staring at her. She wanted to rise, but her legs seemed blocks of stone. The woman ran toward her saviors. Sarah pulled back as a pair of boots stepped in front of her.

"Come out of there," the man who wore those mud-spattered boots demanded. She crept forward and looked up at him, hopeful yet cautious. He had a handsome face, with kind but serious eyes; he held his hand down to her. "No one will hurt you," he said, his tone much softer now.

She crawled from the bushes and grasped his hand. He helped her to her feet. Weak with hunger and from her flight out of captivity, she crumpled forward. Unable to open her eyes or speak, she moaned. He caught her as she fell and lifted her up in his arms.

Exhausted from the traumatic ordeal, Sarah pressed her face into the man's shoulder to hide her tears.

If only it were Alex's.

23

Someone touched her on the shoulder. An older woman in a snowy white cap stood over her. She quickly sat up, staring and feeling a little afraid, forgetting Black Fox was no longer near.

"Be at ease, child. You are safe now."

"Where am I?"

"A place called River Run. Mr. Halston brought you here after he rescued my dear Eliza. Lord, I thought all was lost until I saw him coming across the field with you in his arms and my girl walking alongside him and his blacksmith. I fear to think what would have happened if Mr. Halston had not acted as swiftly as he did."

"I passed out. . . . I do not remember much."

"I am not surprised. Why, you are weak to the bone and starved half to death. Oh, and your poor feet. How you made it this far is a miracle. What is your name, child?"

"Sarah Carr, ma'am. Are you mistress of this house?" Sarah fixed her eyes upon the matronly woman. If she were the mistress, would she send her away, sell her off to another? But the eyes in the woman's face promised a different answer—for they looked at her with concern and kindness.

"My name is Fiona Goodall. I am the housekeeper of the family you are now with. I came from England with my mistress and her husband. They are good people. You will see."

"I am grateful for their help . . . for giving me sanctuary." She looked down at the white chemise covering her. "My dress?"

"I burned the rag. It was beyond saving." Fiona handed a clay mug to Sarah. "Here. It is my best mint tea, sweetened with honey. It will do you good."

The clay against her palms felt warm, and when Sarah tasted the tea, tears sprang to her eyes and she struggled to hold them back.

"Dear me!" Fiona said. "No one has ever been brought to tears over my tea. Perhaps my meat pasties, but never over my tea."

Sarah wiped her eyes. "It is very good, Mistress Goodall."

Fiona sat on the bedside. "But it is more than that, why you weep, isn't it?"

A sob escaped Sarah, and Fiona took the mug out of her hand and set it down. She then drew Sarah into her arms. "There now. You have a good cry. You have been through a terrible ordeal. You could have died out there."

"I would have welcomed death to being taken again to the Indian village." She drew back and looked at Fiona. "When I saw your mistress had been captured by Black Fox, I wanted . . . I wanted . . ."

"I know what you are feeling, child. I hid under the floor with little Darcy, her daughter. I felt so helpless as I worried what they would do to my girl."

Sarah sat back. "I do not understand why such hard things have happened to me."

"Life is hard indeed, and there are things we cannot explain. You may tell me about them if it will help."

"My husband drowned in a cove where we lived in Cornwall. I was with child, and so I went to his sister, and they treated me cruelly. They and another man tricked me. The man said he'd give me a position in his house."

Fiona's eyes widened. "You were kidnapped, weren't you?"

"I was. And I was brought to the Chesapeake and sold to Mr. and Mrs. Woodhouse. I worked for them until debt destroyed his estate and they sold me to another, a trapper. Indians attacked us and killed him and an old woman. They took me captive, and I escaped."

"Poor girl. Do not worry, for you are safe here." Fiona stood. "You must be famished. I will bring you a bowl of stew and some bread. Think you can manage such food?"

Sarah could not believe the kindness. "I would dearly welcome it. I haven't had anything like that in a long time."

Fiona frowned. "What have you had?"

"Venison, wild turkey, and fish. But mostly maize."

"Ah, 'tis why you are so thin. Well, that shall be remedied. You stay where you are. I will be back shortly," and she turned to leave.

Sarah held her hand out to Fiona. "Before you go, have you a brush and something I can wash with?"

"I will bring that, too."

Sarah waited for Fiona to return. As she sipped the tea, enjoying the warmth of it as it went down her throat, she studied her surroundings. A narrow table stood against the wall. Upon it sat a blue and white pitcher and bowl, and a brass candlestick with a short taper in the socket.

The heavenly scent of stew flowed through the open door, and she grew ravenous for it. She swung her legs over the edge of the bed. Afraid to touch the floor, to feel the pain it would bring, she slipped back beneath the covers. She wondered, too, what the people in this house would think about her impediment. Would they frown upon her, be shocked, or have sympathy? She decided she would not conceal it. Nor would she try to duplicate Alex's remedy, as a reminder of what he had done for her, to keep her love for him alive within her heart.

A child poked her curly head around the corner of the door and came into the room. Her eyes were large and bright, her hair chestnut, reminding Sarah of Rose and Lily. She missed them so much. Where were they now? She hoped Mrs. Burnsetter was taking good care of them, and giving them all the love they needed.

Fiona called back into the room. "Darcy, meet Sarah Carr. She is staying with us. Can you not say hello?"

Darcy pulled her finger from her mouth. "Hello, Sarah," she said, tripping over the pronunciation of the letter S.

Sarah smiled. "Hello, little one. I am pleased to meet you."

With a skip, Darcy climbed into the ladder-back chair across from Sarah, and gathered her legs upon the seat Indian-style. "Have you a little girl too?" Darcy's question was innocent, and her eyes searched Sarah's for an answer.

"Unfortunately, I have not," Sarah replied. "I could have once had a son, but it was not meant to be. My baby is in Heaven with his father."

Darcy's eyes widened. "An angel," she whispered.

"I am not sure if that is God's way with people, Miss Darcy. But I do know angels are with us here on earth when we need them, and in Heaven."

"Mama said angels protected her from the Indians."

"Your mama is right, little one."

Fiona squeezed back inside the room with a bowl of steaming stew and hot bread slathered with sweet butter. She set the tray on the table near the washing bowl and pitcher. Then she picked up a horsehair brush and began to untangle Sarah's hair. "My, my. Your hair needs such a brushing. It is as if you ran through a briar patch. So many knots." She leaned over. "It needs a washing."

"They would not let me get it wet when we went down to the river for water or bathing. The Indians thought my locks held some kind of magical power."

"Oh, well they may be right. I cannot see how any man in his right mind would not be taken by the length and color. You are blessed to have such hair. My mistress's hair is as dark as a summer's night."

Sarah placed her hand over her growling stomach. "May I?" she said, glancing at the tray.

"Oh, yes, of course. What was I thinking?" Fiona set the brush down and lifted the tray to Sarah's lap. Digging into the meat and vegetables, she savored every bite of the rich stew. The bread melted in her mouth.

"This is so good. 'Tis like manna from Heaven. Thank you."

Eliza stepped through the door. She wore a brown home-spun dress with a simple kerchief over her shoulders. And in her arms were clothes.

"It is late." Eliza smiled down at her daughter, then at Fiona. "Darcy should be asleep by now." Eliza spoke softly and lovingly to the child. Sarah watched them with her heart aching. *If only things had been different, I might be holding my son.*

Darcy looked over at Sarah. "Mama, is she an angel?"

"I do not think so, my love. She is a young woman God has brought to us for as long as she wishes to stay."

The word *stay* rang clearer in her mind than any other.

With a little shake of her head Darcy said, "I heard angel's wings, Mama, me, and Fonna."

"It must have been wonderful, my darling, for they kept you safe. Now, come. Fiona will tuck you in. I will stay here a while."

"The girl's name is Sarah. Let her eat, Eliza, and do not wear her out with too much conversation."

Eliza smiled with a nod and Fiona left with Darcy. She set the clothes down on the foot of the bed. "These are for you. I am Eliza Morgan, mistress of River Run." She pulled the chair up to the bedside and sat down. "Are you feeling better?"

Sarah nodded with relief, the bedding a comfort over her legs and Fiona's stew warm in her belly. She thanked Eliza for the food and shelter, and promised to repay her through hard work. She told her she had no family, and begged her not to send her away. She had been indentured to a man who was cruel, and although she no longer belonged to him, she worried he would claim her if he knew where she was.

Eliza closed the curtains over the window. "Do not worry. If you like, you may stay with us . . ."

As Sarah ate the last of the bread, she listened to Eliza explain who Halston was—her nearest neighbor, not her husband. Hayward was away fighting. It caused her to think of Alex again. More than likely he had returned to his regiment, to help the sick, wounded, and dying. Her greatest fear rose within her, a weight that pressed heavy upon her chest. He could die in this war.

Please protect him. Shield him from all harm. Bring me back to him.

Eliza blew out the candle and left Sarah alone. Content for the moment, she lay back and stared up at the ceiling. It felt good to sleep in a bed, to have a down-filled pillow tucked beneath her head, to feel safe. But the idea that she had not told Eliza the whole truth, pricked at her. Mr. Woodhouse had been relatively kind, but pitiless when it came to selling her to Mr. Thrasher. And Thrasher had not mistreated her—yet there was no telling if he would have in the long run. Dead, he could not claim her. Mr. Woodhouse, gone to Jamaica, had given her up and had no claim. But the fear Eliza would send her back to the auctioneers gripped her.

She asked God to forgive her for not speaking the truth. She should have told her about Mr. Thrasher, about Black Fox and what she had lived through—and about Alex. Perhaps Eliza would find a way to help her find him.

Convinced she must eventually tell Eliza everything as she had done with Fiona, she shut her eyes. For tonight, she had to let things be as they were.

24

*M*orning broke sunny and warm. Sarah washed the grime from her body and hair. The water in the blue and white china bowl foamed with the cake of lye soap Fiona had given her and smelled of lavender. She hoped that in time she would fill out the dress now covering her thin frame.

She went out to the garden with Eliza, where early vegetables sprouted and sparrows flitted across the grass in search of insects. She stood beside Eliza. "I did not tell you everything last night. I hope to today."

"I did not expect you to, Sarah. But I will listen to anything you now want to tell me. Only I will not press you to reveal things you wish to keep to yourself."

Sarah paused in her steps. "I was kidnapped—after Jamie died. I went to his family and they did not want me. So I was taken against my will and brought to the Colonies. I lost a baby aboard ship." She went on, explaining her situation in greater detail, and with her emotions stirring in her like a coming storm.

Eliza looked stunned—speechless, as if Sarah's pain had become her own.

"They sold me to Mr. Woodhouse of Virginia. I met a man, Dr. Alex Hutton, and fell in love with him."

"Did he love you?"

"Yes, he told me he did. And he wanted to pay my debt, but then Mr. Woodhouse went bankrupt and sold me to Mr. Thrasher."

"Thrasher? Who was he?"

"A trapper. I wasn't long with him when the Indians attacked and killed him. That is how I came to be with them."

Eliza shook her head in dismay. "You have suffered so much. Where is Dr. Hutton now?"

"I am not sure, but I suspect he is with his regiment."

"You must write to him and tell him where you are."

"I do not know the regiment he is with. But I can send a letter to the trading post close by the house he inherited."

"I will give you paper and ink. There is a post rider who comes through here." Eliza looped her arm through Sarah's and they walked on to the patch of tilled earth. "You will find your doctor again."

The sun felt warm and Sarah lifted her face to drink it in as they conversed. Kneeling beside Eliza, she pulled a spring onion out of the earth and dusted it off. Then she set it in the basket beside her.

"You are fortunate to be married and live in such a fine house," she said. "Your husband is a good provider."

Eliza pushed a spade into the ground. "Your husband? Did he provide well for you?"

"He did his best. But we were poor."

"Do you miss him terribly?"

"My heart does not ache like it did in the beginning. He was more like a close friend than a lover. It is different with Alex. What I feel for him causes me great pain."

"I understand the feeling. I cannot wait for this war to be over." Eliza stood, straightened her back, and gathered up the basket. "I miss Hayward so much. How I wish he would come home."

Sarah stood and brushed off her hands. "I wonder sometimes if I shall ever see Alex again. I worry he could be killed."

"We have a common worry, you and I. Perhaps that is why God brought us together, to comfort each other."

Growing more and more at ease with Eliza, Sarah took the basket from her, feeling she should be doing the hard tasks. Darcy skipped across the grass toward them, dandelions in her fist. Every time Sarah looked at her she thought of Rose and Lily, and the baby boy she had lost.

She turned to Eliza. "Darcy is such a sweet child. You are blessed to have her. It is painful to lose one before they can ever call you mother."

"I am sorry for you, Sarah. But have faith. God will bless you with many children one day." Smiling at her daughter, Eliza accepted the rustic bouquet from her petite hand and turned to Sarah. "Set the basket by the kitchen door. I have something to show you."

Curious as to what it could be, Sarah followed Eliza down a narrow brick walk to a cabin situated near the line of woods at the rear of the house. It took some time, for Darcy paused to pluck every dandelion in the grass, to blow each puffball into the wind.

On either side were majestic trees, the boughs of which shaded a porch. On one side, a stone chimney covered with wild ivy jutted out from the logs. Sunshine fell warm upon the windows and turned the mortared chinking from stark white to pale yellow.

"This was the first house built at River Run." Eliza walked up the steps and opened the door. "It is warm in winter and cool in the summer, and it has more space than the sickroom."

Eliza walked inside with Darcy, and Sarah, lifting her skirts, followed. "You mean I am to stay here?" she asked.

"Yes. You can fix it up any way you wish. Fiona has kept it swept and dusted."

Sunshine poured through the windows. Sarah breathed in the musty smell of the hewn logs, the fireplace ash, the hint of tobacco, the old scent of life. Light struck across a cast iron pot, upon the copper kettle on the hob in the fireplace. Overhead the beams and rafters were blackened with age, and the puncheon floor was marred from years of wear.

Beside the fireplace, a shelf held a few cooking utensils, two pewter plates, several cups, and a wooden trencher. A small table and two crude chairs sat beneath one of the windows. Against the wall stood a bed that sat low to the floor.

Sarah's eyes filled and she blinked back tears. "Why are you so kind to me?"

Eliza smiled. "I am kind to everyone."

"To this degree, that you would give them a home? Fiona should live here. Surely she deserves it more than I."

"Oh, no. Fiona is settled in the house, and would never live apart from Darcy and me. "

"It seems too much. My house in Bassets Cove was nowhere near this large, and I had a small room at the Woodhouses half this size. The worst I've ever lived in was Mr. Thrasher's cabin. All three of us shared it and it was very dirty."

"Well, all I ask is that you keep the cabin neat, and do the chores I give you."

"I will. I owe you so much."

"In that drawer, you will find some paper and an inkwell. I will leave you to write your letter."

Eliza stepped back outside with Darcy. She left the door ajar and the breeze passed inside. Encouraged, Sarah sat down and over the next hour penned a lengthy letter to Alex. Each day the wait for the post rider grew excruciating, but when he finally arrived and she handed him her post, she watched him with hope in her heart as he galloped off.

The beat of a galloping horse drove Sarah to the window. She could see the rider in the distance as he rode toward the house. "It is a post rider!" she called out to Eliza and Fiona.

Together they dashed out onto the front porch. The post rider halted his horse and dismounted. His boots were covered in dust, as were his breeches and brown coat.

"Have you come far?" Eliza asked.

"All the way from the mouth of the Chesapeake, ma'am."

Eliza turned to Fiona. "Fiona, please fix this man a plate of food. You are no doubt famished, sir?"

"Yes, ma'am. It's been a long ride—been months since I rode this far west. Got a sack full of letters and messages to deliver on this side of the river and then across to Twin Oaks. I happen to have one for Sarah Carr, River Run. Is that you, ma'am?"

A thrill shot through Sarah. Could it be from Alex?

Eliza took the letter and handed it back to Sarah with a hopeful look in her eyes. "Perhaps it is from Dr. Hutton," she said without looking at it.

Poor Eliza, thought Sarah. She looked disappointed she had not gotten a letter from Hayward. It had been so long since she last had word from him.

Her hand trembling, Sarah shoved the letter into her apron pocket and walked back to the cabin with her heart pounding. She sat down on the top step of the porch in the sunshine, the breeze sighing through the trees, bees humming over the trumpet vine. She took the letter out and saw it was the letter she had sent to Alex. Mr. Pippins at the trading post had returned it. He had scribbled on the back in a poor hand:

Currioman Bay Trading Post. Dr. Hutton gone to do his duty. Hutton House closed up. Return to River Run on the Potomac.

Her heart sank. "He has gone back. The house is empty." She looked up at the flashes of sunlight between branch and leaf. "That means he sent the girls away with their great-aunt. But to where?"

She refused to weep. Instead, she stood and went inside the cabin, grabbed the broom next to the fireplace, and swept the floor with all the vigor in her.

25

The Queen Ann's lace in the fields had not wilted in the early summer heat. Having filled her basket with the beautiful wildflowers, Sarah placed them in a glass jar beneath the window by the front door. The lace blooms spilled over the lip in a cluster of deep green leaves. On the sill, a small blue jar of bachelor buttons drank in the sunshine.

Alex had been on her mind, and the melancholy that fell over her could not be cheered by the array of flowers, the sunshine, or the blue skies above. She prayed. She read from the Bible kept in the study. She took long walks after her chores were finished and sat on the riverbank listening to the tumble and whirl of water, to the songs of birds. She watched the herons perch on the rocks and the mallards skim along the surface near the shore. But nothing helped. Perhaps loving him, hoping to be with him, was nothing more than an unrealistic dream—a forlorn hope.

She lifted her eyes and gazed out the window. Eliza had her arm linked through Reverend Hopewell's, a man of gentle nature who ministered to both poor and rich in the area. Sarah fixed her eyes on him as he and Eliza strolled toward the house, and thought of speaking to him about the sadness she felt, but delayed.

Darcy sat on the bottom step of the staircase playing with her rag doll. Sarah turned to her and handed her down a bloom. "Reverend Hopewell has come to visit, Darcy. I hope he has brought your mama good news about your papa."

Darcy sprang to the window and stood on her tiptoes to look out. "Hurrah! He brings me sugar candy, Sarah."

"Let us hope he has a pocketful, little one. We shall wait in the kitchen and see."

Fiona kneaded the day's bread dough and looked up at Sarah as she came through the door. "Oh, let me help, Fiona. You work so hard."

With a heavy sigh, Fiona tossed the dough into the pan. Then she brushed her flour-covered hands on her apron. "My hands are tired, Sarah. It's age, you know. I cannot seem to work the dough the way I did in past years." She held her hands out for Sarah to see. "Just look how crooked my fingers have become. And they pain me so."

"Poor Fiona." Sarah took each hand in turn and rubbed them gently. Her heart went out to the older woman, who had labored all her life to please others. "Have you tried the salve I made you?"

"It helps immensely. I will apply some later once I am finished rolling out a piecrust."

"No, I will finish." Sarah set the bread pan in the hearth oven, then picked up the rolling pin from the table and ran her hand over it. There were nicks from it being used so much—like her. Then she pushed it across the lump of dough and flattened it.

"Reverend Hopewell has come to River Run."

Fiona's eyes opened wide. "He has? It's a hot day. He'll want something cool to drink." In a hurry, she drew off her apron, patted her cap, then left. Darcy trailed behind her, her rag doll dragging along the floor.

Setting the dough over the pie pan, Sarah crimped the edges. A nagging feeling gripped her suddenly, that all was not well for Eliza. Stepping away from the table, she went to the kitchen door and peered out into the hallway leading to the foyer. A fan of sunlight spread over the floor when Eliza stepped inside with Reverend Hopewell. He drew off his hat and handed it to Fiona, then spoke to Darcy and handed her a brown bag.

The way his smile quickly faded, Sarah could not help but believe he was the bearer of bad news. A troubled look shadowed his otherwise cheerful countenance. Before he followed Eliza into the sitting room, he turned to Sarah. "I have no news regarding Dr. Hutton, Sarah. You understand how difficult it is, don't you?"

"Yes, Reverend, I do. But I shall continue to be hopeful."

With a nod, Reverend Hopewell stepped into the sitting room and closed the door. Sunshine fled the foyer, and a grim silence followed. Fiona looked disappointed, and Sarah turned back into the kitchen.

"He does not want a thing," Fiona said following her through. "It worries me."

"Perhaps he is not thirsty, Fiona."

"If there is one thing I know, Sarah, it is that when a minister visits someone and will not partake in any kind of food or drink, he is there to bring ill news. My poor girl. I am afraid for her."

"Try not to worry , Fiona."

"It cannot be helped. Ah, you have rolled out the crust. Thank you."

Sarah went to empty the bowl of berries into the pan. Fiona stayed her with her hand. "Let me. I need the distraction."

What Sarah sensed was true. Eliza's world was about to come crashing down. Kind Eliza. She did not deserve heartache or trouble. And Sarah wished she could do something to shield her for all the good she had done for her. Hayward was either wounded or dead, the latter being the worst tragedy of all. *Show me what to do. How can I ease the pain she will feel?*

Darcy held the paper sack up for Sarah to see. "See, Sarah. My candy."

"Shall I keep it for you?"

"Yes, please. Keep it safe, Sarah." Darcy rubbed her eyes and yawned. "Abigail is sleepy." She cuddled her doll close.

"*You* are sleepy. Come. I will go with you upstairs and tuck you and Abigail in for a nap."

As she passed the sitting room with Darcy's hand in hers, she heard Reverend Hopewell speaking gently and then Eliza's strained voice. She could not make out the conversation, and she avoided doing so. But then she overheard Eliza say, "I cannot read it."

It had to be a letter, but what kind? Pressing her lips together and gripping the stair rail, Sarah led Darcy upstairs, while an anxious churning started up inside her. The breeze fluttered the curtains in the room, and Sarah drew them closed over the first windows. When a sparrow alighted upon the sill of the other, Darcy ran to it.

"Do not run, Darcy," Sarah told her. "If you wish to see him closer, you must stand still. There, you see—he has flown away."

Part 4

When my heart is overwhelmed:
lead me to the rock that is higher than I.

Psalm 61:2b

26

Fiona's face had lost all color and her hands trembled when she held them out to Sarah. "Eliza left the house an hour ago and has not come back," a worried Fiona told Sarah. "She has received horrible news. Captain Morgan was executed."

A chill raced through Sarah. She understood the pain Eliza felt. "Do not worry, Fiona. I will go find her."

Dark clouds gathered overhead and wind whipped through the trees, bending limbs and sending leaves whirling into the air. As she approached a bend in the road, she spotted Eliza walking in the rain as if in a dream. Her clothes were untidy and soaked through, her eyes like glass as she stared ahead through wet strands of hair. Sarah hurried to her and threw her arms about her. Then, she guided Eliza back to River Run in a storm that battered the land.

In the weeks that followed, not once did she press Eliza about what had happened when she had been at Halston's. But it was clear when her frocks were too snug she was with child.

Eliza did not speak Halston's name, even when the women learned he had joined the Maryland regiment and his fields went fallow. Downy thistles and fleabane overran them and now stood in dried dead stalks beneath cloudy winter skies. It grieved Sarah to see Eliza so low, barely speaking and secluding herself in her room.

On a clear, cold night in 1780, Sarah had come from the cabin carrying the quilt she had finished for Eliza's baby, hoping it might cheer her a little. Stepping over the flagstones, her calf muscle in her shorter leg ached. As she approached the rear door she saw her face reflected in the window glass. The cold reddened her cheeks, and her hair, long and unbound, twisted around her shoulders. Scissors had not touched it since she left the Woodhouse farm, and it now reached her hips in long twists.

She looked up at the stars before going inside the house. How could the darkness of space go on forever? Was Heaven beyond the constellations? The reflections of the moon, huge and bright, surrounded by starry patterns, tripped over the brass handle as she closed her hand over it.

A moment later, she found Fiona in the sitting room sewing by candle and firelight. The fire in the hearth crackled and Sarah welcomed the warmth of the room, a contrast to what the cabin provided. Although it was her own to live in, she grew lonely there, especially for the man she loved.

"Ah! You have finished." Fiona set her sewing on her lap. "Let me see."

Proud of her handiwork, Sarah opened the quilt. "Do you think she will like it?"

"No doubt she will." Fiona examined the stitches. "You do very fine work. The stitches are tight and the pattern so even."

"It is by no means perfect."

"It does not have to be. Such a good use of Darcy's outgrown clothes."

Sarah set the quilt down and sat across from Fiona. "I wish Eliza would talk about things—with you, I mean. You are like a mother to her."

Fiona sighed. "That I am. Her silence and the way she secludes herself troubles me."

"And me as well. She is afraid, and I wonder if she will love this baby."

Fiona picked up her sewing and continued, "Afraid, yes. Loving the child, I know she will. But she feels such shame."

"Whatever she may feel now, let us hope love will come when the baby is born and heal her heart." Thinking of her own baby, Sarah lowered her head. "I loved mine the moment I knew."

"Yes, but the difference was you were married to your babe's father. This is a very hard thing for Eliza. How she will explain this child to others who know Captain Morgan is dead, I do not know."

"She is a strong woman and will bear up under the shame, I am sure."

"Part of me is angry with her for giving in. She should have never gone to Mr. Halston, but stayed here with us. However, the rest of me feels so much pity for her, I can hardly bear it."

Footsteps crossed the floor above, and the women paused to listen. Then all went quiet again.

Sarah folded the quilt and set it aside. "Fiona, you know I was an orphan."

"You told me, Sarah."

"I saw children brought to the workhouse who had families but were unwanted, others with no relations at all. Some were brought in fine carriages and handed out. Those were the illegitimate children of aristocrats."

Fiona frowned and shook her head. "Shameful—on all accounts."

"Yes, they only saw the indignity in the child, not in themselves."

"Do you know who your parents were?"

"No, but the staff at the workhouse would tease me by calling me *Lady Sarah*."

With a lift of her brows, Fiona cocked her head to one side. "Well, perhaps you are higher-born than you thought."

"It is too late now and does not matter." She stood, picked up the quilt and laid it in the cradle beside the fireplace. Keen of hearing, Sarah heard footsteps thump up the steps outside.

"Someone has come." Sarah hurried into the hall, and Fiona followed her. Eliza lumbered down the stairs, her belly great with child, her flintlock pistol in her hand.

"Eliza, my girl. You should not be climbing up and down the stairs. It is too dangerous for you and the baby," Fiona warned in a soft whisper.

Eliza held her hand up for silence as a loud knock fell on the door and a man called from without. His voice, young and strong, trembled from the cold, and he pleaded for her to open up, giving his name and saying Captain Hayward Morgan had sent him.

Captain Morgan? That cannot be!

A chill prickled over Sarah's skin. She clenched the folds of her dress and drew close to Eliza. And when asked to open the door, trepidation filled her. She wanted to disobey the order. She wanted to warn Eliza of the danger of such a person as her hand closed over the cold handle and gripped it. With the other, she pulled back the bolt, swallowing the lump in her throat. Slowly she peered out from the edge of the door. Out on the porch, his face touched by moonlight, stood a lean man in buckskins. He dragged off his tricorn hat and held it between his hands. Eliza allowed him in.

He brought startling news that shook River Run to the very foundation. A letter, dated and signed by Hayward Morgan to Eliza, provoked such a mix of outrageous emotions that the women of the house passed from crying tears of joy that he lived, to trembling with fear that he should return and discover Eliza had given birth to a child not his own.

When Sarah laid her head on her pillow that night, she could find no words of her own to utter in her prayers. She stared up at the rafters, firelight from her hearth trembling over them. The scent of pine filled the cabin, and the pinecones she had tossed in the hearth, crackled as the coals and ash hissed.

"Our Father, who art in Heaven," she whispered, her hands clasped over her breast. "Hallowed be thy name . . ."

The prayer stuck in her throat. Tears blurred her vision. Distressed, she shut her eyes and let the tears drift down her face. She lay silent now, listening to the wind whistle through the cracks in the logs. Desperate for some relief, she sat up then sank down on her knees beside her bed.

"Dear God, forgive me for the oath I have taken if it were wrong. I shall be living a lie, and when Captain Morgan returns, deceiving him. Yet, I cannot bear the thought of what might happen if Eliza were to tell him the truth about the child."

She laid her head against her arms. "Be merciful to us, Lord. Take pity on Eliza. She has been kind to me and is my sister if ever I had one. Allow me to do this for her, with your grace and mercy on me."

Through her tears and her plea, she struggled with what she was about to do, to say she was the babe's mother, to raise and love the babe, all in front of Eliza. And what would she do if Alex found her at last and they were to see each other again? How would she explain the child to him? "I will tell him the truth, God, that I did it in order to protect my mistress—my friend. He will not reject me or the child, for his heart is kind and good."

If only Alex would return to Hutton House, Mr. Pippins would tell him a letter had been sent from River Run and he'd come for her. But as long as the Revolution went on, he would be in the field, attending patriots.

"Please, God. Let this war end soon. Please watch over Alex while we are apart, and the twins and Mrs. Burnsetter, wherever they may be."

The multitude of troubles that came with sacrifice rushed over her like the moaning wind rushing over the barren land outside. She had given her pledge to a reluctant Eliza, along with Fiona, not thinking it all through. Now it was too late to go back on her word even if she wanted to.

Her door creaked open, and when she looked up to see Eliza standing there, Sarah wiped her eyes and got to her feet.

"May I come in and speak with you?" Eliza had no cloak on and shivered.

Sarah drew her inside. "You will catch your death coming here with no covering. Come sit by the fire."

The heat that radiated from the hearth shone on Eliza's worried face as she sat down. Dark circles were beneath her eyes. She had aged, and Sarah feared Eliza would not make it through the birthing of this child.

"I wanted to come and sit awhile. It is the place where you will be raising this baby." Eliza laid her hand over her belly. "It is a great sacrifice you are making on my behalf."

Eliza's eyes filled with tears, and Sarah crouched down in front of her. She took up Eliza's hands and held them. "I wish there had been someone to help me when I was carrying my babe. He might have lived if there had been."

"So much loss for one woman to bear, Sarah. I should not let you do this."

"I want to."

Eliza hung her head. "No, I should take the consequences."

"Think of Darcy. Captain Hayward could send you away, or leave you. Do you think he would let you have Darcy? The law would be in his favor."

"God forgive me." Eliza withdrew her hands and pounded them against the arm of the chair. "Is there no compassion for a woman who thought her husband dead?"

"For some, yes. But you know Captain Hayward better than any of us."

"He would be hurt . . ."

"And feel betrayed, don't you think?"

"Yes, and angry. You are in danger as well, Sarah, if he finds out you were indentured. The law could punish you for hav-ing a child unmarried."

"I understand the threat. I cannot stand to think your hus-band could reject you and this child. Don't you see? I love Darcy. She cannot go through life without you."

"Oh, I am so confused. What I have done has touched everyone." Eliza winced and gripped her belly. "I have pain."

"Is this the first?" Sarah asked, reaching for her cloak. She put it around Eliza's shoulders.

"Two before I came here."

Sarah helped Eliza stand and proceeded with her to the door. Before they went out into the night, Eliza, with pain and sorrow in her eyes, looked at Sarah. "Will God forgive me?"

"He is faithful to forgive us our sins when we ask, Eliza. Do not forget His love for you. Now, we must hurry and get you back to the house."

She gripped Sarah by the arm. "If Hayward questions me with kindness, if he shows compassion and love for this baby, then I shall tell him the truth. Surely, his heart will break, but there is the chance he will not cast me out—if anything, for Darcy's sake and for the sake of our marriage. I am praying he will forgive me."

Sarah did not answer. Convinced Hayward would not be so tolerant, she could not agree with Eliza and give her false hope. Her heart ached that she would live this lie, but if she cared for this child, would it be a falsehood to say she was her mother?

Once inside the house, she helped Eliza upstairs. Fiona rushed down the hallway hastily dressed in her night robe and cap.

"Eliza is having the baby." Sarah paused with Eliza as she faced another contraction.

Fiona's wide eyes caught the flame of the candle she held. "Dear me. Well, I suppose it is the proper time. Come on, my girl. Let's get you to bed."

With care they helped her to her room, and Fiona threw back the heavy coverlet and drew the sheet over Eliza's body. Again Eliza groaned.

"Sarah," Fiona turned to her, "I will sit with her. You go down to the kitchen and boil water. Bring it up here as quick as you can along with the basket I prepared for this birthing."

As quick as her impeding legs could carry her, Sarah descended the gloomy staircase in the dark. She heaved the cast-iron kettle from the table and filled it, then set it back in the fireplace. She fanned the coals and they grew bright red, igniting a log above them. Sitting back in the chair, she clasped her hands together and prayed for her mistress, and the baby that was about to be born.

"Oh, what kind of life will I be able to give her?" she whispered. "Please, God, work in Captain Hayward's heart to love this child and accept her. She belongs to Eliza—and Darcy is her sister. Is it your will that they should be separated? Should she go through life not knowing her real mother or her sister? Hear my prayer. Bless this little one. Help Captain Morgan to love her and be her father."

She covered her face in her hands feeling conflicted. Unable to prevent her body from trembling, she feared a man she had never met. Through her ordeal, she had learned to mistrust. Lem Locke's face flashed in her mind. The way he treated her when he was told she carried Jamie's child plagued her. Mary had been no better. Selfish. Cold.

And then there was Sawyer, and the captain and sailors aboard that horrid vessel transporting souls to a life of servitude against their wills. They had no sympathy for a woman with child.

Her grief rose from the place where she had long buried it. It raked through her, tore, and stabbed. All over again her heart broke, as she remembered the pangs of childbirth, and then the small, white, innocent stillborn, wrapped in a rag and given to the sea. She never saw her child's face, only one tiny clenched fist raised in protest.

Crushed by her sorrow, Sarah hugged her knees and waited for the steam to spew from the spout and wake her out of her misery. By the time she returned to Eliza's room with the hot water, and the basket in the crook of her arm, the babe had started to crown. One push and she came whimpering into the world, black-haired and pink-skinned. Sarah could not remove her gaze from the newborn child. Ilene, as she would be called, quieted when Fiona wrapped her tight in a blanket and held her out to Sarah, whose heart had been instantly stolen.

"You must take her now, Sarah," said Eliza, her chest heaving.

Sarah drew near the bedside cradling Ilene. "Don't you want to hold her?"

"I cannot." Eliza turned her head away. "If you do not take her now, I should want her. It is better this way."

Fiona stepped up to stand beside Sarah. "Eliza is right."

Sad for Eliza, Sarah stepped out of the room into the darkened hallway. Darcy stood against the wall with a bewildered look on her face. She stared up at Sarah with a flood of questions in her eyes. And wanting her to see the baby, Sarah leaned down to show her.

"Is she not beautiful, Darcy?"

"Oh," Darcy breathed, touching the baby's cheek with the tip of her forefinger.

Ilene began to cry, and Sarah went down the staircase to the kitchen, fetched a tankard of milk, and headed back to the cabin. That night, she sat beside Ilene's cradle watching her, and when she stirred, Sarah lifted her into her arms and held her close.

"You are a gift from God, little one, sent to fill a void in my soul and soothe my heartbreak. My prayer for you is that others will know it as I do now."

Unsure when Reverend Hopewell could baptize Ilene, and fearing the social stigma that would follow, Sarah dipped her finger into a dish of tepid water and blessed the baby girl on the forehead.

27

1782

The day Hayward Morgan returned home, Sarah had just finished hanging the morning wash and now stood at the end of the porch, her bare feet in the cool grass. With anxiety building, she watched him ride his horse toward the house along the soft sandy lane. Darcy and Ilene played on the lawn, on a tattered quilt, and she lifted the two-year-old Ilene to her hip.

Glancing at Eliza, Sarah read the excitement in her movements, but fear flickered in her eyes. "Do not worry, mistress. He will think of nothing else but you. Look how quickly he is coming."

"I am happy. It has been so long since I had his arms around me," Eliza said. "But yet, my heart is aching, Sarah. God give me strength."

Sarah placed her hand on Ilene's back, and wondered how long Eliza's secret could be withheld from Hayward. What kind of man would he prove to be? Compassionate? Forgiving? Would he love Ilene if he found out the truth, or would he be harsh and uncompromising?

Ilene whimpered and turned her eyes away from the stranger. Sarah held her closer, felt the warmth of her cheek pressing against her neck. "It is alright, Ilene," she whispered. "I will protect you, my darling."

At all costs.

Ilene was her child, and the love she felt for her rose—no one would harm her girl or take her away from her. Only a mother could feel this strongly. For two years, Sarah cared for Ilene in the quaint cabin. Through times of sickness she prayed and worried over her. In times of want she gave to Ilene before herself. She showed her the kind of affection and love only a mother could. She would sacrifice her own life for this beautiful brown-haired child, and if Hayward ever knew the truth, she would beg to be allowed to remain with her.

"Mama." Ilene put her little hand over Sarah's cheek. And when Sarah saw the pain the word brought into Eliza's eyes when she heard it, she turned aside.

Sunlight crossed Hayward's broad shoulders and touched his handsome face as he brought his horse to a halt. A strand of his dark hair hung over his forehead and he smiled with his eyes riveted upon Eliza. Throwing off his hat, he dismounted and hurried to her. He was not at all what Sarah had imagined. She thought he would be more heavily fleshed, but she could tell by his loose regimental coat that his time imprisoned by the British had weakened what was once a muscular build.

He drew Eliza into his arms and kissed her. Hope for happiness for Sarah's friend heightened. Could this love dismiss their secret? He turned, locked his eyes upon her and then upon Ilene. She grew afraid as he questioned Eliza about her. The beat of her heart quivered in her chest like the wing of a frightened bird. His eyes squinted a moment at the child in her arms, and frowned at the absence of a father. She realized he was not a man to be provoked or crossed as he turned inside the house with Eliza's hand in his, leaving Darcy standing on the threshold.

28

*W*arm days deepened over the next few weeks. Wild daisies, fleabane, and thistle wilted in the heat. The leaves on the trees twisted, thirsty for rain. The Potomac ran low, and in Israel Creek the mill had not enough water to turn the wheel.

The drought hardened the earth and made the river road dusty. Sarah had gone out with Eliza and the girls into the woods to pick wild blackberries. The bushes were abundant with fruit, and her fingers were stained with their sweet juices. As she walked home with Eliza, the girls skipping like lambs across the field, she smiled at Darcy's chatter and how it made Ilene giggle.

Sarah lifted Ilene when she raised her arms to her. "Life is good, is it not, Eliza?"

"It is. Hayward and I are becoming reacquainted. He seems happy."

"I am so glad." Sarah avoided Hayward as much as possible, for she did not like the way his eyes beheld her in Eliza's absence. She paused a moment, her lower lip between her teeth. "I know it has been hard for you—regarding Ilene."

Eliza gave her a sad smile. "Yes, but it eases my heart she has you to take care of her. What would I have done otherwise?"

"Your husband does not question you about her?"

"No. Do not worry. You and Ilene are safe."

"I fear our secret may be a mistake."

"You mustn't say anything to Hayward that would reveal the truth. It would hurt him. And God only knows what it would do to our marriage. You made me a promise. Besides, I have come to realize Hayward would never believe anything other than what I have told him. If you say anything, you risk him casting you out."

"You would stand up for me, would you not?"

"Yes, of course, I would. But I will not jeopardize my marriage or Darcy's well-being."

"No, I would not want you to do that." Still those conflicting feelings lingered.

Eliza touched Sarah's arm. "Then we are all safe."

They walked on, and Sarah, being deeply troubled, lifted her face to the breeze. She looked toward the house and saw Hayward standing in the window. He wore a light linen shirt open at his throat, his hair loose about his neck.

"The air smells of rain. There are thunderheads on the horizon," she said.

Ilene wiggled and Sarah let her down. They stepped onto plowed earth where the seed had not taken. Ilene balled her fist against her eye and began to cry.

Sarah set her basket down. "Oh, is the ground too hot, my darling?" She put out her arms to comfort Ilene, but Eliza stopped her and bent down.

"You are hot and tired, Ilene. But look, Darcy is not crying." Eliza ran her hand gently over Ilene's hair and when Ilene stopped her tears and put her arms around Eliza's neck, Sarah felt a pain dart through her being.

"You should not show too much affection for her, mistress. Captain Morgan stands at the window and watches," Sarah warned.

Quickly, Eliza stood. She and Sarah glanced at the window. Hayward frowned, ran his hand over his face, and moved away. The white curtains rippled, and Sarah questioned the change in his expression. There was no doubt in her mind he disapproved of Eliza's show of affection toward Ilene.

Inside the kitchen, Sarah sorted out the berries while Fiona kneaded bread. Ilene lay down in front of the cold hearth next to Hayward's new dog, a shaggy creature who put his head between his paws and welcomed the child's caress.

"She is tired." Fiona set the dough in a wooden bowl.

"I should take her to the cabin for a nap."

Fiona touched Sarah on the shoulder. "You look troubled, my girl."

"You can always tell, Fiona."

"A gift I suppose. What's troubling you?"

Sarah glanced over at Ilene and breathed out a long, painful sigh.

"Oh, I see. Now, you mustn't worry. God put that child into your hands for a good reason. He will not forsake you or Ilene."

Sarah shook her head. "I am uncertain how long this can stay a secret. Am I sinning by saying I am Ilene's mother?"

"Are you? Who has cared for her these years? Who has loved her more than you?"

"When Ilene is grown, I will have to tell her the truth. She would have a right to know."

"Then wait until that day comes. Now is not the time."

Hayward walked into the kitchen. "Sarah. I want to speak to you. Come to my study." He strode out, and Sarah looked at Fiona, feeling worried.

"Do not keep him waiting." Fiona put her hands on Sarah's shoulders and turned her toward the door. She hurried to the study, through the darkened, cool hallway. His door stood open, and she watched the curtains flutter over the window as they had earlier.

She stepped inside, eyes lowered. "What is it, sir?"

He turned to look at her. "I have spoken with my wife and she has explained to me the circumstances that brought you here. How long were you with the Indians?"

"I lost track of time, sir. Months, I believe."

"And from where were you taken?"

"A cabin in the wilderness."

"And whose cabin was this? Why do you look afraid to answer?"

She looked up at him. "I am not afraid, Captain Morgan."

"Then speak up, girl."

"I was there with a man and an old woman."

"Their names?"

"Jebediah Thrasher, sir. The woman's name was Sally. That's all I know."

"He was your husband, a relative? What?"

She could not lie this time. "He—owned me." She lowered her eyes again, feeling shame.

"You were indentured to him?"

She nodded.

"For how long?"

"He had just," and she swallowed, "acquired me."

"From whom?"

"Simon Woodhouse of Virginia. He was financially ruined and left for Jamaica with his wife. He had to sell everything, including me, to clear his debts." She took a step forward hoping he would listen to her plight and be understanding. "I was kidnapped in Cornwall and brought to America. They sold me against my will."

"You are not a runaway and lying to me?" He seemed not to care what she had been through.

"No, sir."

"We do not keep secrets here at River Run. If you are to remain here, you must be truthful and honest about everything. Do you understand?"

Her heart skipped a beat. "Yes, I understand completely."

"So you, by law, are still indentured to Mr. Thrasher. By law, my wife should have returned you to him."

"He is dead, sir. When Indians attacked, they killed him and the woman . . . even their poor dog. They looted and burned the cabin."

"So there is no proof of his ownership of you, except what is documented in a ledger?"

"I suppose not."

"My wife tells me it was Mr. Halston who rescued you both. Did he visit River Run often while I was away?"

"I cannot say, sir. I did not admit guests into the house."

"Your child does not appear to have Indian blood in her. Her skin is fair. But I suppose that could be how you came by her."

"I do not wish to speak of it, sir."

"I imagine not. The experience was not a good one, no doubt. That is one secret I will allow, Sarah. But having a child, and being unmarried, shall make life hard for you. I am willing to keep you on, if you will serve me well. I will say nothing to anyone about your indentureship."

She looked up at him with glistening eyes. "I will always work hard, sir."

He locked his gaze on her. "Did your former masters expect anything more from you other than hard work?"

A lump formed in her throat. "You mean, was I also their mistress? No."

"It is not uncommon. Even accepted. If I should need comfort from you, and you give it, I shall reward you. You could do with a few new dresses and a bit of money of your own."

Sarah scowled. "I cannot do that. It is an affront to Almighty God. And I would not hurt Mrs. Morgan."

Indifferent to her refusal, he shrugged, then returned to his desk and lifted some papers from it. "I think you will eventually change your mind."

Her courage rallied. "I will flee River Run before that happens."

Hayward's mouth twitched. "You do that, and I will see to it your time of indenture will be lengthened by two more years, and I will sell you off to the worst vermin I can find. I daresay, he will not suggest anything, but take what he wants."

"Your threat is a cruel one, Captain Morgan. Why would you even consider betraying the wife that loves you more than anything in the world just to satisfy your desires?"

His face stiffened, and he said nothing at first. Then he tossed the papers down. "Leave me."

She sped from the room and out into the dim hallway to the kitchen. She would never give in to him, no matter what he promised to do. Her heart ached for Alex. His love was true, pure. He never took advantage of her, but treated her with respect and as an equal.

Fiona looked up with a start. "Dear me, you look as though you have had a fright. What happened?"

"I cannot tell you. Do not ask me."

She scooped Ilene up from the floor and went with her back to the cabin. Closing the door, she could not help but let the tears flow, afraid of what would be demanded of her, afraid he would keep approaching her day after day. The way his eyes looked at her, she wondered if he were capable of taking her by force.

"Alex. Where are you? Why haven't you come for me?" She rushed over to her table and wrote to him. Somehow he must get her letters. She had sent him so many, and they all had been returned from the trading post. The war was over. Hadn't he returned to Virginia? Could he have been killed, forever lost to her?

"No, I will not believe that." She shook her head, and her hair fell forward. "He has forgotten me. No longer loves me. He has probably found someone else and is wedded. The girls needed a mother." She tore the letter to pieces, threw her arms across the table, laid her head there and wept.

She looked over and saw Ilene had fallen asleep, her rag doll tucked beneath her little chin. With a small cry, Sarah gathered her up in her arms and settled down next to her, listened to her even breathing, to the rush of wind through the trees. Weary in body, and low in spirit, she fell asleep.

Little time had passed when the rain began to drum on the roof. A flash of lightning and a rumble of thunder shook the rafters, waking Sarah. So fierce was the blinding light, so deafening the din of the storm, that fear gripped her.

She reached for Ilene. She was not there. Sarah scrambled from the bed. "Ilene!"

She looked all about the cabin. Ilene's rag doll lay on the floor in front of the door, which shifted in the wind. Sarah's heart raced up her throat. She hurried to it, picked it up.

"Ilene!" she called from the threshold.

Rain pelted her face. Rushing out onto the porch, panic struck her. Going down the steps, she saw tiny footprints in the mud. Her heart pounded. She hurried into the house, expecting to find Ilene there.

"She is with Darcy," Sarah said hopefully. She found Eliza and Fiona in the sitting room. Darcy snuggled beside her mother.

Rainwater dripped from Sarah's hair and clothing, and made a puddle on the floor. Dread ran up and down her spine, and she trembled. "I cannot find her!"

For over an hour, a candle burned in a brass socket on the table in the sickroom. Almost within reach of Sarah's hand, its light shimmered across the coverlet. With her head cradled in her arms, she silently wept. The night wore on. Ilene sighed and stirred. Beads of sweat stood out on her face. Sarah bathed it tenderly.

"She will be alright, will she not, Fiona?" she asked, seeking comfort.

Fiona laid her wrinkled hand over Sarah's. "Yes, God willing."

"I should have thought to look for her outside. But I did not think she would stay there—not in the rain, with the thunder and lightening. She is afraid of those things. I do not know why she left the cabin."

"Perhaps she wanted Darcy. They are so close."

"Eliza is worried."

"She looked calm when she left," said Fiona.

"But Captain Morgan is so angry with me. Did you hear what he said?"

"I did. He can be without feeling at times and does not understand a woman's heart."

"He blames me." Sarah turned into the older woman's arms, heard the clock out in the hall strike nine. Looking over at the door, she saw a shadow pass behind it along the threshold. She sensed it was he.

She turned back to Ilene and wiped her flushed face once more with a damp cloth. Ilene opened her eyes and looked up at Sarah with a faint smile. "Mama. Dolly?"

"Oh, yes, my darling. Here she is." Sarah picked up the rag doll from the edge of the bed and tucked it beneath Ilene's arm. It was still damp from being in the rain. "Hold her close."

"Me, too, Mama." Ilene stretched her arm up to Sarah.

With a little cry, Sarah held Ilene in her arms, then set her back against the pillow. She put a glass of water to her mouth but Ilene could not drink.

"Please, God. Do not take her."

Ilene drew in a breath and slowly released it. Sarah caught up her hand and spoke words of entreaty. "You mustn't go, Ilene. Stay, my darling. Do not leave. Do not go."

With Ilene's hand in hers, with her agonizing gaze upon the face of an angel-child from which the light of life slowly faded, Sarah poured out her anguish. She shook with crying and the candle in the room guttered. A whirl of smoke rose from the charred wick.

Fiona put her arms around Sarah, but she refused to be led away.

29

Alex stripped off his deer hide leggings and shirt and stepped into a pool of water up to his waist in the Savage River. As he lowered himself, the current rushed over his shoulders, soothed his tired body. He felt the summer grit wash off his skin.

He'd given all he could for the Glorious Cause, moving north from Fort Frederick to Fort Pitt with the patriots, all this time the memory of Sarah lingering in his mind. His love for her had not lessened, but remained a constant flame.

After eleven months, he requested release from his duty and, having been granted a departure, rode out into the wilderness upon Charger in search of her. Having gone as far as the river through the Alleghenies, he began the long trek home with no success. He had to see his nieces and aunt, to insure all was well with them, and hire another tracker, this time one who knew the woods and the Indians far better than Riddance and had a reputation for finding runaways and captives.

After changing into his military garb that he had kept folded in his saddlebag, he rode east along the National Pike, paused at a tavern for a hearty meal and a good night's sleep in a real bed, then headed for Annapolis in the morning. An hour before nightfall, he saw the town on the horizon bathed in golden dusk. Spurring Charger, he galloped toward it, and the horse whinnied when his hooves crossed over from the dirt road to cobblestones. He rode past red brick buildings, houses, and shops. Along the streets, lamps glowed and people tipped their hats as he rode past. Servants carried baskets of goods homeward, and merchants were closing their shops for the day.

Dismounting in front of his aunt's house, he bounded up the steps to the door and eagerly knocked. A middle-aged woman opened up. Her large ebony eyes glanced him over.

"Yes, sir?" She set her hands demurely over her starched apron.

"Is Mrs. Burnsetter at home? I am her nephew, Dr. Hutton."

Before he could step inside, his aunt came into view. She raised her brows, which skimmed the edge of her white mobcap. "Who is it, Millie?"

He smiled. Millie replied, "He says he is your nephew, ma'am."

"Forgive my tattered appearance, Aunt," he said, dragging off his slouch hat. "I did not expect you to know me on first glance."

"My Lord, it is Alex!" She opened her arms, pulled him inside, and embraced him. With a happy sigh, she stood back. "Millie, take my nephew's hat." She turned to her maid, finger on her chin. "Have we anything left from this evening's supper?"

"We got ham and taters—cornbread biscuits with lots of butter and honey."

Aunt Moria slapped her hands together with joy. "Wonderful! Fix my nephew a heaping plate, and brew some hot coffee. Oh, and what about pie? He must have some pie."

"We got half an apple pie."

Alex could not help but smile at the attention given to his appetite. "Well, Millie, you best bring it on. I am famished and will not give up the chance to try a woman's cooking. It's been some time since I had home fare."

"Oh, poor Alex," cooed his aunt. She poked his ribs and frowned. "Millie's pie is just what you need to put a bit of weight on your bones."

Smiling, Millie threw back her shoulders and put her hands on her hips. "How could I have forgotten that pie? I make the best in all of Maryland, sir. Why even General Lafayette has had my pie. Said they had nothin' like it in all of France."

"When did you ever serve General Lafayette pie, Millie?" said Aunt Moria.

Millie leaned forward. "When he came through Annapolis in secret."

"I believe it is a fable."

"No, it is true, ma'am."

"Someone told you he was General Lafayette and had a French accent and you believed him."

Millie shrugged. "Don't matter. He sure did like my pie though—whoever he was." With a skip in her step, she returned to the kitchen.

Aunt Moria set her hands on Alex's shoulders. "You have had a rough time of it, I see. Your hair has a bit of gray in it now. I'd wager you shall be happy to have a warm bath and sleep in a feather bed." She went to the bottom of the staircase. "Girls, your uncle has come home!"

Down the stairs barreled Rose and Lily. They threw their arms around his legs, and he crouched down to embrace them. "Look at you girls! You are both a little taller since I last saw you. And so pretty, too."

Rose looked up at him with wide eyes. "Did you bring us anything?"

"It is rude to ask such a question, Rose," said Aunt Moria. "Your brave uncle has been away doctoring the patriots."

"Uncle Alex, did you?" asked Lily.

"But of course. I could not come home empty-handed." He reached inside his waistcoat pocket, took out two coins, and dropped one into each palm. Their eyes lit up and they danced about the room holding up their shiny coppers to the light.

Alex laughed. "We will go to a shop tomorrow and you can spend those."

Aunt Moria threw her arms around the girls to keep them from spinning about like a pair of tops. "Calm down, my dears." Immediately they obeyed her, but the excitement lingered in their eyes and wiggled through their limbs. "Now go upstairs and put your coins away for safekeeping. Your uncle is weary from his journey and needs supper."

Off they dashed, thanking him as they climbed the staircase. Lily turned and looked at him with questioning eyes. "Uncle Alex?"

"Yes, Lily. What is it?"

"Where did the lady with the red hair go? I have missed her and you said you would bring her home with you." Her little pout cut him to the quick.

Amazed that she would even remember his words, he gave Lily a sad smile. "I know I did. I have looked for her. But I do not know where she has gone. Someday I will find her."

That night, when he had finished two plates of supper and a hunk of Millie's pie, Alex sat with his aunt in the parlor with his boots up. The girls were tucked in bed, and a gentle

breeze blew through the window. It smelled of saltwater and
cool, misty air. Absent were the scent of hemlocks and rotting
leaves, the songs of woodland birds, and the cries of the bucks,
which he had come to know in the wilderness. His time spent
searching for Sarah had taken the city out of him, and he
yearned to return to his brother's house in Virginia where at
least he could farm the land, set up a practice, and live away
from the bustle of people.

Moria looked up from the pair of pale yellow mitts she was
knitting. "What are you thinking about, Alex? You look far
away."

He stretched his arms behind his head. "What I always
think of."

"Sarah?"

"I cannot help it. My soul is tied to hers."

The expression on Aunt Moria's face was one of deep
concern. "I liked her, I admit. I could tell she was a good
person and one who did not deserve her lot in life. You must
have traveled far in search of her. Was it a hardship?"

"I will not complain. But out there, I saw and heard things
I never had before."

"I worried over you. Some nights I could hardly sleep a
wink."

"Why? There was no danger for you to fret over."

"You are trying to comfort me. I thought of the Indians
. . . the war."

"As long as I had something to offer the Indians, they were
kind. I helped their sick."

"And the British?"

"I had no confrontations with any redcoats that mattered."

"And no word of Sarah?"

"An old squaw told me she had seen her, that she went into
the forest and was never heard from again."

"Oh, poor girl. How could she survive such an ordeal?"

"I have prayed she found people. I am going back to look for her."

"So soon, Alex?"

"The longer I wait, the worse my chances are. I will stay here a few days." He patted her hand and stood, then kissed his aunt's cheek. "I am tired. Good night, Aunt."

She touched his arm. "God's will be done, Alex. I shall pray for Sarah this night, and for you, that God guides your path to her."

30

*T*wo days later, at the break of dawn, Alex rose and pulled on his buckskin jacket and leggings. His moccasin boots reached his knees, tied with four-inch thrums and decorated with blue and red beadwork. His first night home, Millie brushed down his regimental blue coat and hung it in the wardrobe. His beige breeches and linen shirt were folded in the drawer, and his black riding boots sat on the floor beside the dresser.

Over his shoulder he slung his powder horn and bullet pouch, and then slipped his knife into the clout pocket. He picked up his musket, and before walking out the door, caught his reflection in the old, mottled mirror beside it.

He'd changed so much. His hair fell to his shoulders, a touch of silver near his temples. No longer did he appear the finely dressed physician with a silk cravat at his throat. Instead he had been shaped like a piece of clay, conformed to the task he'd been called to. Some would have said he was out of his mind for struggling on to find such a girl. But he knew if he did not, he would be awash with regret the rest of his life.

Without making a sound, he stepped out into the hallway, and walked past the room where his nieces slept. His heart grew tender at leaving them again, and he hesitated a moment, set his musket against the wall, and slipped inside. The girls were sound asleep, with dawn coming through the window and alighting upon the curls of their hair, and he bent down and kissed their foreheads. Rose did not stir, but Lily's eyes blinked open.

"I must go away again," he whispered. "Be good for Aunt Moria. Tell Rose I love her as I love you and I shall return."

"Where are you going?" she calmly asked. Lily was always the levelheaded one, but ever curious. If Rose had awakened, she would have clung to him and cried.

"To find Sarah and bring her home."

"Oh, good." She smiled. "You promise to come back?"

"Nothing shall keep me away. Now go back to sleep." He tucked the covers closer to her chin and she shut her eyes. Then he slipped out and crept by his aunt's room down to the lower level of the house. He smelled coffee and cooking, heard the quick patter of feet come up behind him.

"You ain't leaving without breakfast, Dr. Hutton." A hand touched his shoulder.

He turned and fixed his eyes on a worried brow. "I am sorry, Millie. But I cannot spare the time."

"I knew you would say that. So I packed this sack for you. There are biscuits and jerky in it." For a moment she stared at him with her great, glistening eyes. "I have heard the wilderness is a fierce place. I'll worry about you, and be praying every night to the dear Lord that He protects you."

A grateful smile tugged the corner of his mouth. "Thank you, Millie. I have survived these past years. No need to worry. But I do covet your prayers and those of my aunt's."

"Alex, you are leaving without saying good-bye?" Aunt Moria called from the top of the staircase. The hem of her long silk robe made a soft swishing sound as she hurried down the stairs.

"I hated to wake you, Aunt Moria. It's so early."

"Why? You know I cannot let you go without an embrace from me."

He went to her, and when she took the last step, he put his arms around her. "Please do not worry."

"I cannot help it. Come back as soon as you can with your bride." On tiptoe, she leaned up and kissed his cheek. She rubbed his jaw and smiled. "I am bound to buy you a new razor for when you return. Godspeed, Alex."

Without another word, he nodded, then went out the front door into the morning haze and climbed onto Charger's back. The restless horse stomped its front hooves and paced. He turned the horse and rode south, urging Charger to a gallop. To find a tracker, he needed to head away from the city and villages, into the countryside along the river where trappers were bound to be. The riverbanks were abundant with beaver and otter and the selling of furs was brisk at the trading posts.

The day grew excessively hot. Alex paused to let Charger drink from a stream. He dismounted and filled his canteen, then splashed water over his face and head. By dusk the sky turned magenta and sapphire along the horizon. Swallows darted above the darkening treetops in search of insects, and crickets chirped in the tall grasses.

Along the dusty road stood a log tavern with broad mullioned windows and a smoky chimney. A number of horses were hitched outside, swishing their tails to shoo off the bottle flies. A sign above the door read *The Eagle Ale House*.

Alex looped Charger's reins over the split rail post and went inside. The light coming through the windows sparkled with dust motes. Tin lanterns hung from blackened beams over heavy oak tables and benches where men sat with tankards of ale and pewter plates heaped with food.

The tavern keeper greeted him. "Good evening, sir. Thirsty?"

Alex drew off his hat. "Do you know where I might find a tracker in these parts?"

One man heard his question and stood. "If it's a tracker you need, sir, then search no longer." He slapped his hand to his chest and bowed short. "Christopher Cread at your service."

Cread's eyes, dark as the tobacco in his pouch, gleamed in the lantern light. Deep lines fanned out to his temples. His hair was long, streaked gray and oaken brown.

"May we talk business, Mr. Cread?" Alex moved to a table near the window.

"If you think it worth my time, why sure."

Grabbing his mug of ale, Cread strolled over to the table, his rifle set in the hollow of his left arm. He was dressed in beaded buckskins and a coonskin cap, whose feathery tail fell over his shoulder and blended with his beard.

"Well, sir," he said, scratching his beard. "You look to be a man born to the wilderness and should be skilled enough to hunt elk and deer. What do you need someone like me for?"

"I have been searching for someone—a long time."

Cread sat down and leaned back against the bench. "Oh. Captured by the Indians was she?"

Alex, astonished that Cread surmised it was a woman, nodded. "Aye. I hired a man to find her, but he would go no further than Fort Frederick."

"Why not?" Cread asked, eyeing Alex with frank curiosity.

"Winter. And he thought it would be in vain. He proved right. I tried to find her but had no success."

"Why, I would have found her within six months. That tracker led you down the wrong path. It takes a lifetime of experience to know the wilderness. Where'd he take you—exactly?"

"Up the Potomac on the Virginia side. She had been taken to a cabin owned by a trapper."

"Indentured or kidnapped?"

"Indentured. But before that, kidnapped from England."

Cread let out a low whistle and shook his head. "A bad business. What happened after you found this cabin?"

"She was gone—the cabin burned to the ground. The man was dead, and another woman. Tracks showed it was Indians."

"Shawnee, I suppose. What next?"

"I went on to Fort Frederick, then Fort Pitt. When the war was over, I tried to find her on my own. But I am no tracker."

Setting his arm across the table, Cread leaned in. "What are you then?"

"A patriot and a physician."

Cread slapped his knee and laughed. "Who would've thought? A doctor, dressed like a backwoodsman, tripping through the woods in search of a girl. You must be crazed with love to go to those lengths."

Affronted, Alex felt the blood rush to his face. He gritted his teeth and said, "You mock me, Cread? I will have none of you then." Refusing the tin of ale the tavern maid set down, he stood to leave.

Cread put out his hand. "Sit back down. I meant nothing by it."

"I am easily offended when it comes to that kind of comment, Cread."

"Sorry. Truly I am." Cread held his hand out for Alex to shake. And when he did so, Cread looked more serious.

"You learnt nothin' the whole time out there?"

Alex slowly resumed his seat. "I found an Indian village of old men, women, and children."

"And what did they tell you?"

"They said an Indian named Black Fox had a woman with red hair, that she escaped and he and another brave went after her. They were never seen again."

Cread squinted. "And where was this camp?"

"Along the Youghiogheny."

"Well, they do move around. Most likely they ain't there now, but west of the Ohio. I doubt they could have told you any more than they did. I bet she headed east to the Potomac and those warriors caught up with her."

Alex's gut twisted. "Then she is dead you think?" he said with quiet sadness.

"They'd punish her, not kill her. But if those warriors did not return to their village, they're no more. That much I can say with certainty."

"Can I rely on you?"

"Ask any man here what they've heard of Christopher Cread, and they'll give you two words— honesty and talent. I can find just about anything."

"Even a girl who was taken captive years ago?"

"I'm sure of it. I helped a settler find his wife and two children six months ago. They were in bad shape, but he was glad to have them back. Part of it has to do with reading the woods, things left behind. What did you pay the last man?"

"Four gold pieces."

"Well, I don't want money. I thrive on the experience alone. Pay me in food and supplies, and I'll do it."

"You are a man of honor, if money is not your goal."

"I don't need it." Once more, Cread reached out his hand and shook Alex's. "We'll start on the Maryland side of the river first. Hope you don't mind if I bring my dog, Scout."

From under a table a spotted hound whined. "He's got a nose that can sniff out a weasel in a mile-long hole in the ground. Can't ya, Scout?"

Wagging his tail, Scout stood and stretched. Then he threw back his head and howled.

31

$\mathcal{O}$n a wooded hillside, Sarah waited behind a maple tree. She peered down the grassy slope to a field studded with wildflowers. At the far end were two graves, one for Addison Crawley, who had been the Morgan's farmhand, and the other for Ilene. To see the small mound of earth brought tears to her eyes. Ilene was with God now, and there was no bringing her back. Even with thoughts of Heaven, of its splendor and peace, Sarah longed for the child, to hold her in her arms again.

She saw Eliza standing in front of Hayward—his horse a few yards off. They were arguing, and Sarah watched Eliza move out of Hayward's shadow. She gripped her arms as if cold, and he grabbed her. Then, jerking away, Eliza made her way to the hillside that led back to the house. Sarah frowned at the way Hayward treated her friend, and she wished she could stop him. A husband should not be so unkind. But Eliza had warned her not to interfere.

Hayward's anger was clear. Fearing he harbored suspicions about Eliza's show of emotion over Ilene, Sarah pressed closer to the tree, feeling the bark bite into her hands. She watched him mount his horse, kick its sides, and ride up the slope toward her. Fearing he would see her, Sarah sucked in a breath and hid behind the massive trunk. Then she breathed out as soon as he rode past her.

Dashing the tears from her eyes, she sank to the base of the tree. Sunlight flashed through the limbs above, and she watched it a long while with her knees drawn up to her chest. She had not spoken to anyone in days, but had secluded herself in the cabin after finishing her chores. She would pass Eliza's room, hear her crying, and then find Darcy sitting on the floor in her room alone, cradling her doll.

When she had left the cabin, she had gathered a fistful of wildflowers. Rising from the mossy ground, she looked around the tree and saw Eliza slip over the hilltop. As fast as her legs could take her, Sarah stepped down the slope, flowers in hand. Her limp felt worse these days, her feet heavy as lead.

Reaching Ilene's grave she stood stark still. A lump formed in her throat. Without a sob or whimper, she allowed her tears to fall down her face. With no strength left to stand, she went down on her knees and set the nosegay on the red earth. Unbearable pain raked through her, as if a hand had reached inside and squeezed her heart and torn it from her chest. Agony clawed up her throat and escaped in a ragged cry. Her body shuddered and she fell forward, gathered the clay in her hands and clenched it hard.

Why had she lost all the children she had ever loved? Why had she lost Jamie and been carried off? Why had she lost Alex and been separated from the twins?

"Will you not have mercy on me, God? I can bear no more." She stayed there as the sun sank behind the mountains, as dusk softly fell and the world grew dark. A voice called to her and she lifted her head to see Fiona walking toward her, lantern in hand.

Soon Fiona's hand rested on Sarah's shoulder. "Come away, my girl. It grows dark and rain is coming."

"I do not want to leave."

"I understand. But you cannot stay out here and get a soaking."

"I do not care if the rain comes. I hope it drowns me."

Fiona set the lantern down and drew Sarah up. "Do not speak so." Fiona's motherly hands brushed Sarah's hair back from her face. "Dry your tears and let us go up to the house together."

"You are good to me, Fiona. What am I to do?"

"Carry on, my girl. 'Weeping may endure for a night, but joy cometh in the morning.'"

"I have not stopped weeping."

"You do not have to stop. Weep as long as need be."

"I shall never have joy again. Never."

"Oh, I do not believe that to be true. Now come with me."

Arm in arm, they climbed the hill together, and walked across the grassy meadow back to the house. Inside, Fiona insisted Sarah eat. A few bites, and no more, and then Sarah kissed Fiona on the cheek and wished her a good night.

Soft rain began to tap against the windows of the cabin the moment her hand closed over the latch and pushed the door in. She paused a moment on the threshold to listen. The rain murmured at first, then fell hard. It did not drive her inside. Instead, she turned, went to the edge of the little porch, and lifted her face to the deluge.

Pelted by raindrops, she pushed her fingers through her hair and drew in a long, deep breath. Her body trembled as she thought of the day Ilene had wandered out into a similar storm. How afraid she must have been—how cold.

"Heal me," she whispered, opening her eyes and looking into the whirling clouds. "Deliver me."

She looked down at the patch of ground beneath the tree where Ilene loved to play. Rain had made a few puddles there, and although she grieved, Sarah felt a bit of joy touch her heart that God had given her the gift of knowing motherhood, and had brought Ilene into her life.

The wind blew her door in and she turned. Strange, she had not left a candle burning on the table when she left. She would never be so careless. A shadow rose in the corner and Hayward moved out of the darkness toward her.

"I wondered when you would return." He strode to the door and shut it. "You will catch your death. Your hair is soaked through."

She moved away. "Why are you here? Am I needed in the house?"

"You just came from there, didn't you?"

"Yes, sir."

"I know because I saw you and Fiona in the kitchen."

"She gave me a little supper."

"These have been sad days for you, have they not, Sarah?"

She nodded. "They have. God will help me through them."

"I hope so." He sat down in a chair near her fireplace. "I need to talk to you. You can sit if you wish, or remain standing before me." His eyes roved over her, and she realized he admired the way the candlelight touched her. She set the candle on the mantle and sat across from him.

Hayward lifted his hand away from his chin. "Have you noted the grief Eliza is showing? It is unnatural."

"She loved Ilene. We all did." *Except for you.*

"Yes, but she behaves as if Ilene had been her child."

"It proves how deeply a woman can love."

He shifted his eyes away from hers and did not speak for a full minute. Then he looked back at her. "I know the truth," he said. "I know Eliza's secret. Ilene was not your child. She belonged to Eliza, didn't she?"

Fear raced through Sarah. How did he know? Had Eliza given herself away? Had she broken down and told him?

Standing, Hayward moved close. She stiffened and looked up at him. His eyes looked down into hers, hard as a pair of flints, but not without a glimmer of pain.

"I am sorry she forced you into lying for her. It was a selfish thing to do."

If she replied, she would fall into his trap and confirm his conclusion. She looked away, silent.

He touched her cheek. "Won't you speak to me?"

"I need to see Reverend Hopewell." As she began to stand, he took her by the forearms, his grip tight, and drew her up.

"There is no reason to be afraid of me, Sarah. I only want to help. Your secret is safe with me, that you are a bondservant. Understand?"

She shook her head. "No, I do not."

"Eliza is the one to blame for all this. You were only doing as you were told in order to protect her and Darcy. You were all afraid of what I might do. Eliza should have been honest with me from the start. Instead she concealed the truth from me, and that I find more disloyal than going to Halston."

He stepped back, leaned against the table. "So you see she told me everything and has destroyed what love I felt for her. Betrayal after betrayal. Lie after lie. Is it too much to ask for your comfort in exchange for my protection now that I know what you are?"

Sarah clenched her fists. "It is, and it would be wrong. I don't care if you turn me in or send me away to be auctioned off. I won't give you what you want from me."

Hayward stared at the floor, his brows pinched into a single line. Then suddenly he walked out, his face inflamed and his breath heaving. As soon as she heard the click of the latch, Sarah pulled down the heavy wooden bar over the door.

32

*S*hortly after dawn the next morning, Hayward woke Darcy, rallied the household, and left with her on horseback. He swore to a pleading Eliza she would never see the child again, and no amount of begging from her, or Darcy's tears, could change his mind.

Frustration that she could do nothing mounted in Sarah, and watching Eliza and Fiona grow pale and silent as he rode off, she begged God to take the pain away and bring Darcy back. The three women stood in the morning haze together, and when the sound of Hayward's horse faded into the distance, Eliza turned out of Fiona's arms and staggered back inside.

Sarah gripped a post. "He cannot do this, Fiona."

"He always does what he wishes without thought of anyone else, Sarah."

"But how can he be so cruel to Eliza—and to Darcy? She needs her mother."

"Believe me he will regret it one day."

"He needs to regret it now. I wish there were something we could do." She sat down on the top step and wrapped her arms around her legs.

"Eventually he will come to his senses," Fiona said. "My poor girl—that she would have to bear this breaks my heart."

Sarah glanced back over her shoulder at the elder woman. Sorrow flooded Fiona's eyes and etched deeper the lines of her face. "I will sit here until he returns."

"Get up, Sarah. Sitting there will not change a thing."

"This is my fault."

"We are all to blame. But what else could we have done?"

"Our hearts are sorry, are they not?"

"Indeed they are."

"Then whatever wrong we have done, as long as we repent with a heavy heart, we are forgiven. But never again will I do such a thing."

Sarah then fixed her eyes intently on the place where the lane met the river road. "I shall pray hard, Fiona, that this is made right."

"And so shall I. There is nothing else to do. You have made enough sacrifices."

Sarah pressed her balled fists against her eyes. "It was no sacrifice to be Ilene's mother."

"It was honorable the way you loved that child and how you kept your word to Eliza."

As if a dam broke within her, the heat of emotion flushed her face. "But look what has happened."

Fiona set her mouth hard. "It is plain enough to me. Day one he would have taken revenge on her. The Almighty only knows in what way."

Sarah pounded the post with her fist, and when Fiona's hand touched her shoulder, she stopped.

"I see now," said Fiona, "what this is truly about. Eliza will bear up and Mr. Hayward will come home with Darcy sooner or later. He will eventually forgive her and their lives will go on. But you, Sarah, you loved that child as your own, and losing her broke your heart. It is a thing you may never get over."

Sarah moved into Fiona's arms and wept. A moment later, she wiped her face dry with the back of her hand. "I must somehow reach Dr. Hutton. I can no longer live without him."

She stepped through the door and went up to Eliza's room. Fiona trailed behind her. Together they sat with Eliza through the long hours into nightfall. For all the comfort they could give, Eliza cried herself into exhaustion and silence. Nightjars murmured along the riverbank as if they mourned with her.

Seeing Eliza's condition worsen, Fiona drew on her shoes. "I must set out for the inn."

Sarah urged her not to go. "In the dark. No, Fiona. Let me."

"I will take the mare. She knows the way there and back."

"But . . ."

"No buts about it, my girl. You stay here with Eliza. Captain Morgan will listen to me."

"At least take Eliza's pistol with you for protection."

"Wise thought, but I shall not need it. Try to get her to drink some water."

And as Fiona hurried out, Sarah reached over and held Eliza's hand. "I am sorry, Eliza—sorry for everything."

✒

The heat of the day lingered into the night, and the crickets in the hedgerows seemed louder than usual. A cloudless sky yielded to a full moon that bathed the land in a blue haze, as if dawn would break early.

From the window, Sarah spied out a pair of horses. They drew closer and she saw through the moonlight that Fiona had convinced Hayward to return. In front of him sat Darcy, her legs dangling over the side and her head resting against her father's chest. Fiona rode behind him, leading Eliza's mare.

Her heart pounding with the hope all would be well, Sarah fastened her eyes hard upon Hayward. She disliked the way he sat straight as an arrow in the saddle, proud as a lord entering his castle.

If only she could stand up to him and tell him what she thought, that he was a hypocrite. He had touched her too many times and had looked at her in a wanton manner. In his heart he had been unfaithful to Eliza. Had he any right to cast stones?

Eliza called to her, "Has he come home, Sarah? Please tell me he has."

Sarah sat on the bedside. "They are just now coming down the lane."

"With my darling Darcy?"

"Yes, mistress."

Eliza looked white as death in the glow of the candle near the bed. A weak smile touched her lips and she spoke low as if she had aged into an old woman. "I am glad. I prayed he would. He has forgiven me."

Even if he had forgiven her, Sarah knew he would not forget. She pitied Eliza, for unless Hayward's cold heart would warm, everyone under his roof would suffer. Perhaps the time he had spent away, though short, had allowed him time for reflection, and he would make life tolerable for them.

"Here, drink some water. It will help." Gently she lifted a glass to Eliza's mouth. "Rest easy. He will come to you in a little while. Everything will be alright. You will see."

"Have I thanked you for all you have done for me, for Ilene and Darcy too?"

"Hush now. You are not well and should not be speaking." Sarah set the glass on the bedside table.

Eliza reached up and placed her finger on a ripped seam along Sarah's sleeve. "Your dress is torn. You are not hurt, are you?"

"I went out to get water and caught it on a branch. Not to worry. I will mend it."

"I am sorry, Sarah, for the pain I have caused you. Will you forgive me?"

"Gladly, but there is no need to forgive you for anything. We did not imagine life would turn out this way."

"I hope Dr. Hutton and you will find each other again. God knows you deserve to be happy."

Sarah shook her head. "It may be too late. It has been so long."

"It is never too late for love," said Eliza. "I will not be surprised if you learn he has been searching for you."

"I have thought of it. But if he would just go back to Virginia and stay in one place long enough, I could get a letter to him."

Weary and pale, Eliza closed her eyes. Sarah laid her finger on Eliza's wrist. Her pulse seemed weak, and Sarah hoped Hayward would not delay coming upstairs. Stepping lightly from the room, she went downstairs, opened the front door, and watched Hayward lift Darcy down from his horse.

"What she faces, Lord, help her little heart to bear," Sarah whispered.

Climbing the steps, Darcy held out her hand to Sarah. Hayward drew her away, his face chiseled hard in the gloom. "How is she?" he asked, looking into her eyes then away. "Very sick? Near death's door as Fiona has led me to believe?"

"She is not at all well, sir. But now that you and Darcy have come home, she will recover."

He went on, then paused at the door after Fiona passed him. He looked back at Sarah and one corner of his mouth lifted. "I am glad you are here, Sarah. You must promise you will never leave me."

"How can I make such a vow?"

"Just speak it, and I will believe it." He held Darcy's hand and proceeded with her into the house.

Inside, Sarah paused in the foyer, watching him go up the stairs. Fiona drew beside her.

"He plans to take her away for a while," she said. "To mend matters, and then send her to his mother in England for a visit. He will not allow me to go with her. He needs me to stay with Darcy."

"You are free to go, Fiona. He cannot stop you."

"I believe he can and he will if I try. Besides, I cannot abandon Darcy. Eliza would not want me to."

"I suppose I am glad for it. That way I will not be left alone here with him. I would run away otherwise."

Hayward called from the top of the staircase, and Fiona hurried up the steps to Eliza's room. Angered by the plans he had made, Sarah strode back to her cabin, her leg aching as the night air finally cooled. She sat down on the top step of her porch with her chin resting on her fist. She could see Eliza's window and the dim candlelight behind it. She wondered what words were being spoken, if Hayward was being kind. Shadows moved behind the curtains, and the candlelight grew weak.

She prayed all would be well after tonight. Was not their love, their marriage, stronger than the wrongs done? Yet she feared Eliza would die with her heart so broken it could not be mended by words of forgiveness or love.

"Foolish girl," she said aloud to herself. "How unwise you were to agree to be something you were not. Look at what a lie has brought."

Tears streamed down her cheeks. She covered her face with her hands, shivered, and wept. She could not stay apart from her friend and so went back to the house. As soon as Hayward left Eliza, Sarah went in and sat in the window seat of Eliza's room and stayed until dawn.

When she awoke, she turned her eyes to the world outside her window. The leaves on the trees were bright green in the morning light. Fiona brought in a tray.

"He was not kind or forgiving to my girl. I am worried what might come of him sending her away."

"Does she know?"

"Not yet. And we will not be the ones to tell her. Let it be upon his shoulders, between husband and wife."

She raised herself up to see Hayward drawing his horse out onto the lane and galloping away. For what reason he was leaving she cared not, but felt relief they all would be free from his anger for a time.

33

$\mathcal{L}$ess than a week later, when the first golden streaks of dawn crept over the mountains to the west and brightened the river, Sarah stepped out of her cabin door and lifted her face to the sun. She had dreamed of Alex during the night, of his handsome smile and his warm eyes. He would never treat her the way Hayward had treated Eliza. She would never deceive him.

Once again, her letters had come back with a note from Mr. Pippins begging her to stop. It was futile, and a waste of paper and good ink, he had written on the back of her most recent missive. Perhaps he was right. Obviously, Alex was not returning to Virginia. It broke her heart to think of it, to bear the thought he might be lost to her forever and she would never see him again. Yet God knew where Alex was, and she could still believe in miracles in the face of grim reality.

She paused to listen to the sounds of the morning. Usually she could hear Fiona banging pots and pans in the kitchen, and Darcy's little voice chattering away through the open door. But there were no sounds, just the chirping of goldfinches in the trees. She made her way down the rickety steps and across the span of grass to the house. She did not hurry, but walked with a slow, uneven gait. For her first chore of the morning, she paused at the well, lowered the bucket, and brought it up again sloshing with water.

Walking through the kitchen door, she found the heavy oak worktable swept clean, the hearth cold, every spoon and bowl in its place. Not even the teakettle simmered over a low fire. She emptied the water into the oak barrel and closed the lid tight. Where could Fiona be? Breakfast would be ever so late.

She set the bucket down by the door, and went out into the hallway. The front door stood wide open. A fan of sunlight crossed the floor and the breeze rippled the curtains over the windows. Out front, Hayward's horse swished its tail against the blue bottleflies. Eliza's mare shook her shaggy mane and whinnied. Both horses were saddled. Hayward, dressed in traveling clothes, his hair neatly tied back in a queue, turned to look at her. She read the expression in his eyes. He was about to do something she would not approve of. He motioned to her with his hand.

"Sarah, come wait outside the door for your mistress."

She obeyed, but paused on the threshold and turned. "Both horses, sir?"

"Yes. You will know soon enough why, if Eliza has not already told you."

"She has told me nothing. It is a fine day for a ride along the river."

One corner of his mouth lifted into a devious grin and he looked back, up to the top of the staircase. Footsteps creaked upon the floorboards above, and Sarah looked up, too. After a moment, Eliza came down the stairs dressed in a plum frock with her cloak draped over her arm. Behind Eliza followed Fiona and Darcy. Darcy's hand clutched her mother's dress, and Fiona held her apron up to her nose.

"It is too warm for her to carry her cloak. Why is she taking it with her?"

"She will need it on her journey to England," said Hayward.

"England? You *are* sending her away. You cannot do that, sir."

He turned a stern stare toward her. "I can do as I please. I am the lord and master of this house and of my wife."

It could not be true. Sarah watched as Eliza bent down and held Darcy close, speaking sweetly in her ear, and then embraced the deeply grieving Fiona. *He has kept all of us from her, worst of all Darcy.*

"Mistress," Sarah said, wiping her eyes.

"Do not be sad, Sarah. My husband's mother is in need of me. I shall be back in a few months. It is my duty to go to her. She has no daughter." Eliza went on to wish Sarah well in finding the man she loved, and then went down the stairs to her horse.

Indeed, Sarah had no right to question Hayward's decision. Perhaps a time apart would bring them together again. But this meant she would be without Eliza's protection from Hayward. She gripped the fabric of her tattered dress, and struggled down to the steps and headed out into the meadow. Tall grass swished against her legs. She shambled through it, her fists clenched, her head down.

On the hilltop, she waited, listened as the horses rode off. Then silence. She went on, down the slope to the level plain and sat by Ilene's grave until the sun went down.

✣

Eliza had been gone a fortnight the afternoon a wagon pulled by two horses rumbled down the river road. Sarah lifted a hand to shade her eyes while in the other hand she held the string of bass she had caught for the evening meal. Trotting alongside the wagon, a brown horse with black stockings shook its mane against the pull of the rider's hands. Hayward had returned.

The wagon turned at the lane leading to the house, the rear loaded down with crates and barrels. Hayward drew up in front of Sarah. "A nice catch of fish, Sarah. I daresay you are a better fisherman than I ever was." He waited for her to speak. "Are you not going to welcome me home?"

"Welcome back, sir," she said dryly. "Did you have a fair journey? Did Mistress Eliza do well setting sail without you?" Her voice hinted of sarcasm as she gripped the string tighter.

"She did very well and was anxious to see my mother. You know what they say about the absence of one person causing the heart of another to grow fonder, don't you?"

She swung away and walked toward the lane. He followed on his horse. Sarah could not be sure of his meaning, whether he hoped he and Eliza would grow closer by the separation, or whether he meant that Sarah's heart had grown attached to him. One thing she knew for certain, her love for Alex would never change. She belonged to him, not Hayward.

"Well?" Hayward said. "Can love grow when people are separated?"

She glanced back at him over her shoulder. "I had not believed it until I met Dr. Hutton. My feelings for him have not only been constant but have grown."

"Ah, a confession at last," Hayward said. "I am surprised. . . . I guess you are wondering what all this is about." His eyes directed her back to the wagon.

"It is none of my business, sir."

"My half brother has brought his family down from New York and has settled in a comfortable house along the river not far from River Run. You and Fiona are to stock the barrels with whatever we can spare from our larder. I will give her a list of household goods to pack in the crates."

"'Tis generous of you, Captain Morgan. I hope, however, that when your wife returns she will not be unhappy you have given her things away."

"She will not care. . . . Tell Fiona I am starved and to prepare an early supper." He turned his horse and trotted down the lane. Darcy sat on the floor of the porch with her dolls, and when she saw Hayward she jumped up and hurried back inside the house.

34

$\mathcal{S}$arah retreated to Israel Creek, hot and sweaty, longing to strip off her clothes and bathe. The creek opened into the Potomac with forests on each side. An enormous sycamore shaded the bank and cooled the ground beneath the soles of her shoes. The Potomac ran shallow here, and she walked on until she reached a pool between two large rocks deep enough to rise above her waist. She pulled off her shoes, then her dress, and stepped into the water in her chemise. Down on her knees she leaned back and soaked her hair.

She sighed and dug out the sand in the bottom of the river and rubbed her skin clean with it. Running her fingers through her hair, she broke tangles and knots free, and gazed up at the sky. Pale with a hint of blue, great cumulus clouds hung above, their peaks starkest white, lined with shades of pink and purple in the waning light.

A chill rushed through her at the sound of footsteps crushing the flora. She hoped it was simply a deer, but when she turned she saw Hayward standing on the bank looking down at her.

"You had not come home and I began to worry."

"It was so hot and I . . ."

"Stand up, Sarah." He held his hand out to her.

"I will not. You must go away."

"Afraid? There is no reason to be. I was going to help you climb the bank. If you did not want me to see you, then you should not be bathing in the Potomac."

She frowned. "I am clothed, sir."

"Yes, but soaked to the skin. A pretty sight—a wet chemise clinging to a woman's body."

Sarah narrowed her eyes, and looking away she sank lower in the water. Weary of the things he so freely said to her, she wished she had the courage to unleash her tongue and put him in his place. "I am not ready to go back."

"Alright, I will leave you be. But I want you home in a quarter of an hour. My boots need to be polished, and Fiona needs help in the kitchen."

After he walked away, Sarah huffed. She gathered her hair and squeezed the water from it as hard as she could, her eyes fixed on the spot where he had stood. As she started up the bank, she heard the whinny of a horse on the opposite shore. There the riverside ascended higher, formed into forested hills with trees so ancient little grew between them.

It had been a while since she had seen travelers near the river. Two men on horseback passed through the forest, both dressed in buckskins. Cautious, she slipped behind a tree and peered out, unable to make out their faces for they were too far off. A dog bounded ahead of the horses, sniffed the ground and ran in circles. He looked across the river directly at her, then howled. A man's voice called to him and the dog jerked away.

One horse appeared to be the same shade and height as Charger, and for a moment she imagined it were Alex in the saddle. Sad loneliness filled her as she watched the riders disappear into the thick woods. How she missed him.

Gathering up her shoes she drew them on, remembering the remedy he had made for her. Then she slipped on her dress and trekked back to the house. The heat of the day and the sun dried her hair quickly, and it felt silky over her shoulders. Even the chemise dried to a soft dampness beneath her cotton dress before she reached the kitchen door.

"Thank goodness you're back." Fiona plopped bread dough into a pan and set it aside.

"I was down at the river."

"Yes, I heard." Fiona began to beat egg whites in a bowl. "*His lord and master* wants a large supper. I'll need your help."

Sarah grabbed an apron and tied it on. "It is too hot to eat, let alone for you to slave over the fire. I'll baste the chicken."

Fiona wiped her forehead dry. "Thank you, Sarah. 'Tis kind of you to think of me."

Sarah, cloth in hand, lifted the cast iron lid and steam rose from the pot. She dipped a spoon into the juice and dribbled it over the chicken. "Ah, it smells good, Fiona. Did he say why he wants so much food?"

"No, he tells me nothing." Fiona wiped her hands along her apron. She snatched a potato out of the basket on the table and scrubbed it with vigor. "I should put hot pepper in his pudding for sending my girl away. I worry over her every minute of the day."

Sarah put her hand on Fiona's arm. "So do I, Fiona. I keep Eliza in my prayers every night."

"I miss her, Sarah. I would walk out that door this minute and sail back to England if I knew she weren't coming back."

"She will return soon. You just have to wait out the time."

Hayward strode through the kitchen door. Sarah noticed he had not changed his clothes. "I need to talk to both of you."

Sarah moved closer to Fiona and waited. Fiona worked faster, potato peels falling in a heap on the table. "I am doing the best I can, sir, with what we have. Nothing is wrong with a plump chicken and a—"

Abruptly Hayward raised his hand. "It has nothing to do with what you are cooking, Fiona. I have come to tell you I am leaving River Run in a few days."

Fiona stopped peeling and stared at him quizzically. "Business, sir?"

Hayward set his hands on the edge of the table, and a strange smile crossed his lips. "In a way it is. I have business with God."

Sarah drew in a quick breath. She had never heard him speak in such a way. Had Hayward come to realize the error of his ways? With all her heart, she hoped he had.

Fiona shook her head. "I do not understand."

"You do not have to, Fiona," Hayward said. "But it is something I must do."

"When will you come back? In a week? A fortnight?"

"I will not be returning—not for a long time."

A potato fell from Fiona's hand and rolled across the table. "Does this mean you are going to England, to my girl?"

"No, I am not going to England, and I am not bringing Eliza home. I have other plans."

Sarah touched Fiona's arm when she moaned in disappointment. And when she saw Fiona blink back tears, she grabbed her hand. "Perhaps Captain Morgan will sort that out while he is away, Fiona. Eliza will be home eventually."

"No, she is staying in England until I decide otherwise. You must get her out of your minds."

Fiona gasped. "What about Darcy? She has missed her mother. You can't keep Eliza in England. And now you are going away. Have you thought how your absence will affect your daughter? Hasn't she been through enough?"

Hayward set his mouth and drew in a breath. At least he tried to control an impulse to lash back. "I am sending Darcy to my half brother, William, and his wife. It is best they raise her for now."

Fiona slapped her hand on the table. "You have separated her from her mother and now this?"

Hayward's eyes blazed that she would dare question him. "Darcy has no brothers or sisters," he said, rushing his words. "Her cousins will be the best companions for her."

Sarah stepped around the table and faced him. "But River Run is her home. Leave her here with us."

"With servants? I cannot let her live in this sad place." He turned to leave. She grasped his sleeve, and he looked back at her, shocked by her action.

"But when Mistress Eliza eventually returns—"

"She is not coming back."

"Heaven above, Captain Morgan. Are you in earnest?" said Fiona.

"I am."

Sarah wanted to shake him, cause his heart to break open to the reality of what he was doing. Instead, she fastened her eyes on his and leaned forward. "When will you ever stop punishing those who have offended you?"

His jaw shifted as he clenched his teeth. "Punish them? I am the one being punished, Sarah. I am going into the wilderness in order to accept my punishment."

"The wilderness? No, sir."

He grabbed her arms and she gasped. "Let it fall hard upon me. Let it break me!"

Confused, she stared into his enflamed face, his desperate eyes. She felt pity slowly creeping into her heart. His soul was tormented. He breathed out and let her go.

As he stepped away, Sarah said, "Are we to remain here, or will you be sending us away too? Will we go with Darcy?"

"I am sending Fiona to England to be with Eliza." He spoke over his shoulder. Fiona let out a little cry and threw her hands over her mouth.

"Do not look so surprised, Fiona," said Hayward. "And do not ask me a string of questions about my decisions either."

Fiona twisted her hands in her apron like a nervous mother. "Oh, but Darcy, sir. Please, let me take her with me."

"Why ask me when you already know the answer?" His eyes shifted to Sarah. "Sarah, come into the sitting room." He walked out the door.

Before Sarah followed him, Fiona held her back. "Be careful, Sarah. I did not miss the way he looked at you. He seems to have forgotten Eliza altogether."

"I hate his stare," Sarah said, watching the door close. Then she gave Fiona a reassuring look. "Do not worry. I will not let anything happen. Even if he were to threaten me with death, I will stand up to him."

35

A steady breeze blew through the windows in the sitting room, and the heat grew intense. Hayward bid Sarah to close the door behind her when she stepped inside. He sat on the settee, his arms resting over his knees, his fingers clasping and unclasping, his expression downcast. She stood a few feet in front of him and waited, her body erect, her head high.

"Come near me, Sarah. You may sit across from me if you wish."

She kept her place. "I am more comfortable standing."

"I am sorry it makes you uneasy to be so close to me." He glanced down at her limbs. "It does not hurt you to stand, does it?"

"I am used to it."

"It would grieve me if I knew you were suffering. So, please. Sit."

Cautious, she moved to a chair and lowered herself into it.

"I have things to discuss—my soul to bare." Appearing nervous, he continued to clasp his hands together. She could not help but look away. Why he should want to expose his heart to her, she refused to consider.

"You have already made your mind known to us. You are sending Darcy away, as you did her mother, and leaving for only the Lord knows where."

"The frontier," he said quickly looking over at her.

"Does this mean I am free to go?"

"It might."

"What do you intend to do with me?"

"To treat you kindly, Sarah. I have forgiven you."

"I am grateful for that, sir. But I have no regrets when it comes to Ilene. I loved her very much."

"Of course, you did. How could you not?"

Swallowing her grief at the mention of Ilene, Sarah caught her lower lip between her teeth. "You do realize that by leaving River Run, and shutting up the house, it could fall into decay. And what will become of the mill and—"

"William has promised to look after my property. He will insure it goes to Darcy upon my death. The condition of the house will not matter. What is important is the land. No one is to live here until then."

"I do not understand why you are doing this. It was your dream to build an estate, was it not?"

"The memories are too difficult to bear. I am going to lose myself in the wilderness—to find God."

"You can find Him anywhere. If you go down to the river at twilight or just before dawn, and sit on the bank—"

Abruptly he stood. "Don't you see? I want you to come with me."

"Into the wilderness?"

"Yes—beyond the valley. Beyond the river and mountains. As far away as I can take us."

Sarah felt her heart contract. She remembered her life with the Indians. "I have lived there before and do not wish to go back for any reason."

It seemed as though he did not hear her. She knew all that mattered to him was the fulfillment of his own desires, not hers. Was he afraid to be alone?

He remained silent. His hand on the window frame, he stared out at the land. Then he lowered his head and spoke softly to her. "I loved Eliza, but what I feel for you is different. I cannot go on without you near me . . ."

Stunned by his confession, Sarah stood and backed away. "I do not want to leave with you."

He turned to look at her. "You have some better place to go?"

"Yes. To Dr. Hutton. I am to be his wife, not his mistress, as you would have me be," she snapped back.

He grabbed her arms and crushed her against him. "You took Eliza's place before. You can do it again."

Sarah shook her head. "No, I cannot. No one can take her place. She is your wife, until death parts you. You are asking me to be your mistress? I cannot. I will not."

"Better that than a bondservant."

"I will be neither."

"I suppose you think your Dr. Hutton will show up any day now—a knight on a white horse to rescue you. Men forget women over time, and he is no different."

"Do not mock him. He is nothing like you."

"Then why hasn't he come for you?"

"I have faith he will find me one day." She laid a trembling fist against her heaving breast. "I feel it here."

"He has forgotten you. More than likely he is married and settled somewhere."

"No matter what you say, you will not cause me to lose hope."

His fingers brushed her hair at the back of her neck. Passion burned in his eyes as his mouth steadied close to hers. "How long has it been since a man held you in his arms, since you were kissed, and felt the heat of love? Do you miss it as much as I do? Do you not crave to be touched—to feel loved and wanted?"

Tears welled in her eyes and she shook her head forcefully against his words. "There is only one man I think of."

"You must forget him and move on with your life."

"Like you have forsaken Eliza?"

"It is not easy for a man to confess how much a woman has injured him," Hayward said. "But confess it I must. Eliza broke my heart to the point I despaired of life. Have some pity on me, Sarah."

She stared back at him, on the brink of letting the tears fall, but not without anger coloring her face. "I have compassion for the pain you are in," she said. "But I cannot be what you are asking me to be. You are Eliza's husband, and I will not betray her or sin knowingly against my God for anything in the world. Nor will I betray my love for Alex Hutton."

Hayward's jaw tightened and the look in his eyes seemed to tell her he realized how wrong he had been. His harsh grip on her eased and he released her. Sarah ran her hands over her tender forearms.

"You could change everything," she said. "Go to England and bring her home. Mend your family and let the past die."

He hung his head and reached for her hand. She drew back. When he finally claimed it, he brought it to his lips and kissed it. "Forgive my anger. Please come with me, Sarah. You will have no worries. No longer will you be a servant."

She jerked her hand from his. "No."

For a moment, he looked at her shaken. Had he expected her to willing obey him? She knew he realized what he asked of her was wrong, for in his eyes she saw guilt and shame emerge. She hoped he would leave for his time in the wilderness, and be humbled, and repent of all the wrong he'd done, for the cold and unforgiving heart he had portrayed.

The tread of horses beat over the hard road above the river, grew out of the distance as they trotted down the lane toward the house. Hayward stepped over to the window and looked out. He grabbed his musket as if he were clenching the throat of an enemy, and stomped out into the hallway.

Sarah threw her arms around her waist and bent forward. Could she tell the riders? Would they show compassion and help her flee River Run?

Distraught, Sarah peeked around the corner and watched Hayward cross the foyer to the front door. Sunshine flooded inside and fanned across the wall. The haze blocked her vision of him, outlining his silhouette. Moving slightly forward, she caught sight of the horsemen, each dressed in dark brown coats and breeches, riding boots, and tricorn hats. One rider lingered behind the other with his head down, while the other raised his hat from his head.

"Good day, sir," the man said in an earnest drawl. "Am I right that this is River Run and you are the owner of the place?"

"You are correct, sir. I am Captain Morgan." Hayward relaxed his musket against his arm "What brings you?"

The man inclined his head. "My name is Laban Thrasher."

Sarah gasped. Mr. Thrasher's brother had found her.

Hands trembling, she drew back inside the sitting room. At the window, she peered out for a closer look. And indeed, from this position she was able to see the face of the other rider when he lifted it to acknowledge Hayward. Instantly her fingers dug into the painted wooden frame. A cold sweat broke out over her body as if a wintry wind had suddenly passed over her. A taut breath trembled over her lips and she stared at him in disbelief.

What her eyes beheld was the face of evil. Her knees gave way, and she propped herself against the deep sill to keep from falling. Her worst nightmare had come to River Run. A man more dastardly than Hayward Morgan, more feared than Black Fox. Sarah locked her eyes on his face and backed away.

Terrible memories sprang up. Her hand flew to her throat. She listened attentively to them speaking. The words were low and unclear, but she knew the danger that ran through them.

The rider who hung back drew off his hat and wiped his sweaty brow. His hair lay in a neat dark ponytail at the nape of his neck, where a stark white neckcloth wound around his throat. His eyes, close-set beneath wispy brows, held an arrogant gaze, the same expression they held when she first laid eyes on him. The deceiving good looks of his face and the proud manner in which he sat upon his horse she could never forget—nor what he had done to her.

"Sawyer!" The whispered name tasted bitter on her tongue.

36

*G*ripping tight the fabric of her gown, Sarah made to hurry away. But when she saw the men dismount, she slipped back inside the room. Footsteps treaded toward her out in the hall. Along with the scraping of boots across the hardwood, the sound of their voices caused her to snatch her hand away from the doorknob—that brogue spoken by Cornish gentry blended with the less-refined inflection of a Maryland planter.

It was too late to flee the house, so she stood back from the door. It opened and Hayward came through first, then the men, Sawyer being the last. His self-important gaze fastened upon her and an instant recognition sprang within them.

Alarmed and speechless, Sarah stood in the heat of the sunshine that flowed through the window. She could feel it burn onto her neck through her hair. Yet she shivered with cold fear and looked away, toward Hayward, for the first time longing for his help.

Sawyer swore under his breath.

"Leave the room at once," Hayward ordered her. "Tell Fiona to hold supper."

With her eyes down, she stepped past Sawyer, careful not to touch him, not even to have the hem of her skirt brush across the toe of his boot. If only she could tell Hayward how ill he had treated her, and exactly who and what he was, perhaps he'd throw him out. She paused and opened her mouth to speak, but when Sawyer laid his hand on her arm, her throat tightened.

"Your name, girl?"

She shook him off, as if sudden and mortal danger had reached out and snatched her.

"Excuse me, sir. I will not permit such liberties with my serving girl," Hayward said. "Remember your place in my house."

Raising his brows, Sawyer made a short bow, and shifted his eyes back at her. She clasped her hands together. "Captain Morgan, I—"

"Go, Sarah."

She hurried through the opening and closed the door, then set her ear against the wall, desperate to know what they were saying.

"I beg your pardon," she heard Sawyer say. "I was taken off guard. It isn't every day a man sees a redheaded beauty like your servant. She is yours, is she not?"

"She is."

"Well, be assured, Captain Morgan, Laban and I are anxious to hear how you came by this woman. I would assume at auction, or by a private sale. Is that how you acquired her?"

"My wife took her on while I was away fighting the British."

"I see."

"Why does she interest you, and why have you come to River Run? I do not recall ever meeting you, or you, Mr. Thrasher." Sarah noted how Hayward emphasized the man's name, as if he were annoyed by his presence.

"No, sir. I have not had the pleasure of coming this far west," Laban Thrasher said. "I reside on a farm along the eastern shore."

"And you, Mr. Sawyer. You have a thick Cornish accent. You are not native to America."

"No I am not, sir. My business in Cornwall got too close for comfort when it came to the King's laws. And so, I immigrated and picked up my trade, where it is safer."

"What is your trade, exactly?"

"I provide a service to farmers and plantation owners. They cannot run their estates without able bodies—able bodies they must keep."

"Ah, so you are a slaver? It is a trade I do not look favorably upon."

"I would not call myself a slaver, sir."

"Then what would you call your occupation?"

"I help find runaways, or in this case lost property. I have been hired by Laban to help him regain what is rightfully his according to the law."

Sarah swallowed the hard lump in her throat.

"What has this to do with me?"

"We were informed you have an indentured servant here by the name of Sarah Carr. We discovered her whereabouts from a Mr. Pippins who runs the trading post near Currioman Bay in Virginia. Miss Carr has been sending letters there in hopes they will reach a certain person who quit the area long ago. By law, she belongs to this gentleman."

Sawyer took a step forward. "Mr. Pippins was at the tavern we visited and thought it a good story to tell. Call your girl back in, sir. I recognized her the moment I laid eyes on her."

A short pause followed and Sarah prayed that Hayward would not give her over. Then he spoke.

"From where do you know her, Mr. Sawyer? Cornwall? Did you have something to do with how she came to America?"

"How I know her is of no importance. You cannot deny it is she, Captain Morgan. She can be noticed by her uneven gait, a flaw that was overlooked with kindness by the men who bought her."

"You will have to convince me she belongs to you, Mr. Thrasher. Can you not speak for yourself, sir?"

"Oh, certainly, Captain Morgan," said Laban Thrasher. "You see my late brother bought her at auction fair and square. I have a copy of the bill of sale here in my pocket."

"May I see it?"

Another tense pause followed. Sarah clasped her hands tight. She had thought the bill of sale destroyed in the fire. But she had not counted on a copy.

"My brother, Jebediah, was killed by Indians, and not long ago I was notified that he had bequeathed his property to me," Laban said. "There was no sign of the girl, and so logically it was concluded she escaped."

"And you have been looking for her?"

"Yes. The property is a sweet plot of land and I have been able to acquire over five hundred acres attached to it. The cabin is a heap of ash. And I am glad for it. It saved me from pulling it down to build a large house. I am a rich man and the plantation that shall emerge out of the ashes is my golden phoenix. It will make me even wealthier."

"And you want Sarah? Why, when you can acquire all the labor you need elsewhere?"

"Then you admit the girl we just now saw is she?"

Sarah bit the inside of her lip against the fear rising higher. She pressed her hands against her tearing eyes.

"I admit that is her name. And will you compensate me, Mr. Thrasher, for the time I have provided for the girl?"

Tears burned her eyes and she shut them. Just moments ago he had said he could not live without her. Would he now give her to this man? Would he punish her for rejecting him?

"We thought you would be reasonable, sir," said Sawyer. "That we could negotiate this situation as honest men should."

"Honest men, certainly," Hayward replied. "But I shall not give her over to you so easily. How can you claim to be honest when you participated in the kidnapping of innocent people, shipped them over here and sold them off like cattle against their will?"

Laban Thrasher huffed. "Well, I had nothing to do with that, Captain Morgan. That is another matter entirely."

Sarah imagined Sawyer was now red in the face with anger. Any moment she expected Hayward to either throw him out on his ear, or that Sawyer would storm out on his own. When she heard footsteps and saw the knob turn, she backed into the shadows.

"Sarah," Hayward called.

She stepped forward, putting on a brave face to hide her fear when she met his eyes.

"Ah, you have been listening haven't you? Then I do not need to explain the gravity of the situation. Come inside."

"That man, the one called Sawyer," she began.

"I know who he is. And what he is." He took her by the elbow and moved her through the door, then shut it behind him. Sarah hung back, hands in fists at her side. Instead of weeping, she gathered all the inner strength she had and looked at the men proudly.

"Sarah, this gentleman claims to be your former owner's brother. He has inherited his property, which by law includes you." She said nothing, only prayed silently that all would turn in her favor.

"She looks fit," said Laban. "But it is true what Mr. Sawyer said. Why does she walk that way? Has she been injured?"

Sarah lifted her chin and locked her eyes on Thrasher. "It is how I was born."

He frowned. "Hmm, I see."

"It does not keep her from doing her work, Captain Morgan?"

"No, you little sot."

"No need to be insulting, sir."

Sawyer stepped closer. "She is prettier than I remember."

Sarah narrowed her eyes. "I will not hear any words of flattery from you. You brought me to this wretched life."

Once again, Sawyer smirked. "I was not cruel to you, Sarah. I sent you away to begin a new life."

"Kidnapped me, you mean. Deceived me!"

"Your brother-in-law was on the brink of tossing you out. You would have starved, and as I recall you were with child. Yours would have suffered in poverty and more than likely died."

She cried out. "What do you know of my baby? God will hold you responsible."

"Quiet, Sarah," Hayward ordered. He moved her behind him and looked down at the two men.

Laban Thrasher held his document up, his hand shaking. "I have shown you proof. Give me my property at once!"

"I absolutely will not! I can make an account of what it has cost me to take care of *your property*. I have clothed, fed, and cared for her these past years. I will not stand for such insolence."

"You have no rights to her, Captain Morgan," said Sawyer.

"I say I do."

"If you do not hand her over immediately, we shall be back with a constable and a warrant. Then you will see."

"Leave my house and get off my land." Hayward picked up his musket and the two men stormed out to their horses.

Sarah waited in the shadows of the hallway trembling. What would she do now? Her mind reeled. She struggled to breathe and her heart pounded. As the men galloped off in a cloud of dust, Hayward turned, locked eyes with Sarah, and then walked back inside. He leaned toward her to speak into her ear, his breath hot against her skin.

"Now . . . you . . . owe me."

He walked past her, leaving her to stand alone, between freedom and him.

37

The cabin had become Sarah's sanctuary, a place of refuge. She retreated to it, sat on the top step of the porch, and thought long and hard about what to do. Her choices were few. Go away with Hayward into the wild frontier. Face Indians, poverty, and hardship. Be his mistress. Or wait for Laban Thrasher and Mr. Sawyer to return with a constable. She pounded her fist on her knee. She could not, would not accept either. There had to be another way.

If she ran away, her servitude would be doubled if she were caught—unless Laban Thrasher took pity on her. But what were the chances of that? She put her face into her hands, felt hot tears gather between her fingers. She prayed a gentle plea, her heart aching in her breast.

She had escaped the Indians and journeyed through a hostile wilderness on her own. Black Fox had hunted her down. This time it could be dogs and slavers if she ran. Dashing the tears from her face, she knew she could face the danger. She had to try.

The birds ceased singing. The house was quiet. Usually Darcy would be outside on her swing or romping in the yard where Sarah could watch her. She could see the tree's limbs stretching past the house out front, and the swing motionless in the summer heat. Long she watched it, until she heard the clopping of hooves.

In the haze, she saw Hayward draw his horse out of the barn doors and into the grass. Darcy ran up to him in her white cotton frock, her rag doll clutched in her hand. Fiona walked slowly behind her. Sarah tried to absorb what she saw, but it seemed surreal.

"He is taking her away, and then leaving her for good."

She hurried down the steps and struggled to run, to reach Darcy before Hayward rode off. "Please, sir. Let me say good-bye to her," she called out.

He turned his horse toward her. Sarah reached up to Darcy and brought her down. On her knees she embraced the child. "I love you, Darcy," she whispered in her ear. "Your mother loves you, too. Never forget her. Never forget me. Be happy."

Darcy stroked her palm over Sarah's cheek. It felt warm, smooth. "Do not cry, Sarah. Papa says I will be happy living with my cousins."

A curl tumbled over Darcy's forehead and Sarah brushed it back. "Certainly you will, darling. It will be like having sisters."

"Come visit me when Papa comes."

"Yes, Darcy."

Hayward dismounted, placed his hands on Darcy's shoulders and drew her away. He lifted her onto Gareth's back, then climbed up behind her. Darcy's white-stockinged legs dangled against the soft brown of the horse's coat Sarah stepped back, and wiped her eyes.

"I will be gone overnight." Hayward's eyes were upon Sarah. "Have your things packed for when I return. I am giving you Eliza's mare."

She lowered her head and turned away. Would he bestow what possessions remained behind of Eliza's to her as well? A bitter taste rose in her mouth, and she set her teeth. She glanced up at him and his eyes shifted to Fiona.

"Fiona, I want all of Darcy's belongings packed in a trunk for you to take to her when you leave. I have ordered a carriage for you, and the driver will know where to go. It will be here in a few days."

"It will do my heart well to see Darcy is settled," Fiona said, her body stiff. "But please, won't you reconsider and allow me to take her to her mother?"

His mouth twisted at her request. "You are to leave the keys to River Run with my brother. You are not to stay, but take the carriage on to Point Lookout. Here's the money for your fare and expenses." He reached inside his pocket and handed her a moneybag.

Sarah stood beside Fiona. Perspiration trickled down the nape of her neck into the back of her dress. The heat seemed as oppressive as Hayward's plans. For a moment, he locked eyes with her, and drew his horse away, toward the lane at the front of the house, then out to the river road.

Sarah heaved a sigh. Tears pooled in her eyes. Dust from the road kicked up behind the horse and soon she saw them no more. Fiona's hand touched Sarah's shoulder. "Come inside out of the heat. We've work to do."

"Will I ever see Darcy again, Fiona?"

Sadness etched the older woman's face. "I do not know. I pray she will grow up happy, and not regret her parents."

"And poor Eliza. It is cruel he denies her of her child."

Fiona drew in a long breath and looked out at the trees along the edge of the land. "Hayward Morgan may never return, and even if he does, he will not be able to keep them apart forever.

Perhaps his stepbrother will send Darcy to England when she is grown, so she can reunite with her mother."

In silence they walked on. Then Sarah halted. "I have to leave, Fiona."

"What do you mean? Captain Morgan expects you to go with him, not that I approve."

"I have been called away. That is all I can tell you."

"Called away? Did you hear from Dr. Hutton?"

"No."

"Then what is it? You have no place to go."

"God will lead me to where I need to be. I shan't be alone or afraid."

"Let me speak to Captain Morgan when he returns. I will tell him you are going with me to England. Why shouldn't he allow it?"

"Because he believes he owns me."

"Oh, dear child. Then we must hide you somehow and see to it you meet the carriage on the road." Fiona pulled Sarah by the sleeve toward the door.

Sarah twisted away. "I cannot go with you. I will be considered a runaway and you would be an accomplice. I will not have you risk prison for me."

Fiona paused, her hand over her heart. "Oh, those men that were here. I had forgotten them."

"You need not know any of the details." Sarah set her finger against Fiona's lips when she opened her mouth to reply. "Say no more."

Fiona stood motionless, her eyes filling. Sarah knew how hurt she felt to be separated from another person in her life. Ilene was taken from them so young. Then, Eliza and Darcy were carried off. Now Sarah was going away, too.

"Remember to protect yourself, Fiona. Tell Captain Morgan I slipped away without you seeing. Do not let anything prevent you from leaving America and going to Eliza."

"You are right in what you say." Fiona wrung her hands. "But are you sure this is the right thing for you to do?"

"I am. You forget, I escaped Indians, trekked through the wilderness on my own, and survived."

"But where will you go, Sarah?"

"Where He leads me." She threw her arms around Fiona's shoulders and embraced her. "I will never forget you."

"Then, if this is how it must be, I will get to the kitchen and fix you a bag to take." A sad smile lifted Fiona's mouth. "I will not have one of my girls fainting on the path she is to follow."

$\mathcal{L}$❧

Sarah stood in a fan of sunlight that poured through the cabin window. She ran her eyes over the room one last time and said farewell to the memories. Most dear were the ones of Ilene. She saw her at play on the floor, sitting in the chair by the fire, drinking from the tin cup that now sat on the mantelpiece. She felt her huddled in her arms as she told her stories and rocked her to sleep. She heard the sighing of the tiny bundle curled up in the bed next to her, her little hands holding her doll, her hair over the pillow.

The small quilt she had stitched for Ilene's cradle still lay at the foot of the bed. She walked over to it and ran her fingertip across one of the red squares. "I shall love you always, Ilene," she whispered. "I will never forget."

Before turning away, Sarah pinned the tiny quilt to her skirt, wanting a reminder of the adored child to take with her. Past the threshold, she pulled the door closed and headed for the forests above the river.

38

A mile from River Run, beyond the stone mill at Israel Creek, the path Sarah followed grew narrow. Ancient sycamores dwarfed white ash and maple. Sunlight twinkled between the branches of the trees. Birdsong echoed through the woodland.

Her fears lifted as the beauty that surrounded her settled into her soul. She leaned against a fallen oak, the bole taller than she, draped with bright green lichen. Easing down to the ground she listened to the sigh of the breeze, the rustle of leaves, and the murmur of the river flowing over the rock terraces below.

Slowly she drifted off to sleep, and woke from the chirps of chickadees above her head. For a moment she watched the tiny birds dart from branch to branch, their black eyes glancing down at her and their heads turned as if they wondered what sort of creature she might be. They did not seem to fear her, and she reached inside the bag Fiona had given her, took out a bit of bread, and scattered it on the ground. The curious onlookers dove to the forest floor and flew back into the trees with morsels in their beaks.

Standing, Sarah dusted off her dress and trudged on, but not without noticing the sun had sunk lower in the sky. It would be dusk soon. She remembered how it felt to spend the night in the woods, where fear would jar her awake at the slightest sound or movement.

When she escaped the Indian village, she would lie in beds of leaves under wild vine and the shelves of great rocks—alone and afraid. Even now, she could hear the owls call to one another, and feel the eyes of some woodland creature watching her.

She moved on until, through the trees, she spotted an inn situated on the road below in the waning light. It may have been the one Hayward had retreated to with Darcy, but she could not tell. Too weary to go any farther, Sarah hobbled down the slope and reached the scullery door. She knocked and a woman dressed in a dingy cap and apron opened the door just enough to peak outside. Her cautious eyes latched onto Sarah.

"What is it you want?"

"Could I rest here? It is going to be dark soon, and—"

"Go around the front to my husband and pay."

"I have no money."

"We are not a charity." She started to shut the door. Sarah stretched a hand out to her.

"I will work for it."

The woman pressed her lips together and eyed her. "Hmm. I suppose by the state of you, you know how to work." She opened the door wider. "Let me see your hands."

Sarah held them out and the woman turned them over. "Well, they certainly are not the hands of a lady, that's for sure."

"I can clean and cook. Do most anything."

"Surely you can. I see the calluses. I should probably ask where you are coming from, or rather is it running from? You do not have to say if you don't want to, as long as it will cause no trouble to us."

How could she assure it would not? "I am very tired. I have walked a long way. I promise I will not be any trouble."

"Well, come inside." The woman stepped back. Sarah entered a large kitchen. The hearth covered an entire wall. "I could use another pair of hands for a day or two."

"I only wish to stay long enough to get my strength back. I will not burden you."

"No burden to Christian folk. Call me Mrs. Sadler." She went to a door that swung out into a large meeting room. "George, my dear. This girl is traveling alone and is in need of shelter for the night. I am putting her to work for it."

A foyer led to the desk where Mr. Sadler kept an enormous ledger for guests to sign. On the corner sat a silver bell, a brass inkwell, and white quill. Coming around to take a closer look, George Sadler adjusted his spectacles and paused to glance Sarah over.

"Wash your face and hands, girl. Cleanliness is next to godliness."

She curtsied. "Yes, Mr. Sadler."

"What's your name again?"

"Sarah, sir."

"No last name?" He scratched his chin. "Well, you must have your reasons for not giving it. I do not care who you are or where you are going. Don't want lots of talk. Just work. Understand?"

Sarah nodded. Mrs. Sadler turned her back into the kitchen. She gave Sarah a bowl of stew and a hunk of brown bread. In no time, she felt her strength return. The minute she finished, Mrs. Sadler handed her a bucket and brush.

"The floor needs doing, Sarah. Think you can finish by the time we all will be abed?"

"I can, Mrs. Sadler." She emptied water from a pitcher into the bucket. The lye soap within it foamed. If she could have stretched out on the floor, she would have fallen right to sleep, so weary was she from her journey. But she rolled up her sleeves and got down on her hands and knees. The water felt cold, but she did not mind for the heat of the day had lingered into the night.

As she pushed the bristles over the flagstones, she heard the patter of feet. She looked up to see three children grouped together. She knew they were curious about her and so she sat back on her haunches and smiled.

"Hello," she said.

"Mama says you are a gypsy." The girl looked to be no more than six years, her hair yellow as the bowl of golden apples on the table. Her staring eyes were bright blue.

"I am not a gypsy," Sarah assured the children. "My name is Sarah."

"Sarah was a princess in the Bible," said the girl's older brother.

"Indeed she was. But, I am no princess either."

"What are you then?" asked the girl standing in the middle.

"I am just a girl. Just Sarah," she answered.

Mrs. Sadler burst through the door. "Out with you. You have had your supper, now off to bed." One by one they headed up a small flight of stairs to the upper floor and the family quarters.

Sarah shoved the brush across the floor. "They are your children, Mrs. Sadler?"

"All three, yes." She snatched up an apple and sliced it in two. "Each more precious to me than gold. Janet is the baby and quite spoiled by her pa. Our son is a good lad, and our Nan is growing up fast. I suppose you noticed how different she looks to her brother and sister, her hair being so dark and her skin tanned right down to her bare feet. She takes after my dear mother."

"They are fine children. Such a blessing they must be."

"Indeed they are. Now, I am fixing a tray for a gentleman that is seated out front. You are to take it out to him. You can finish the floor later. This is more important."

With a little effort Sarah stood, then untied her damp apron and set it across the back of a chair. Mrs. Sadler gathered dishes onto the tray, then spooned a helping of boiled fish onto a plate. "Are you sure you can manage a tray? You do not walk so well."

"I have learned to compensate for my flaw, Mrs. Sadler. No need to worry. I shall not spill a thing."

"I would not want an accident in my dining room." Mrs. Sadler moved the tray across the table to Sarah. "Now, be nice to the man. He is a widower and comes here every night to get away from the memories. Served under General Braddock in the French and Indian War, then under George Washington. He has a few scars to prove it."

"I shall be kind." To help Mrs. Sadler's task to go faster, Sarah set a fork and knife on the tray.

"Yes, be kind, but also attentive. Mr. Blye is a sad man who misses his wife." Mrs. Sadler sliced the apple pieces again and placed them on the plate of fish. "He does love apples."

"Did you know her?"

"Who, Sarah?"

"Mr. Blye's wife."

"I did. She was a sweet soul. Died last winter of consumption." She waved Sarah away. "Go on. We do not want his food to grow cold."

Sarah heaved the tray to her hip and left the kitchen. She knew Mrs. Sadler kept an eye on her from the doorway.

"Remember not to spill anything," she called in a hushed voice.

The dining room extended across the entire front of the inn. Along the wall were oak tables and benches with a few Windsor chairs. Although no fire burned in the fireplace, the scent of charred ash and cedar lingered in the air.

An older man sat at a table with his hands around a mug of ale, his head hatless and bowed low. He did not look up when Sarah approached him.

"Your supper, sir." She spoke softly, and when he finally glanced up to see her, she saw the grief in his eyes. "Smells good, does it not? Mrs. Sadler prepared it especially for you."

"Venison stew? It is what I always have."

"Not today, sir. Mrs. Sadler has provided fish. And fresh bread, too."

He removed his eyes from her, picked up the fork and dug in. Sarah turned, but he stopped her by touching her elbow. "I have never seen you before."

"I am new here. But not for long."

"Is that so? Why?"

"I am on my way to the man I am to wed." *If I can find him.*

Mr. Blye's eyes lit up. "Ah. That is good indeed. But why did he not come for you himself? 'Tis ungallant for a man to make his bride travel alone. Are you alone?"

She gave him a slight smile. "Shall I bring you another mug of ale, sir?"

He chewed his food and swallowed. "I have plenty, miss. But if Mrs. Sadler has any pie, I would like some. Apple suits me best." He popped an apple slice into his mouth and bit down.

Mrs. Sadler would be put out that she could not persuade him to take more fish. She turned once again and went toward the kitchen door. But at the sound of horses drawing up outside, Mr. Sadler called her over.

"We've more guests." With a wide grin, he craned his neck to see out the large bay window. "You must be good luck, Sarah. Go tell my wife."

39

*B*efore Sarah could carry out Mr. Sadler's order, the inn door swung open. The hot breeze touched her face. The lantern in the post outside flickered as three men stepped inside.

"Good evening, gentlemen," Mr. Sadler said, anxiously making his way around the counter. "You wish rooms or refreshment? Oh, beg your pardon. I did not realize it were you, Constable. How are you, sir?"

"Well as can be, Sadler. It has been some time since we last saw each other. Refreshment if you please."

Sarah felt a chill race up her spine. She turned to retreat to the kitchen and out the back door before they could see her. But before she could take five steps, a hand grabbed her arm and swung her around. Her eyes met Sawyer's. Cold and hard, they bore into her. Surprised, he curved his mouth into a cruel grin.

"What were the chances we'd find you here?" he laughed.

With a moan of fear, Sarah tore at his fingers and twisted away, but she was helpless against his strength and he jerked her forward. Her hair fell over her eyes, and when she looked up she came face to face with a man a head taller than the others, broad-shouldered and heavily armed with two flint-lock pistols in his belt.

"What have you here, Sawyer?" the constable said.

"Sarah Carr," Sawyer snarled.

The kitchen door banged against the wall behind her. "Let that girl go, you ruffians."

Quickly, Sarah looked over her shoulder to see Mrs. Sadler, a pot raised above her head.

"I will strike you down if you do not."

The constable stepped up to her. "You would not strike an officer of the law, would you, Mrs. Sadler?"

Her angry face went blank. "Oh, dear. I am sorry, sir."

"Not to worry. Lower the pot, if you please."

She obeyed him immediately. The constable turned to the third man. "Well, Laban. The girl has saved us the trouble of going to River Run and dealing with Captain Morgan." Then his gray eyes narrowed at Sarah. "So, you are now a runaway?"

Mrs. Sadler gasped. "A runaway?"

Mr. Sadler slapped his hand on the counter. "I knew it. We had nothing to do with it, Constable. She came here of her own accord."

"I believe you." The constable then stood aside. Behind him stood Laban Thrasher. "You have found your property, Laban. What do you wish to do with her now? Put her in irons so she will not escape?"

Laban Thrasher turned his hat in his hands. "Well, I suppose that is the thing to do. But not too tight, sir, for I would not want her injured."

All eyes were upon Sarah, even the old widower's. She clasped her hands together in a plea. "Please, sir, do what any good Christian man would do and let me go. I am to be married and I was on my way to him." She hoped he would have sympathy for her, but by his unmoved stare she knew different.

Laban Thrasher huffed. "Married? I doubt your story, girl."

"It is true. His name is Dr. Alex Hutton. He is a physician."

The men laughed.

"I swear it is true. The war took him away, and when your brother bought me, he did not know where I had been taken. I wrote to him—"

Thrasher waved his hand. "Yes, I know. Mr. Pippins told us all about it."

Sawyer drew up behind her, so close she could smell and feel his hot breath laced with rum on her neck. Dread rippled down her spine and she felt faint.

"It is over, Sarah. Give the constable your wrists."

With no one to defend her, she resigned her hands, tears pooling in her eyes. Her heart beat in her breast like a caged bird's. She closed her eyes and prayed. If this was God's will, she had to let go. Faith seemed to be all she had left. But even it wavered. The anchor had been lifted from the bedrock, slipped, and she had to find a way to hold it fast before all she believed, all she hoped, drifted away.

Thrasher looked her over once she was secured. "Your clothes are in tatters. A reflection of your poor life, I would say. Wouldn't you like a new dress?"

Ashamed, she lowered her head and did not reply. Her hair fell over her face, a veil to keep him from seeing the tears in her eyes. She cared nothing for a new dress, or anything from this man. She wanted to be free, to go on, to find Alex and be his wife. So much time had passed, and now the hope of finding him, being his, seemed a futile dream.

"I will not extend your time for running away," Thrasher said. "I do not blame you, with all you went through. But it is a good thing you got away from Captain Morgan. He would have made things very difficult, if he had not already. We learned he sent his wife to England. You are such a pretty girl, and I hope he did not take advantage of you. He didn't, did he?"

Sarah blinked, glanced up at Thrasher from behind her locks. "No. *Your property,* sir, is unscathed."

"Have you ever been wedded?"

She paused, took in a breath, and said, "I am widowed. Sawyer did not tell you?" and she jerked her head back at Sawyer.

"I do not recall him mentioning it." Mr. Thrasher shook his head. "Well, a nice dress will soothe your woes, surely, and a new pair of shoes. I will pay top price for them."

"Is she worth that much to you, Mr. Thrasher?" Sawyer stepped in front of Sarah. "Guess you mean to make her more than a servant."

Mr. Thrasher smiled. "I assure you, a servant is all she shall be. But she is a woman and deserves a bath and a nice frock. No property of mine shall be seen in rags."

"Seen? There is only one reason why you would waste your money."

"Indeed that is true. Make a small investment and you may gain a large profit. You should know all about that." Thrasher ran his beefy fingers through Sarah's hair. Sarah shivered and jerked away from his foul touch.

"Why a female like this will bring me enough cash to buy two men to work on my plantation. I will need field laborers, not house wenches. And a field laborer she is not."

"Perhaps, but do not overlook her flaw." Sawyer ran his eyes down her body. When he looked back at Thrasher, Sarah thought she saw jealousy rise in his gaze. "You may not get as much for her as you are hoping."

"Speak of me as a child of God, not an animal you can buy and sell," she cried, her fists clenched. "Constable, you must see how wrong this is. Let me go."

"I am only an instrument of the law. Mr. Sadler, have you rooms?" the constable asked.

Mr. Sadler swallowed and looked uneasy. "I do."

"And, we will need a place to secure this girl. If not a room, then a closet will do."

Mrs. Sadler stepped forward. "See here. I'll not have any human being in my establishment, indentured or not, treated like that. Locked in a closet indeed. You should be ashamed of yourselves, gentlemen."

The constable leaned in toward her. "Have you a spare room for this girl? Preferably without a window so she may not climb through it."

Mrs. Sadler shrugged. "No, sir."

"Then show me the way, madam."

With a frown, Mrs. Sadler turned on her heels and went through to the kitchen. She opened the pantry door. Spacious for its kind, she went in and moved crates to the back wall, then looked at Sarah with sad eyes.

"I will fetch a blanket and pillow," and she stepped away.

Sarah sat on one of the crates, her face in her hands. There was no point in speaking. Mrs. Sadler returned with a soft woolen blanket and a down pillow covered in a white linen case. "I am truly sorry, Sarah. Is there anything I can do? Anyone I can send word to?"

Sarah looked up at her, clutching the blanket. "There is no one."

Mrs. Sadler crouched in front of her and picked up Sarah's hands. "I shall pray for you this night. As they say, there is a silver lining to every storm cloud. I hope you find yours."

The door closed and with dread Sarah listened to the key turn in the lock. A narrow window was located at the top of the wall, but it was too narrow for her to climb through, too high for her to reach. Moonlight shined through it and bathed the walls around her. She drew the blanket close and lay down on the floor with the pillow beneath her head. Very still she lay, listening, hoping she would hear within her one word of comfort. Then, *be still*, sprang into her heart.

She shut her eyes and let the tears slip from them. She heard the men speaking, a muffled laugh outside the door. She sat up, crawled forward, and set her ear against it.

"Perhaps you would like to buy her for yourself, Mr. Sawyer. We could make that transaction right now," she heard Laban Thrasher say, his tone firm.

"I have no time for a female servant in my line of work," Sawyer grunted.

"You should have a woman to cook and mend for you. I have Dina. She's a Creole and does everything for me. I really do not need another woman, just laborers."

She heard Sawyer slap his hand on the table. "Why must you repeat yourself, sir? I understand you do not want to keep her. I understand you are in need of laborers."

"You do not understand the economy of the thing."

"So you said before."

"Go to bed, the pair of you. I'll keep watch," the constable spoke up. "Argue in the morning."

A moment later, when all went silent, she heard the constable snoring. Sarah buried her face in her arms and cried herself to sleep, but not before Alex's name settled on her lips and she whispered prayer after prayer.

In the morning, the smells of breakfast made her stomach wrench. The door creaked open and Mrs. Sadler handed her a bowl of porridge and a tin cup of coffee.

"I owe you so much, Mrs. Sadler. How can I pay?"

"Do not worry about that. You earned it. I have the cleanest floor this side of the Potomac thanks to you."

Sarah shook her head. "I never finished it."

"You may think that. One day when you are free, come see me again."

Sawyer stood behind the constable as the man stretched his arms. "Time to go, Sarah. Let us not keep Mr. Thrasher waiting."

He took her by the arm and led her out into the yard. Gray clouds massed along the horizon and promised storms by late afternoon. The heat pressed upon her, causing her to sweat beneath her clothes. Her hands trembled, and she could not look Mrs. Sadler in the eyes when she walked past her and the children. Mr. Sadler lingered on the porch.

"I wish you well, Sarah," Mrs. Sadler called out. "You have been treated very ill. God will have His justice one day. You can depend on that."

Coarse hands lifted her onto a horse. And so, crushed by shame and defeat, Sarah said good-bye to what she believed were misguided hopes.

Part 5

Hold up my goings in thy paths, that my footsteps slip not.

Psalm 17:5

40

A few miles north of River Run, a shallow stretch of the Potomac rippled over stones and driftwood. Flanked by oaks and elms, it lay in shadow, except for the few places where the trees did not reach overhead to darken the water.

Anxious to cross, Alex nudged Charger down to the water's edge. Stepping high, the horse placed his hooves into the river, snorted, and splashed his way to the other side. Cread followed, with Scout sitting on his lap.

The warm day turned leaf and bloom, settled the dust from the road on the flora as they traveled southeast. Drawing in a breath, Alex looked up at the sparks of sunlight shining through the trees. He smelled the rot of last autumn's leaves and heard the cry of a jay in the recesses of the woods.

He turned in the saddle. "The old men spoke of following this well-worn hunting path," he said to Cread. "Would you agree?"

"That I would," said Cread. Scout leaped down and bounded alongside the path. "But I got this nagging feeling if we find nothing within the next five miles, we've reached a dead end."

"Do not give up so easily."

"I will stay positive for as long as it seems right."

"It seems right to me now."

"But those braves that went after her never returned. You know what that means."

"I do, but there must be signs. I will not give up—not until I know for certain."

On they rode until Scout stood stock-still, pricked his ears, and whined. "What ya smell, Scout?" Cread said. "Go on, show us, boy."

At first, Scout ran in circles, sniffing the ground. Then he took off like a shot into the woods. He leaped over fallen trees, scooted around boulders and bracken, pushed his nose along the ground. Then he dug through the leaves with his paws.

Alex dismounted and crouched next to him. From his leather sheath he drew out his hunting knife and moved aside debris. He stopped, stared, chilled at what he had uncovered. With the tip of his blade, he lifted a patch of deer hide.

He looked up at Cread. "A loincloth. Looks like we've stumbled onto something gruesome."

Cread swung off his horse. But before he made it over to Alex, he stubbed his toe. "Dang! What is this?"

Bending over, he lifted from the ground a tomahawk, the wooden handle rough and pitted from lying on the ground for so long. "Well, look at that." Cread took it in hand. "A tomahawk." He brushed it off and studied it. "See these marks? Says it belonged to a chief."

"I wonder if he could be the one who went after Sarah."

"Hard to tell, but it's not impossible. Someone caught up to him and stopped him."

"And—may have rescued her."

"Or she escaped him beforehand."

Alex examined the ground around him with close attention. He prodded something with his boot. "And here—human bone. Not much else. Animals have scattered the rest."

Cread scratched his head beneath his coonskin cap. "Well, you would know bein' a doctor and all."

"You cannot tell the difference? Come and look."

Cread strolled over and, placing his hands on his knees, looked down. "Yep. It ain't a bear bone or even a deer's."

"By its size, I would say it were male."

"Hmm, and Indian."

"Yes—the loincloth would say as much."

"How long you think it's been here?"

"Several years. I am sure we would find more if we looked hard enough. But let us leave well enough alone."

"I agree." With a groan, Cread straightened up. "I don't like disturbing the dead."

"Nor do I." Alex placed his hands on his hips and looked around. "There are plenty of reasons for what could have happened here. We will press on."

He strapped the tomahawk onto his saddle and raised his eyes to the cloudless sky, then swung onto Charger's back. He took out a bit of jerky from his bag and rewarded Scout. They rode on, not more than a mile, to where the river widened. The hunting path curved and met the river road.

Off in the distance, an hour before dusk, a large house came into view. Forests fenced in the green meadow it stood upon. In the rear, beneath a shady bower, stood a cabin. There were no people, no cattle or horses in the field. A swing hung motionless from a tree, and all the shutters on the house were closed. Quiet prevailed as Alex's boots stepped up to the door. He knocked several times. No one answered. Then he tried the handle.

"Locked," he said, coming back down the steps. "No one is at home."

"Nobody closes their shutters in this heat."

"Unless they are away or afraid."

"I heard of this place. They call it River Run, the farthest estate of its kind this side of the Potomac before you reach Fort Frederick." Cread leaned low in the saddle. "There's been a horse here, and a coach. Looks like the people abandoned the place."

"Perhaps not all. I am going around the back to that cabin."

Alex strode off. Cread followed him on horseback. Scout raced ahead. Again no one greeted them, and this time they found an unlocked door. Alex went inside. A faded quilt covered the bed. A small pillow lay against the crude headboard. Upon the table that stood beneath the window, a glass jar filled with dried wildflowers sparkled in the sunlight. A candle stub had melted over a brass socket.

On the table were two books, neither of which he looked at. The paper beside them drew his attention and he picked it up to read it.

Do not search for me—signed, *Sarah Carr*. His heart pounded. His breath heaved. At last he had found her. "Sarah."

He searched the cabin for more signs. There were no clothes, no brush or comb left behind. She had lived here and was gone. To whom had she written that message and how long ago, he could not tell. Outside, Cread sat on his horse, hands over the pommel of his saddle. Alex stepped out into the sunshine, folded the paper and tucked it away.

"What did you find in there?" Cread asked.

"An empty cabin, except for a message with her name inscribed on it. She was here, but has left. God alone knows where to." He gathered Charger's reins. "I am thinking she walked away from this place to escape something. Downriver there are churches and villages. Someone must have seen her."

Cread wiped the sweat from his forehead. "Well, it will be night soon. I'm dog-tired and hungry."

Alex agreed with a nod. "I am as well. We will spend the night here and leave in the morning."

Venison jerky hardly seemed enough to fill the belly. He found food in the icehouse, and after a more substantial meal, he stretched out to sleep. Cread took the floor. Scout curled up beside him.

Alex's mind twisted and turned. Restlessly running his hands along the side slats of the small bed, he suddenly felt a stack of papers tucked along the mattress—the returned letters that Sarah had sent to him. By candlelight he read the letters, savoring her words as he searched for any clue that might lead him to her. Finally, the wick sputtered and the flame died. Moonlight streamed through the cabin windows. Hoot owls called to their mates, and a fox barked at the night sky.

Tired, he ran his hands over his eyes and gathered her quilt over him. He could smell her scent—the smell of a breeze after a spring shower. He realized she had not been gone long. Tonight she would be alone, perhaps sleeping beneath the stars, hungry and afraid. As his thoughts turned, he wondered why she had been set on such a path. Somewhere soon that path had to come to an end, and he prayed to God he would be there for her.

On the floor in front of the fireplace, Cread snored. His dog rolled over on his back, legs in the air, and sighed. Alex shut his eyes and drifted off to sleep, sensing that Sarah was closer to him than ever.

41

*L*ed into the tobacco barn after a two-day journey, Sarah ached to the bone. Her stomach heaved from the repulsive, tasteless gruel given to her earlier. She wanted to sleep, to lay her head on a soft pillow. She wanted peaceful silence instead of wolves' howls, and to feel Alex's warm touch as opposed to rough hands.

Tonight she was the only woman to be auctioned. Laban Thrasher kept his word and bought her a homespun dress and a linen chemise from the auctioneer's wife. Sarah looked down at the shoes. Made of kid leather, they were soft. But she despised them.

She could have refused all this, but out of fear of punishment, she complied. Not once had she felt a riding crop across her back, and she did not wish to invite it now by being rebellious. Roving eyes fastened on her, made her tremble. Who among these men would bid for her—possibly be the end of her? Would it be the obese man in dark blue, whose buttonholes on his waistcoat separated over a barrel-shaped belly? Or perhaps it would be the taller one in the buckskin leggings and brown hunting jacket.

The frightened stares of poor Africans ripped from their homeland and outcast whites snatched from England's shores stabbed her heart. Shackled in their bare feet, they shuffled up to the platform.

Sarah turned her eyes away—desirous for tears. All men were created equal, were they not? Then why were some not treated as such? If only men would follow the Lord's commandment to love one another, the world would be a better place. A frown creased her brow, for she knew how it felt to be taken against one's will, sold like livestock, live at the beck and call of a master or mistress. But she had also come to know the friendship and compassion of others, like Eliza and Fiona. Could she find such persons among this motley crowd of planters and plantation owners?

"They frighten you, Sarah?" Sawyer stood beside her. She did not answer. "They look hungry don't they?" He leaned closer.

She clenched her teeth. "Do not speak to me."

He leaned into her ear. "You may speak to me in that haughty manner now. But after tonight, your pride will be humbled."

She jerked away and shot him a startled glance. "What do you mean?"

"You will see." With a smug smile, he stepped away and joined the others at the foot of the platform. He crossed his arms over his chest, set his legs wide, and stared back at her.

"The best of the lot, gentlemen," the auctioneer announced. "Which of you need stronger laborers? Who will start the bidding?"

Sarah watched Laban Thrasher shoulder his way through the crowd. She knew by the gleam in his eyes that he was anxious to gain money by her sale. "Auction the girl first," he called out.

The auctioneer looked down at him with his brows pinched. "Why, Mr. Thrasher? It makes no difference."

"With the money I get for her, I can bid on those big fellows. I am in need of hardy men who can work my fields." Proud of himself, he threw back his shoulders. "I have acquired a large tract of land in Virginia that will be one of the most prosperous plantations that side of the Potomac."

"Have you now? Bid for them and pay when we are finished with the auction."

He held out his empty, greedy hands. "How am I to know how much to bid if I do not know how much money I have made?"

"Do any of you gentlemen object?" the auctioneer asked, craning his neck and looking the crowd over.

"I agree with Laban," said the man whose waistcoat stretched across his belly. "It will save me time, for I am in need of a healthy woman."

"I think we all are, Mr. Krude," said the leaner man. His comment caused a round of laughter. "But my wife wouldn't like her. She'd be jealous. Bring her forward and let's see what happens."

"Very well." Giving in, the auctioneer made a motion to move the others off the platform. The manacles on their ankles and wrists rattled, deepening Sarah's sorrow. How could men be so cruel to other men? How could they treat a woman in the same manner used when they bought a horse or cow, and not pity her misfortune?

With a sweep of his hand, the auctioneer then bid her to come up the steps. She stared up at him and stood. Then lifting her dress just above the soles of her feet, she made her way slowly up the steps.

42

*I*n the heat of the night, and in the glare of the lanterns, Sarah stood beside the auctioneer. She fixed her eyes on the doors at the far end of the barn. They were slightly open, and she could see the sway of the torchlight outside in the gloom. Someone had to come through them and redeem her— someone had to rescue her, else she would die on her feet.

A hand raised her chin. "Well, gentlemen. Here is the girl Mr. Thrasher is so quick to be rid of. Surprising, isn't it?"

Forcing back tears, Sarah let a breath pass between her lips. The humiliation was too great to bear all over again. Her eyes cleared and she turned her face away from the hand that held it in an attempt to rally some pride. They could own her body, but they could not own her soul, she told herself. It belonged to God, and she could not be snatched out of His hand as long as she cleaved to Him.

"Indeed it is astonishing." Krude's eyes bulged in a steady stare. "She is even prettier up close. Irish or Scot?"

"Neither. She is English. Dare I say she knows how to keep a man warm on winter nights?"

Krude giggled, then plucked a handkerchief from his waist-coat and dabbed his sweaty neck with it. Disgusted, Sarah looked away. But where could her eyes go to avoid the salacious stares of the others? She shut her eyes tight.

God help me or let me die. I can take little more.

As if her life had come full circle, the memories of those days when she had been taken by deception and forced to stand on this very spot, flooded her. It all began with Jamie's foolish choice. Then the heartless plans of Lem Locke and Mary's lack of courage to stand up to him. And she blamed herself most of all for being so gullible and trusting. But she could not erase the past, or the mistakes she had made. Still, one face lingered, one voice spoke of loving her, one touch comforted her. She had believed his heart true, and even if she never saw him again, the memory of his unconditional love gave her strength.

Alex. Alex.

She kept her eyes closed, pictured him riding into the yard, carrying her bucket into the kitchen, placing a gentle kiss upon her lips, and declaring his love for her. Her dream of seeing him again, of him redeeming her from a life of misery, shattered.

She opened her eyes and looked down, caught the lustful gleam in Sawyer's eyes. She knew then what he was about to do—the man who led her away with promises too good to be true, tempting her with a better life for her and her child.

As if a knife twisted in her breast, the painful remembrance of her stillborn babe and of the one she called daughter pushed her to tears again. She pressed her bound fists to her eyes but could not hold the tears back. Silently they slipped down her cheeks. Her knees buckled under the strain. The voices of the bidders ran together. As she began to fall, the auctioneer's aide grabbed her arm and held her up.

"What's wrong with her?" a man shouted.

"'Tis the heat that makes her faint," said another.

"Or hunger," Krude said. "Maybe Mr. Thrasher did not take good care of the girl like he should have."

"I have not neglected her, sirs," cried Laban Thrasher. "Auctioneer, give her water. The heat weakens her."

A ladle touched her lips and she drank a bit. Then she took in a deep breath and faced the men once more.

"How many owners have owned this girl?" one man inquired.

The auctioneer shifted on his feet. "Makes no difference, but three."

"Used goods. And I bet her back saw the lash often enough."

The auctioneer glared at the man. "She is unmarred."

"Well, I want proof before I bid," said Krude.

The auctioneer shrugged. "If you must."

He nodded to his aide, who placed his hands on Sarah's shoulders and turned her around to face the crowd. She trembled, knowing what would come next. They would expose her flesh for all to see. The aide drew out a small knife and cut her stays. He placed the knife in its sheaf and then pulled open her dress to reveal her back, leaving her shoulders bare.

Disgraced and humiliated, Sarah hung her head.

"You see, gentlemen," said the auctioneer. "Smooth as a white silk stocking. Not a mark on her. Skin as fair as a gentlewoman's."

Thrasher moaned. "Ah, I paid good money for that dress. You will add it into the price, sir."

"Do you want her sold or not?"

"I do indeed."

"Then please, no more comments from you," the auctioneer said. "Now who will start the bidding?"

"One more thing," said Mr. Krude.

"What now?"

"She has a strange way of walking. Let us see her limbs. She could have a club foot or bowlegs." All over again, Sarah felt the heat of blood rush across her face. She wanted to run and hide herself from their eyes.

"She has neither. True, her gait sets her apart from the weaker females that toil in your fields. But she will make a good house servant, or even a wife. Look closely."

The aide turned her around. She kept her eyes down. A staff touched the hem of her dress and lifted it above her calves to reveal her legs. The flush deepened and a cold chill swept over her. For a moment, she looked out at the men, saw lust spring into their eyes, watched them swallow with desire. She knew what any one of them would do to her if they owned her.

"Beautiful. Compare them to the tanned limbs of the girls working in the tobacco fields. Which would you prefer? Skin tough as leather, or smooth as silk and the color of cream?"

"Well, I have seen enough. She's healthy and enchanting." Krude smiled, his eyes flickered and his lips puckered. "I bid ten and five."

"An insulting offer," said the auctioneer.

"Twenty then," Krude said with a wiggle of his stout fingers.

"I doubt that will satisfy. Higher, good sirs."

"Thirty," called out another man.

The auctioneer looked annoyed. "This girl has qualities any man would desire. Her fair skin alone should bring that price."

The lean man scoffed. "Red hair and a temper to boot, I bet!"

"An old wives' tale, gentlemen. What you see here is not an ill temperament but a virtuous disposition. She will work hard to please you, comfort you when you are sick, and praise you when you are not."

"Alright then. Forty pounds," cried Krude.

"Fifty," cried another.

"One hundred pounds is not too much for such a woman, sirs."

"One hundred." Sawyer stepped between the bidders. He set his hands on his hips and turned to look at them with proud eyes. "I doubt any could go higher for this girl."

Sarah whirled around to meet the eyes of the auctioneer. "I will not be bought by this man."

"Be quiet, girl. You are not allowed to speak."

"Please. Not him. He is the one who kidnapped me from England. He deceived me into leaving with him."

Sawyer laughed. "I have never seen this girl until Mr. Thrasher and I located her, she being his deceased brother's servant."

"Liar!" Sarah could not hold back. "I would rather die than go with you!"

"You will hold your tongue, girl," the auctioneer warned. "Any more outbursts and I will have you whipped."

Dreading the thought of the lash across her bare back, she could speak no more. The idea that Sawyer wanted her for his own, for whatever reason—desire, vengeance—made her blood run cold. The thought of his hands upon her could not ever be. She glanced at the doors and then looked back over her shoulder at the way out behind her. Could she run? Could she escape to the hill above and slip into the dark night?

Again she hung her head knowing she would be stopped before she could reach the bottom step. And even if she were able to escape, they would search for her with torches and dogs.

"Bids, gentlemen." The auctioneer waited. During the tense pause, Sarah prayed that Sawyer would not have her.

"One hundred and ten," called out Krude. Sarah hoped his would be the final bid.

"One hundred and twenty-five." Her heart sank at the sound of Sawyer's insufferable voice. The pride. The arrogance.

She looked down at him, watched the ire grow in his eyes. She knew what it meant if he were to own her. He would abuse her, work her from before dawn until long after sunset. And worse of all, he would force his wicked desires upon her.

"Going once. Going twice. Sold to—"

"Two hundred in gold for her freedom," cried a voice in the rear. All the men turned in surprise. Murmurs passed from lip to lip. Necks craned and heads turned from side to side to see who had called out such an offer.

Strangely thrilled, Sarah raised her eyes to see a man dressed in the garb of a frontiersman. He leaned back against the barn doors and crossed his arms over his chest. The wide brim of his hat and a day-old beard darkened his face. A hush fell over the crowd and she waited for the auctioneer to answer. Was this her redeemer sent to rescue her out of the mouth of the lion?

43

The auctioneer motioned with his hands for the crowd to quiet down. He narrowed his eyes and looked directly at the man near the door. "Did I hear you correctly, sir? You bid two hundred?"

"Yes," the man answered as he made his way to the front.

"In gold, you said?"

"Yes, in gold."

"You have it in hand?"

"I do, and I am quick to be rid of it and free this girl from the misery she has lived."

The bidder's voice arrested Sarah. It sounded familiar and struck a chord within her heart. She drew her dress closer over her shoulders and watched him step forward. From his jacket he produced a pouch and looked up at her from beneath his hat. When their eyes met, her heart raced and she drew in a ragged breath and smiled at him. "Alex?" she whispered. At once fear left her. Her tears turned to joy, her body became light with happiness.

The years had made him older, but he was as handsome as ever. His eyes were the same kind and loving ones she remembered, his smile as warm and tender. After all this time, he still loved her. Sarah saw in his gaze a fire that burned like a rising sun. She wanted to leap off the platform and fall into his arms. His smile said he wanted her to, but to wait a few moments more.

Thrasher leaned up to the platform to speak to the auctioneer. "Take it, for goodness sake. No one will go any higher than that. I can buy three laborers with that kind of money."

With a wave of his hand, the auctioneer addressed the crowd. "Does anyone bid higher?"

"Two hundred and one." Sawyer set his boot upon a crate, drew out a moneybag and tossed it in his palm. "In gold."

"Two hundred and five."

Sarah's mouth fell open and her senses reeled. She took a step forward. He had to win her, free her from Sawyer. Alex drew his eyes away from hers and looked at the auctioneer. "I can go higher, if this gentleman will. But I will outbid him."

Abruptly Sawyer stepped forward, white with fury. "Blackguard!"

Alex's eyes shifted to Sawyer. "I will pay any price to keep her out of your filthy hands. I know who and what you are."

"We can settle it outside if you wish . . ."

"We will settle it now, fair and square. I have no wish to kill you, sir." Alex looked at him without an ounce of fear.

Sawyer's eyes locked with his. "You dare to—"

"I dare nothing, though you deserve a horsewhipping for your crimes. The higher bidder wins her. It is as simple as that."

Sawyer's mouth twisted. "A lashing, is it?"

"Some would say a rope would be more appropriate."

Sawyer dragged off his hat and threw it down. Then he sprang at Alex with his hand on the hilt of his pistol. Sarah cried out and fell to her knees at the edge of the platform. This could not happen to her beloved. Not now!

With teeth bared Sawyer drew his weapon, but before he could take aim, Cread threw his arms around Sawyer from behind and held tight. "Oh, no, you don't!"

The flintlock fired, missed its mark and hit a post. Men yelled and moved back.

"Let go of me, you oaf!" Sawyer twisted back and forth.

"Do as he says, Cread," said Alex. "Let him go."

"Alright. But if he tries something again, I'll toss him in the river." Cread opened his arms and Sawyer stumbled forward. Grinning, Cread drew out his hunting knife and touched the point of the blade with the tip of his finger. "You do not intend to reload that pistol, now do you, Mr. Sawyer?"

Sawyer went to retrieve it, but the auctioneer's aide set his foot upon it then picked it up. "You are not supposed to fire weapons in here, Mr. Sawyer. I will have to hold it for you until you step outside."

Then the auctioneer bent over the platform. "Have you a higher bid, Mr. Sawyer?"

Mr. Krude shouted, "Throw him out. He is a menace to us all."

Others joined in. Outnumbered and in danger of being hauled from the tobacco barn, Sawyer brushed off his hat and set it on his head. "I withdraw my bid. She is not worth the trouble or the money." Then, shifting his eyes among the men around him, he stormed off, his face scarlet with rage. It was then Sarah knew she would never see him again.

Alex tossed the moneybag up to the auctioneer and held his hand up to Sarah. She grasped it tight and he guided her down the steps.

"Alex! Alex!" Laughing with joy, she threw her arms around his neck. She nuzzled her face against his soft deer hide jacket and gathered it in her hands. To be so close to him made her feel safe, rescued. No man would ever call her his property again. No man would call her his servant.

She looked up into his eyes. "You let him go."

"Believe me, my blood is hot for revenge. But he will be dealt with one day, whether in this life or face-to-face before God's throne."

With a swagger in his step, Cread approached the couple and drew off his hat to Sarah. "He never gave up his search for you, miss. I'm happy this all ended well."

"Thank you, sir." She looked up at Cread, fascinated by his rugged appearance and stalwart ways. "You helped him?"

"Aye, my dog and I. I've got to give old Scout some credit." His eyes turned to Alex. "I'll go out and be sure that rascal is on his way and not there to cause any more trouble." He set his rifle in the crook of his arm and walked out through the milling crowd.

Alex escorted Sarah outside, leaving behind the haggling of the auctioneer and the bidding of Thrasher for laborers. For a moment, Sarah paused at the barn doors and looked back at the men on the platform. She wished there were a way to free them all. As she watched them, she knew then she would dedicate her life to exposing the horrors of this trade with her pen and her wits.

A light breeze stirred across the moonlit yard. Alex led Sarah to his horse. "Charger! You still have him." She caressed Charger's neck.

Torchlight danced across the wall of the barn and over Alex's shoulders. He held the bill of sale up to one of the torches. It caught fire and when he set it on the ground, they watched it burn to black ash.

"You are free," he told her. "And where do I begin? I searched and searched for you everywhere."

"I knew you would. And I wrote to you, but all the letters came back."

"That is because I left Hutton House."

"I prayed we would find each other again." She reached down and took his hand. "The girls?"

"They are fine. Lily insisted I find you. She made me promise."

"Where are they?"

"In Annapolis, with my aunt. She is well, too."

"I am so glad. How did you know I would be here?"

"I found your note in a cabin at River Run. We went on to the inn along the river. The good lady there told us what had happened to you, and we determined they had brought you downriver to this place. My word, Sarah, you are as beautiful as the first day I saw you."

A little cry broke from her lips and she brought her arms around his shoulders and wept. He caressed her hair. "Tears of happiness, I hope."

"Yes. Tears of happiness, finally."

He looked over at Cread, and then moved Sarah around the side of the barn into the shadows. He touched her cheek, her hair, and drew her into his arms.

"I belong to you now," Sarah whispered in his ear.

"Only as my wife." Alex cupped his hands around Sarah's face, lowered his head, and pressed his lips against hers.

44

$\mathscr{M}$oria Burnsetter's red brick house had become a new sanctuary for Sarah. It lacked the lush forests and the wildness of the frontier, but the sleepy breezes that blew in from the bay and the soft clang of ships' bells out in the harbor eased past hardships. Peace had settled into her soul, and she found happiness in the busy household.

The day they arrived, Alex carried her in his arms through the front door. The twins ran down the staircase, shouting, "It's Sarah!" and it seemed that all the embraces they gave were not enough.

Aunt Moria had not aged a day. She threw out her arms in greeting, "Sarah, 'tis you! I knew Alex would find you. Oh, but I wish to hear every detail." And she drew Sarah into the sitting room smiling and breathless, like an anxious mother.

Millie greeted Sarah with the kind of warm affection that made her think of Fiona.

"Whatever you need, Miss Carr, I can do," she said with a little curtsey. "I suppose Dr. Hutton has told you I make the best pies. You name the dishes, and I'll whip them up for you in a jiffy."

Aunt Moria concurred. "That's right, Sarah. Whatever you need, you have but to ask." She clapped her hands together. "We should have a huge feast tonight to celebrate."

In the days following, Sarah settled into her new life. She watched the twins at play, which stirred memories of Ilene and Darcy romping in the yard beneath the great oak at River Run. Moria's kindness made her think of Eliza. She would forget no one, and remember the good.

As for Hayward, she did not wish to hear another word about him. Yet, she prayed he would find a way to forgive and be forgiven, and repent of his cruelty toward his wife.

During the past month, she and Alex each shared the hardships they had endured while separated, and how their hearts had ached for each other. The banns had been read, and now, three weeks later, they would at last be husband and wife.

The day dawned bright, the sky cloudless and blue. The rector of St. Anne's Church married her and Alex in the parlor. The windows stood open and the breeze fluttered the white gauze curtains and the ginger tendrils of her hair along her throat. She came to him dressed in beige brocade, a nosegay from Aunt Moria's garden in her hand. He smiled and held his hand out to her.

When Alex slipped the knotted gold band that had been his mother's over her finger, tears of happiness welled in Sarah's eyes. And when he kissed her, the tears eased over her lashes and down her cheeks. He drew his lips away and looked into her eyes. He had shaved off his shadow of a beard, and had cast off his buckskins for a new suit of navy blue, buffed black boots, and a crepe ribbon to tie his queue.

He whispered, "Now we have each other forever."

Millie flung open the front door. Neighbors waved their handkerchiefs and cheered for the good doctor and his new bride from their windows and front porches. Guests made their way inside to shake hands and congratulate them.

Millie had laid out a bounty for the wedding feast in the dining room. Upon the table were tureens of crab chowder, platters of fried oysters, roast duck, potatoes, pole beans, and buttery rolls. On the sideboard, she placed bowls of spiced cider punch and ginger beer. On a separate table in the center of the room stood Alex and Sarah's wedding cake, rich with dried fruit, nuts, cinnamon and nutmeg.

By noon, the festivities ended. Dr. and Mrs. Hutton, the twins, and Aunt Moria prepared to leave the portside town for a quiet life in Virginia. Sarah's gown, made of pale blue lin-sey, swished across the cobblestones. Her large-brimmed hat shaded her face. Bronze ringlets cascaded over her shoulders and caught the sunlight.

The coach, festooned in ribbons and silk flowers, awaited them out front. The horses, too, were decorated, the lead horse being Charger. She knew it to be extravagant, but Alex had ordered it, he told her, just for her. She had come to America aboard a rat-infested hulk, and she deserved to travel home in a coach fit for a queen, or more appropriately, a president's wife.

In addition to this, he bought her a trunk load of new clothes, linen chemises, day frocks and silk gowns, stockings, and a burgundy wool cloak for when the cold weather arrived. And for each pair of shoes he bought her, he had made and affixed padding so she could walk easily again. She fell in love with him even more, and wondered how deep love could go before one was completely consumed.

Now, with the packing done, the house closed up for a new tenant and the keys returned to the owner, a wagon waited at the rear of the coach, filled with the goods they would carry to Hutton House.

"I doubt they have ever seen a more beautiful bride than you, Sarah," Aunt Moria said when Sarah sat across from her. Dressed in her best gown and *Bergere* hat, Moria placed Lily and Rose on each side of her.

"You are too kind to say so, Aunt Moria."

"I do not say it to be kind but to be truthful. I have seen plenty of weddings in my day." Moria wiggled her head, smiling. "And Alex. So handsome."

"Yes, he is very handsome."

"What is he waiting for?"

"He is speaking to the driver."

"To be sure he drives gently, no doubt."

"I am sure that is what it is."

"God bless him. He knows how sensitive my old bones are. It is not easy to be tossed about in a coach at my age."

"That is true. Are you comfortable?"

"With Lily and Rose beside me, I am."

"The neighbors are staring at us," said Rose.

Sarah understood why. "They are happy for us, darling."

Moria pursed her lips and shook her head. "Tittle-tattle breeds curiosity, you know. In a good way, in this case."

Sarah smiled. "So I have heard."

"We cannot blame them," Moria said. "It does not take long for a love story like yours to get around town, especially when it involves a handsome young doctor and a lovely girl kidnapped from her homeland and sold into servitude, and how he searched for her the miles over, until he found her. Not to mention the hardships you faced."

"I shall write your story in a book when I grow up." Lily's smile lit up the interior of the carriage. Enthusiasm sparkled in her large eyes. "And Rose can help. She draws pictures very well."

Moria shook the girls' hands in her grasp. "Of course, you can write it Lily. And Rose indeed excels at drawing. This is a story that should be passed down through the generations. . . . What is keeping Alex? He has stepped away."

Sarah looked out the window. "He is now speaking to the wagon driver." She placed her hand on top of her hat and drew back inside. "I wish we had room for Millie to ride with us."

Aunt Moria raised a corner of her mouth into a knowing grin. "Millie is happy just where she is. The driver is a freeman—fought under General Gage and wounded at Yorktown."

"Really? They like each other, do you think?" Sarah asked, hopeful for Millie.

"I do not doubt it for a minute. I have never known Millie to look so shyly at a man before she met Jim. Alex did right in hiring him."

"I noticed how gently he treated her as he lifted her to her seat."

"Yes, and always with his hat removed. Ah, here comes Alex at last."

Alex climbed inside and relaxed next to Sarah. "Are we ready?"

"We are, my love," she said. "Let us go home."

"Yes. Tell the driver to move on, Alex," said Moria. "We are all anxious to get to Virginia. The house will need a good airing, and I shan't sleep until every cobweb is cleared away."

Alex tapped the coach roof, and the horses high-stepped over the cobblestones and moved out into the center of the street. The wagon followed.

Sarah's heart fluttered as she pulled on the embroidered mitts Aunt Moria had made her for her wedding day. Alex closed his hand over hers. She felt the band around her finger press against his, and then leaned her head on his shoulder.

"When we reach home, I should like to plant a garden," she said.

The adversities she had lived through had tried to kill hope. But as spring overcomes the harshness of winter, love had triumphed over all.

And now abide faith, hope, love, these three;
but the greatest of these is love.

1 Corinthians 13:13
"NKJV™"

Glossary

Ginger fairing: A sweet and spicy ginger cookie.

Pasties: Chunks of beef, potato, swede (yellow turnip), and onion wrapped in pastry glazed with milk or egg white.

Molasses dumpling: A type of doughnut fried in oil and dipped in hot molasses.

Stout porter: Strong beer.

Brickbat: An antique form of paving that made use of the inevitable accumulation of broken bricks at a colonial house.

Bergere: (French for "shepherdess") A flat-brimmed straw hat with a low crown, trimmed with ribbon and flowers.

Discussion Questions

1. Sarah wanted to trust Jamie's judgment in advising her to go to his sister if anything should happen to him. What changes did her decision bring? What could she have done differently?

2. Sarah made the choice to conceal Eliza's secret by claiming Ilene was her child. Are there times when hiding the truth, keeping a secret, to protect someone is justified?

3. Compare Dr. Hutton's devotion to Sarah to Hayward's lack of forgiveness toward Eliza. What qualities did Alex portray that Hayward did not?

4. Discuss the difficulties women of lower rank faced during the American Revolution.

5. What makes a man a hero and a woman virtuous? Which characters had these traits?

6. Sarah had the challenge of a disability. How did this mold her character?

7. How important was Sarah's faith to her? Discuss how faith can be shaken in times of adversity and what it takes to make it through the storms in life.

8. What kept Dr. Hutton's love for Sarah and his desire to search for her alive?

9. Were you surprised to learn that men, women, and children were kidnapped in England in Colonial days, and indentured servitude was not always voluntary?

10. Discuss the importance of patience when waiting for the right person to marry. What are the benefits of

patience and trusting in God to bring a relationship together?

11. Was Sarah brave or foolish to escape the Indians and face a journey through the wilderness? Was she foolish to flee River Run? What would have happened in the story if she had not made these bold moves?

12. The title of the novel is a metaphor. What does it mean to go beyond the valley? How can you apply this to your own life? How can you help others get beyond their valley?

Want to learn more about author
Rita Gerlach and check out other great fiction
from Abingdon Press?

Sign up for our fiction newsletter at
www.AbingdonPress.com/Fiction
to read interviews with your favorite authors, find tips
for starting a reading group, and stay posted on what
new titles are on the horizon. It's a place to connect
with other fiction readers or post a
comment about this book.

Be sure to visit Rita online!

www.ritagerlach.com
http://ritagerlach.blogspot.com

Abingdon Press fiction
a novel approach to faith

Plan your escape.

What They're Saying About...

The Glory of Green, by Judy Christie
"Once again, Christie draws her readers into the town, the life, the humor, and the drama in Green. *The Glory of Green* is a wonderful narrative of small-town America, pulling together in tragedy. A great read!"
—Ane Mulligan, editor of *Novel Journey*

Always the Baker, Never the Bride, by Sandra Bricker
"[It] had just the right touch of humor, and I loved the characters. Emma Rae is a character who will stay with me. Highly recommended!"
—Colleen Coble, author of *The Lightkeeper's Daughter* and the *Rock Harbor* series

Diagnosis Death, by Richard Mabry
"Realistic medical flavor graces a story rich with characters I loved and with enough twists and turns to keep the sleuth in me off-center. Keep 'em coming!"—**Dr. Harry Krauss,** author of *Salty Like Blood* and *The Six-Liter Club*

Sweet Baklava, by Debby Mayne
"A sweet romance, a feel-good ending, and a surprise cache of yummy Greek recipes at the book's end? I'm sold!"—**Trish Perry,** author of *Unforgettable* and *Tea for Two*

The Dead Saint, by Marilyn Brown Oden
"An intriguing story of international espionage with just the right amount of inspirational seasoning."—*Fresh Fiction*

Shrouded in Silence, by Robert L. Wise
"It's a story fraught with death, danger, and deception—of never knowing whom to trust, and with a twist of an ending I didn't see coming. Great read!"—**Sharon Sala,** author of *The Searcher's Trilogy: Blood Stains, Blood Ties,* and *Blood Trails.*

Delivered with Love, by Sherry Kyle
"Sherry Kyle has created an engaging story of forgiveness, sweet romance, and faith reawakened—and I looked forward to every page. A fun and charming debut!"—Julie Carobini, author of *A Shore Thing* and *Fade to Blue.*

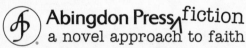
Abingdon Press fiction
a novel approach to faith

AbingdonPress.com | 800.251.3320